There Will Be Blood

by

Jonas Saul

&

Rania Stone

PUBLISHED BY:

Imagine Press Inc.
Ebook ISBN: 978-1-927404-69-0
Paperback ISBN: 978-1-927404-96-6
Hardcover ISBN: 978-1-998047-14-7

Chapter 1

ROXANNE DUPONT CLIMBED ON top of her man and rocked her hips rhythmically. It was her turn to be in control, which was her preference. She leaned down to kiss and nibble on his lips.

She quickly bound his hands with a strip of nylon from the bedside table. Arms up, his hands wrapped as one, she felt his desire for her physically as she dominated their final moments together as a couple.

Her wicked grin didn't need to be concealed as she lifted her dress up over her head. He would think her smile was part of the act, but her malicious intent had her ecstatic at what she was about to do. She tossed her dress far from the bed—she didn't want to get blood on it.

As predicted, he stared at her breasts, enjoying the view of her hardened nipples, yet unable to grasp or suckle them as his hands were tied.

She lowered her upper body, nuzzled his neck, then kissed his ear. After the requisite kisses, she pushed back into a sitting position and unbuttoned his pants. She wanted to feel him inside her one last time.

Moments later, she moved up and down on him as they became one.

It was time.

His eyes closed, and soft moans escaped his lips.

Roxanne leaned over and felt around the edge of the mattress. The weapon was exactly where she'd left it.

"Baby?" she whispered.

"Yeah?" His word came out in a moan.

"I have a surprise for you." She held the knife in both hands raised over his sternum. "Open your eyes."

He did.

They widened when he saw the knife. His hands struggled to come undone as he bucked his hips to kick her off.

She tightened her thighs and dropped the façade of the loving, grateful girlfriend.

"I told you you'd pay for what you did."

Roxanne thrust downward, the knife entering her boyfriend's chest. Even though he fought hard, his eyes wrought with pain and fear, she was able to get the knife in his flesh over a dozen times before he slipped out of her, softened by the trauma. Then, able to maneuver better, she repeatedly stabbed until he wasn't moving, his eyes wide in death, his body a mass of rips, tears, and blood.

Breathing heavily with the effort, she looked down the length of her naked body. A shower was in order. To the side, her dress lay by her panties and bra. Luckily, they were far enough away to avoid any blood spatter.

Her smile wasn't fake this time as she climbed off the bed—it was satisfaction.

Peter had hacked sensitive information—dangerous data on the whereabouts of high-ranking officials and criminals—then told her bosses back in France what she planned to do with it.

She'd warned Peter how dangerous this business was, how dangerous the information could be to them.

It could get them killed.

And, well, now she was the only one who knew everything. Peter's digital tracks were erased, and the information he'd gathered was deleted at the source.

It was time to go, time to sell, time to move on, and sadly, he wasn't part of the future plan. The cash was hers and hers alone.

Everyone had figured they were the perfect couple.

They had been dead wrong.

Chapter 2

ROXANNE DUPONT CRACKED OPEN the car door, and a wave of heat assaulted her as she exited her vehicle. A gentle summer breeze caressed her cheek, pushing her auburn hair off her face. It was hot, almost too hot, but that's what made Greece so palatable.

Every year, she visited the island of Rhodes, one of her favorite destinations. Lindos was a cute village on the island, one she looked forward to all year. Here, she found the missing part of her soul while overlooking the Greek sky and sea.

As an artist, she'd chosen the Lindos Palace and Resort Hotel location to present her work to the world. Invitations had been sent to some of the most important people in the art world, and many confirmed their attendance, saying they would come and celebrate her talent.

And on this hot, sunny Saturday in Greece, her tomorrow

would be determined—without her naïve boyfriend Peter tagging along.

She left her car keys with the valet, entered the lobby, and headed toward the reception desk.

"Good afternoon, Miss Dupont," the receptionist said. "Good luck with your art exhibit this evening, although I'm sure you won't need it."

Roxanne reciprocated the woman's kind smile. "Could I speak with Mr. Diakos for the moment?"

"Let me call him." The woman grabbed her phone, dialed out, and placed the receiver at her ear.

"He isn't answering," she said after a moment. She set the phone down. "Perhaps he's coordinating things for tonight. They're in the big room preparing for the art display last I looked. Do you want to wait for a bit to see if he shows up or take a look around for him? I can certainly try to call him again soon and buzz your room when I reach him."

"It's okay. Thank you. I'll look for him later." Roxanne winked and headed toward the exit.

She glanced out the side windows at the blue sea rolling in on the soft breeze, which made her stop. Just to her left was the large ballroom. Maybe a short look inside would comfort her anxiety about tonight, so she wandered over to the cavernous room, which was bustling with waiters and assistants, all busy at work arranging the tables and chairs for the night's art event. They were placing them according to the plan she had emailed to the hotel manager, Mr. Diakos, the day before. If she hadn't had the forethought to order the preparation, most of what she had planned for this evening wouldn't happen.

The popular art critic, Mr. Nikolas Kovak, had repeatedly

asked her to show him one of her pieces on the way from the airport. Still, she refused, leaving him at a neighboring hotel so he wouldn't linger around here, snooping for an early peek. If she had allowed him any sort of an early preview before the event, it might have been construed as favoritism.

In the center of the room, the hotel manager, Mr. Diakos, stood talking to a man who held blueprints.

Diakos had gained her confidence. He was doing everything he could to help make the presentation successful, even though she'd rebuffed him recently. His pleasant smile and professional aura calmed her doubts and fears about the show and him.

Without further delay, she made her way over to him.

When she was a few feet away, he glanced up. "Good afternoon, Miss Dupont. As you can see, everything is going according to your wishes. The exhibit space remains covered, and we're arranging the chairs now. The champagne and appetizers are being set up over there." He pointed at a table on the side wall. "I'm sure we'll be ready to begin your presentation as the sun sets as planned."

Roxanne smiled wide for Diakos's benefit. "I can't thank you enough, Mr. Diakos, for everything. You've all done a wonderful job." She met his gaze. "I'm going to head to my room for a short rest to have the strength for this evening's event."

"As you wish. Whatever you need, we are here for you."

She nodded and thanked him again, then stepped away. As a hotel guest for almost ten days, Mr. Diakos had been as accommodating as he'd been a prick. Not every hotel manager had a dark side, but this one did, and she'd learned to manage it—well, manipulate it was closer to the truth.

Moments later, she exited the side door of the main building and then strode along the outdoor path to her room. Once she was locked away inside her small bungalow-like room, she tossed her purse on the couch and opened the patio door for air. The warmth hit her hard enough to make her retreat to the huge bed, where she laid down, took a deep breath, and stared out at the serene landscape. After several seconds, she closed her eyes and turned off the world for a while. She focused on her breathing, with thoughts about her dead ex-boyfriend. She had to keep the story straight in her head.

What she had to do tonight would take patience, which involved much planning. Everything was in place, with the art show being a perfect cover because she was *literally* an artist.

Her eyes popped open, and she stared at the ceiling, wondering where she'd put her vanity mirror. How could she forget it?

She got up, grabbed her suitcase and placed it on the bed, then tore at the zippers to open it. She rummaged through her own belongings like a crazy woman, shoving her hand to the bottom and running it along the inside corners of the case, under her shoes, her folded dresses, the small pile of panties and bras—everywhere, but to no avail.

She had a job to do, the last one, and then she would go on with her life as a retired artist in South America, hidden away from the world.

If only she could locate that damned mirror.

***

Brian Miller adjusted his elbows on the rough ground, then returned the binoculars to his eyes. He watched Roxanne Dupont's every move from the side of the hill, in a recess in the mountain overlooking the hotel. Fortunately, the woman had opened the curtains before lying on the bed. From his vantage point, he could only see the lower part of her legs from the knees down, but he was grateful for at least that. It was enough to confirm to his boss that she had returned to the hotel and was in her room. As far as he could tell, it had been almost ten long days of watching her, and no meeting had occurred yet. Which meant it had to take place in the next twenty-four hours.

He eased the binoculars away from his face, set it gently on its case on the ground, and then pulled out his cell phone. After he dialed, he returned to his position, the phone at his ear, the binoculars pressed against his eyes.

On the second ring, it was picked up.

"Wait until I confirm the line is secure," his boss said.

Miller didn't mutter a sound in response.

While he waited, Roxanne rose from the bed in some kind of hurry. Miller frowned as he watched her toss her suitcase on the bed and rifle through it.

"Line is secure. Give me your report."

"Subject back in the hotel. I have eyes on her in her room."

"Any trouble?"

"None."

"Do you anticipate any difficulties in retrieving the item?"

"None expected, sir. No sign of hostiles nor the buyer."

"Very good. Confirm once you have it in your

possession. Do it tonight. She's set to check out soon. I'm on a flight in several hours. I will have more men with me."

"Good to hear. Consider the job accepted and done, sir. Will call in confirmation once I've obtained the package."

The line died.

He lowered the phone, the Greek heat getting to him. His collared shirt was drenched in sweat as he watched Roxanne frantically search for something.

Darwin Kostas, his boss who was operating this mission out of Italy, expected results.

If what Roxanne Dupont was searching for was the item Darwin needed, then heads would roll. He sure hoped she had not lost it. If she did, Roxanne had better locate it before he arrived in her room later that evening to retrieve it. Darwin would kill him if he didn't deliver it to Darwin personally.

Roxanne was pretty, so naturally, Miller didn't want to hurt her or, worse—kill her for it, but the item was simply too important. Killing Roxanne would be such a waste.

Dirt crunched beside him.

Too close, too heavy.

In that second, he understood the mistake he'd made. Being so engrossed in Dupont's frantic suitcase search and the phone call to his boss, he had temporarily lost focus on his surroundings.

He lowered the binoculars and turned slowly toward the sound.

The men had approached from the sunny side, making their faces hard to see.

It didn't matter anyway. By the time he had pivoted all the way around, Brian Miller was already leaking blood into the Greek dirt profusely.

Chapter 3

ROXANNE HAD FIFTEEN MINUTES until the art show began. She fiddled with last-minute adjustments to her pieces while thinking over lines she'd memorized for the presentation.

Many guests had already arrived and were sipping champagne, while others were still approaching the valet area. The sun had lowered in the west, and the blue palette in the sky had given way to soft pinks and light reds. The heat outside hadn't dissipated, but the hotel's air conditioners kept the inside cool and comfortable.

The art critic, Kovak, stood out from the rest of the crowd. He was dressed well this evening, wearing thick glasses and a beret. When he entered the room, the maître d' signaled a waiter to serve him immediately. This kind of attention drew Roxanne's eye.

Kovak scanned the large room until his eyes landed on her. He nodded slightly and started toward her. She waited near the front of the large room as a waiter cut through several guests to get to the man in the beret, a tray held high in his hand. Just before Kovak made it to Roxanne, the waiter caught up to him.

"Good evening, sir. Here's a Smirnoff in a low glass with two ice cubes and a fresh lemon. On the house, sir."

Kovak didn't seem surprised by the interruption, like he'd arranged all this for the benefit of anyone watching him.

He took the beverage, sipped it, and nodded at the waiter, who spun on his heels and sped off.

It was obvious to even a casual observer that this beret-wearing man was used to being cared for. Everyone gave him their utmost attention because he was an art critic—that had to be the reason for his dramatic performance.

None of that mattered to Roxanne, though. As soon as the art show was over, she had plans for her future, and they didn't include ever seeing the art critic Nikolas Kovak again.

With slower steps now, the man approached the wall where Roxanne had displayed her paintings. In the corridor where the hotel had a fountain display with large glass slabs protruding from the water, she had exhibits covered, waiting to be revealed. There would be no early preview of those pieces by anyone.

White light was suffused into the room by a large sphere suspended from the ceiling. The sphere consisted of small pieces of glass that looked as if they were being moved by air. Light emitted from the core where a long, narrow lamp was held in place. It offered her paintings the exact lighting conditions required to understand her passion and message better.

All her creations raised questions about life, death, and

human existence. One had a storm-like background that seemed to be constantly changing, and at the bottom, it had a section that resembled a Dalí piece. Hans Memling influenced the second painting from his work, *Triptych of Earthly Vanity and Divine Salvation.* Hers offered a piece that revealed life and its fragile mortality.

Startled out of her reverie, the sound of wind and waves from the sea roared through the hotel's speakers. The luminous sphere above the crowd changed color, becoming a soft pink-red, making the room appear the hue of cotton candy. Then, the large glass doors eased closed after the staff guided the guests in so that the presentation could begin on time—at sunset.

Roxanne glanced across the room at the young man who stood by the front window. After several deep breaths, he lifted a violin with great care and placed it into the crook of his shoulder. With the same gentle hands that would hold a mistress, he caressed the instrument and began to play. The violin strings vibrated with his touch, quieting the audience.

Roxanne watched all this as her eyes surveyed the crowd, staring at all the faces of the attendees who had come to see her presentation. She studied them to see if anyone stood out for one reason or another but couldn't see a single anomaly. They all looked like art show visitors, anticipating a wonderful evening.

Following the start of the violin, an angelic female voice began to narrate the lyrics she'd prepared, enchanting the audience. Letters appeared on the far wall while the woman read them in a sing-song voice, with the accompaniment of the violin. The experience was majestic, as if the song was being whispered upon a soft breeze.

"Light gives way to darkness, and then again from the beginning in the cycle of life. So is our soul for others mortal, that is eaten by darkness for others *immo*rtal, that is received by light. For some, it's a life that simply changes form and destination; yet, for others, it's an end that finishes nothing. What should you believe? What *can* you believe?"

When she stopped speaking, the glass sphere in the ceiling opened like a flower in bloom, and the intense light it emitted made the crowd squint.

Seconds later, the light diminished until it went out, the sphere dark. The regular lights of the conference room came on, casting the area in a soft amber glow.

One of the covered exhibits swayed under a sheet. It wasn't a sculpture or a painting. It looked like a man who acted as if he were trapped. Roxanne, dressed all in black, stood next to him barefoot, her feet in a small pool of water.

The room was silent, held rapt in anticipation of what they were about to witness.

"Thus, the soul remains trapped in the body," she said, loud enough for everyone to hear. "Whether it wants to or not, whether the body agrees or not, this entrapment accompanies them, body and soul, until death."

With these words, the body under the fabric disappeared, and only the cloth remained, now on the floor and soaking up water.

A collective gasp rose from the attendees.

Roxanne stepped farther into the water and stood next to the second exhibit.

"Anima Mundi," she said, then lifted off the cover to unveil her art. A caterpillar-like body of pipes that gradually made a sound reminiscent of a sea wind was revealed.

"If the soul resides in nothingness within the body, does it live in non-existence, or does it unite with the vast universe? Is it reborn in another body and continues forth? Or does it go to the immortality of infinite light?"

On her last word, colored water ran behind the body of the caterpillar-thing in the shape of butterfly wings, rising from and coloring the water Roxanne stood in.

After several moments to allow the audience to take it all in, she moved to the third and last exhibit and revealed it without delay. It was a glass statue depicting her naked body —not her *actual* body because her body had ugly scars from a shooting accident many years ago—but the flawless body she had desired to have in this lifetime.

The violin slowed its soft rhythm, then stopped. As soon as it fell silent, Roxanne addressed the crowd.

"Ecce homo. Memento Mori," she said, loud enough to be heard by everyone. Then she threw the statue, with all its virtues and flaws, into the water. As the glass head broke, a robotic firefly was released. It emitted a small light as it flew to stand on the sphere suspended from the ceiling. At that moment, the room's lights were switched off, and the sphere re-ignited, casting the room in a heavenly glow.

The presentation was over. She'd done it. Her last art show.

The audience applauded her veraciously, some with wet cheeks, as she'd moved people emotionally.

She bowed, heat rising to her face as if there was a fire close by. As planned, a waiter brought her a pair of slippers and a bathrobe on a tray to help her cover the wet clothes she'd endured during the presentation.

"I'll come back," she muttered to him, then jumped off

the stage to head to her room for a quick change.

The art show had succeeded with flying colors, so to speak. The guests' eyes were fixed on her, their hands still clapping wildly. As she meandered through the throng of people, some offered friendly pats on the back while others whispered positive comments. Maybe she had finally succeeded with her artwork after all these years, only to give it all up in one night.

The guests were pleased, getting drunk on champagne and migrating to the buffet. One last look to survey the room revealed everyone admiring her talent and creativity and discussing the show. Heads nodding, glasses raising, smiles widening—her last vision of a life she'd wanted for so many years but could never attain.

The new life she had been waiting for had begun.

It was time.

To punctuate that thought, the violin rose on a happy note, the atmosphere positive.

The man in the beret—Kovak, the art critic—was the only one out of place. He seemed annoyed, staring at his watch, looking up, and glancing around the room. She should not have left him for so long. No one lets an art critic wait. Yet, she wasn't about to speak with him, covered in water and donning a bathrobe.

Actually, in fifteen minutes, she wasn't about to speak to any of them ever again.

Roxanne Dupont stepped away and disappeared out a side door.

***

The hotel manager, Mr. Diakos, glanced up as a man in a beret approached him.

"Please," the man said in a clipped tone. "Can you inform Miss Dupont that I will be leaving soon?"

"Absolutely, sir. Just give us a moment to locate her."

Mr. Diakos gestured for a waiter to join him. He leaned in and whispered the message to find the artist woman. The waiter left and informed the front desk to call her room. Diakos watched as the girl dialed out. Their eyes met, and the girl at the reception desk shook her head.

No answer.

"Please, sir, if you'll give me a moment."

Mr. Diakos excused himself and moved to the counter.

"Notify housekeeping. Go to her room and knock. She must return posthaste."

Diakos spun around and pointed when he saw Kallonis, his head of security.

"Come with me."

Kallonis nodded, and together, they exited a side door and headed toward Roxanne's room. Less than a minute later, Mr. Diakos knocked on her door and identified himself. When there was no answer, he used his master key to unlock the door.

"Miss Dupont," he called before turning on the lights.

Still no answer.

Diakos frowned and glanced back at Kallonis. Then he shoved the door open wider and turned on the lights.

The room was empty.

He stepped in without touching anything, pushed open the bathroom door, looked behind her bed, and then grabbed the room's telephone to call the front desk in order to tell the receptionist to keep an eye out for her.

"Follow me," Diakos said to Kallonis as they exited her room, closing the door behind them.

He led Kallonis back to the art show and scanned the crowd in case Roxanne had stayed behind to talk to someone, but he failed to see her anywhere.

After fifteen minutes, Mr. Diakos called the staff on-site to mobilize them in an effort to look for her throughout the common areas of the hotel.

There was no reason to panic in such situations, but finding the esteemed Miss Roxanne Dupont was of great importance. Yet, for all their efforts, as the first hour ticked by, she was nowhere to be found.

Miss Roxanne Dupont had disappeared from the Lindos Palace Resort Hotel.

Chapter 4

Mr. Diakos made the call to hotel security so they could help search the outdoor areas, including the beach. Five security personnel exited the hotel to scour the outside areas. One by one, they confirmed over their radios that they couldn't locate Roxanne Dupont anywhere.

Infuriated, Diakos felt the stirrings of losing his temper. A cold sweat ran down his back. This was so unlike Miss Dupont. Why perform brilliantly at her art show, then step away only to disappear? Where could she have gone? Was she in her lover's hotel room somewhere and not willing to speak to her admirers?

He moved away from the reception area in the lobby and stepped into his office. He wanted to do the right thing and inform the authorities, even though it might be too early.

Something he had to consider was the impact on the hotel's reputation. If word got out that something had happened to one of his guests, the hotel would be talked about in a bad light, and that wouldn't bode well for the owners, Mr. and Mrs. Markakis.

He poured himself a whiskey from the side table, then plopped down in his chair to contemplate his next move.

Before he got his first sip, someone knocked on the door.

"Enter," he shouted.

The door opened, and Christos Kallonis, the head of security at the hotel, stepped in. With a grim expression on his face, the man moved to Diakos's desk and took a seat opposite him.

"We can't find Miss Dupont anywhere, sir. It's as if the Earth opened and swallowed her whole. I suggest we notify the authorities."

Even though he was just thinking that exact same thing, he said, "We can't."

"Why not, sir?"

"Because she's not considered a missing person until at least twenty-four hours."

"Sir." Kallonis leaned forward. "She may be missing. We don't know for sure. But calling the authorities because we suspect something may have happened to her is something entirely different. Also, that twenty-four-hour thing is a myth. The authorities will investigate earlier if you can provide evidence that foul play may have taken part in her disappearance."

Diakos sipped from his glass, watching his security man. "Are you saying something criminal took place here?"

Kallonis sat back. "That is exactly what I'm saying. Sir, she just did an art show, then what, she walks out of the hotel leaving everything behind?" He shook his head. "Doesn't add up, sir. Why wasn't she in her room? Why wasn't she back mingling with the guests in a timely fashion? I mean, that's the whole point of putting on a show, right?" Kallonis clasped his hands together. "Something happened to her, and the sooner we discover what that is, the sooner we can help her."

"You think she's still alive?"

"I have no idea whether she's alive or dead, but I sure hope she's alive, as much for her sake as for the hotel's."

Diakos took another sip from his drink, glanced down at his desk, and slowly shook his head. "We didn't do anything wrong. We can't know the exact location of all of our guests. We are not a prison. We're a hotel."

"Everyone will understand that, sir. You're upset, but I'm quite aware of our limitations, and as things are, we can't handle this search on our own." Kallonis kept his voice calm, resolute. "We have to call the police, sir. There's no other way. What if someone kidnapped her? Whatever's happened, the leads are still hot. We could use the help."

Diakos shook his head again. "No, nothing happened to her. Dupont made the guest list herself. No one on that list could possibly cause her harm. She wouldn't've invited enemies."

"How do we know who she invited? Whoever's on that list doesn't automatically give them a free pass. We either locate Miss Dupont safe and sound or call in for help. As head of security, that's my stance on this matter. I've been hired to do a job, and I feel the proper authorities are needed at this juncture."

Diakos drank the rest of his beverage in one pull, then slammed the glass down.

He grabbed his phone and called the front desk.

"Has anyone reported that they've seen Miss Dupont?" he asked, then exhaled in frustration when he got the answer.

The phone back on the desk, he met Kallonis's gaze.

"She has not been found."

"Then we call the police. Worst case, they tell us to call back tomorrow."

Diakos nodded. "Okay." He snatched up the phone and dialed.

"Rhodes police, what's your emergency?"

"I'm the hotel manager at the Lindos Palace Resort Hotel."

"Name?"

"Adonis Diakos."

"How can we help you?"

Diakos detected the man yawning on the other end of the line.

"One of our guests has disappeared."

"Did they bolt without paying their bill?"

Diakos frowned and stared at Kallonis. "No, their belongings are still in their room."

"Okay, start at the beginning. What makes you think they've disappeared if they left their things in their room?"

"I'm talking about Miss Roxanne Dupont, the artist. She was here this evening for her art show. When it was over, with people lingering around to wait and speak with her, she left to get changed and did not return."

"How long ago was this?"

"About an hour ago."

There was a pause on the other end, long enough that Diakos wondered if the cop had hung up.

"Hello?" Diakos said, the phone pressed into his ear.

"Sir, you can't call in about a missing person when they are only gone for one hour unless you can attest to witnessing something of a criminal nature. She probably went for a walk on the beach, slipped into a friend's room, or is having a late-night drink in a beach taverna somewhere—"

"That isn't the case with Miss Dupont."

"Are you connected to her in any personal way to back up that statement?"

"What sort of question is that?" Diakos stifled his volume, not wanting to shout, but he couldn't restrain his shocked tone.

"I'm trying to ascertain why a hotel manager would be calling about a missing guest when you aren't connected to that guest in any way other than to have offered her a room. For example, are you aware of her personal itinerary and her agenda? How can you be certain she wasn't meeting with a married man or she left for a nightcap in another room? That being said, I feel you should call back in the morning. Report her missing then—"

"Wait," Diakos gasped, cutting the guy off as he leaned forward in his chair. "I'm reporting it now. We have people waiting for her, expecting her. She did an art show—"

"As you were saying, but there's nothing we can do—"

"And when that show was completed, there was an art critic she was supposed to meet. Her behavior is highly irregular. Something has happened to her, I assure you." Diakos paused to catch a breath, then continued. "I went to her room. It's empty."

"Wait, you entered your guest's room after being unable to locate her during the past hour?"

"I did, along with my head of security, Mr. Kallonis."

"Who is this woman again?"

Diakos heard something drop on the other end of the line like the cop had grabbed a pad of paper and slammed it down on his desk.

"She is a celebrity of sorts, an important person with influence. If something has happened to her, and your department failed to even respond to my phone call, the bad publicity would hurt this island for years to come, not to mention the viability of my hotel."

"Okay, okay, take it easy. I've got a cruiser in the area. I'll send them over, but you should know they'll tell you the same thing I'm trying to tell you. Nothing will happen due to the time span as she has to be—"

"Fine, send them over. In the meantime, I'll keep everyone here for interviews. Someone knows something."

"Uhm, as you wish. You're evidently the guy in charge."

"That I am." Diakos slammed down the phone. "What an asshole."

Kallonis raised his eyebrows, gawked at him momentarily, then lowered them. He probably hadn't heard his hotel manager cursing out the cops before.

"You heard me," he said. "Secure the building. No one leaves. The police are on their way."

Kallonis jumped to his feet and exited the office.

Diakos watched him leave, then grabbed his glass and brought it to his mouth, but it was empty.

"Dammit," he muttered, then got up to pour some more.

Ten minutes later, Diakos left his office and entered the lobby to ensure the front doors were secure.

The art critic was still there, looking as impatient as

before. In fact, the man appeared angry in the way he glared at Diakos.

"This is unacceptable!" he stammered. "No one has treated me with such disrespect." Veins corded in his neck, and one pulsed on his forehead above his reddened face.

Diakos nodded at the man without replying. He saw no purpose in arguing the point. It would be better to address everyone at once as they moved into the huge expanse of the hotel lobby.

"Can I have everyone's attention, please? We are currently trying to ascertain Miss Roxanne Dupont's whereabouts. Immediately after the art presentation, she exited this area and headed to her room for a change of clothes, but she never returned here. We can confirm she is not in her room at this time. My staff have searched the entire hotel and couldn't find her anywhere." He paused to let that sink in.

Kallonis was at the back of the assembled guests, corralling them tighter with his fellow hotel security officers. Housekeeping and room service staff gathered closer, too.

Diakos cleared his throat. "For this reason, the authorities have been notified and will be here shortly. The faster we deal with this situation, the better our hopes of finding and helping Miss Dupont. So, with that in mind, we are asking for your cooperation. The police have requested that everyone remain on site until they arrive and assess the situation. They will be looking for statements from some of you if you spoke to or saw Miss Dupont prior to her disappearing this evening."

Many of the assembled guests' faces slackened at the mention that the artist was missing. Smiles gave way to grim expressions, the cheerful atmosphere now muted.

A soft din rose as guests whispered to one another.

Diakos raised his hands for calm. "Please, I need your attention." The commotion lowered several notches. "Let us serve you coffee, sandwiches, whatever you may need for your extended time with us this evening."

When he finished speaking, a police siren squawked once in the distance.

"The authorities are almost here. Please feel free to order something on the house while you wait."

Moments later, two police officers stepped up to the locked front doors, pulled on them, then knocked.

Kallonis let them in.

Diakos approached the officers through the thick crowd as the noise increased again. As he passed one couple, they blurted out a question about time, asking how late they were expected to remain at the hotel. He ignored them and kept pushing through to the cops.

Kallonis was shaking their hands when he got there.

"Mr. Diakos is our hotel manager," Kallonis said as a way of introduction. "He's the one who called your station."

"Diakos," the taller cop said. "I'm Officer Samaras. Is there somewhere private we can talk?"

"Sure, my office. It's right over there." He pointed at the end of the reception desk. "Follow me."

Samaras turned to his partner. "I'll be back in a few moments. No one leaves."

The other officer nodded and remained by the front doors.

Once settled in Diakos's office, Samaras asked, "How sure are you that this particular guest has disappeared?

Couldn't she have made a grand exit after her art show simply for attention?"

"We can't be sure of anything at the moment. But the fact remains—she made the presentation, then left to change her clothes and didn't return."

"Has anything happened that's out of the ordinary, like a note left behind, a strange phone call, or anything related to this guest in any way? Something that would cause you to have a suspicion as to her whereabouts or safety?"

"No, nothing. My staff would've alerted me if such an issue arose."

"You have to understand that there's not much we can do at this time. A person can't be declared missing because she left her hotel room—"

"But Officer, she's—" Diakos interrupted.

Samaras raised a hand. "Let me finish."

Diakos crossed his arms over his chest and nodded.

"Is she a Greek citizen?"

Diakos shook his head. "No, she isn't."

"Well, these things have a procedure. Because she's a foreigner seemingly disappearing on Greek soil, I'm willing to entertain this scenario for now, then revisit it tomorrow morning if she still hasn't shown up. Step one, can you seal her room until we locate her?"

Diakos nodded. "Yes, we can do that."

"No one goes in or out until she is located or begins a proper investigation. If she's indeed missing and we suspect foul play, a forensic team will need access to her room."

"Understood."

"Next, I'll speak with the guests so they can return to their rooms. We mustn't have everyone waiting for hours to be interviewed when there's a high chance your guest isn't even missing."

Diakos glared at the cop, his heart racing. "Her name is Roxanne Dupont."

Roxanne was missing, and the arrogance of the Rhodes Police Department was going to ruin him, along with his hotel.

Without responding to Diakos—did he even hear her name?—the tall, dark-skinned Officer Samaras, a man in his early forties, turned and strode to the door.

Diakos followed him without a word as he exited the room and moved out in front of the assembled crowd.

"Ladies and gentlemen," Samaras shouted to get everyone's attention. When the room quieted to some degree, he smiled at them. "Good evening. It has come to our attention that the whereabouts of Miss Roxanne Dupont are in question. So, instead of keeping you all here for an extended period, we ask that you leave your names and contact information with hotel security. Then, you will be free to go about your business. This is merely a procedural request in the event that Miss Dupont does not show up. We may be in touch at a later date. Please allow me to divide you into two groups. Group one to my right will comprise people who knew Miss Dupont personally. Group two to my left will be those who came to meet her or see her for the first time."

Whispers rose from the crowd as people moved toward Kallonis's security officers, who had already pulled out pads and started jotting down names and phone numbers.

Diakos edged to the side of the crowd, already yearning for another shot of whiskey. He scanned faces in search of the art critic but couldn't locate him.

Officer Samaras watched as everyone gathered without protest to offer their personal details, then turned back to Diakos.

"That's the best we can do at the moment."

"Well, it's not good enough." Diakos couldn't hide the contempt in his tone. "The hotel owners will be quite upset with this development."

Samaras grinned wide, his upper teeth popping out. "Sir, with all due respect, I am not employed by your hotel nor care about how your superiors may feel." His phone rang, cutting him off. He picked it up. "Samaras." He paused, then said, "Yes, sir. I understand, sir." He stared at Diakos. "Yes, sir, I'll tell them." Samaras hung up and slipped his phone away.

"Looks like you're in luck."

"How so?" Diakos asked.

"We won't have to wait until the morning to continue this investigation."

"And why's that?"

"The main inspector of this part of southern Greece, Inspector Petrakis, will be here soon. As it happens, he's vacationing on this island and heard our sirens. After calling our station to inquire about the particulars, he expressed interest in Miss Dupont's whereabouts and wanted to visit your hotel. He will be here shortly."

"See, now these are the sorts of results I was hoping for."

"Before Inspector Petrakis's arrival, will you allow me to ask you a few questions?"

"Please, go ahead."

Samaras motioned to the side, then led Diakos to several unoccupied chairs. He pulled out a small recording device and clicked a button. "Can you state your name and occupation for the record?"

"Mr. Adonis Diakos, hotel manager for the Lindos Palace Resort Hotel."

"When did you last see Miss Roxanne Dupont?"

"When she left the art exhibit to go to her room for a change of clothes a little over an hour ago. She was wet from her art presentation, which involved water."

"Can you tell me if you noticed anything unusual going on, like someone acting oddly or aggressive?"

"I detected nothing untoward whatsoever. Everything went as planned. The guests were on time, the food and champagne were excellent, and the presentation went off without any technical problems. Miss Dupont's performance was flawless. I just can't believe she disappeared."

"When did you notice she was missing?"

"When an important guest complained about her tardiness."

"Who was this important guest?"

"He's an art critic. I understand his name is Nikolas Kovak."

Samaras stopped the recording. "I will need your details, like your full name, address, and date of birth. Then I'll need everything you've got on file for Miss Roxanne Dupont. I'll need to know when she checked in when she was planning to check out, and if you took her passport number upon arrival. Everything you can give us will help."

Diakos rose from his seat at the same time Samaras did. "I will prepare everything for you."

"Now, if you'll point me in the direction of that art critic, I'll be done until Inspector Petrakis arrives."

Diakos stared at the crowd but couldn't pick up the critic's beret anywhere. "I don't see him." He turned back to Samaras. "Maybe he gave his information and left already."

Samaras eyed him warily.

In other circumstances, Diakos would address that look and call the man out for it, but since they treated Miss Dupont's disappearance as more serious, he decided to hold his tongue.

"Get me what you have on her, Mr. Diakos. Then meet me by the front doors. I must have a word with my colleague."

Officer Samaras stepped away to navigate through the few remaining guests. The groups had thinned to less than half, but many people were still offering their information to hotel security.

Five minutes later, with Miss Dupont's details printed off and in his hand, he approached Samaras at the front doors.

"Here's what we have on her. Now, what happens?" He handed the papers over.

"We wait for Inspector Petrakis," Samaras said. "If this becomes his case, he'll direct us from there."

"The guests are leaving. He'll have a large list of names and phone numbers to go through. That'll take too much time. Shouldn't they have been interrogated before they left?"

Samaras shook his head. "We don't *interrogate* people, Mr. Diakos. We interview them. A lot of that can be handled over the phone." He cleared his throat and stepped closer. "We're dealing with the disappearance of a foreigner. If she's actually gone, the impact on this community could be immense. So, with the threat of the media blasting this all over the Greek news and international news, I don't intend to do anything more this evening."

Diakos fumed on the inside. How could Samaras be such an asshole?

"Sir," Diakos said, his tone measured. "We have a guest missing. I'm unsure why this wouldn't inspire you to do your job."

"Mr. Diakos, I'm a cop, not an inspector. I'll be handing this case over to Petrakis as soon as he walks through this door, and you know what I'll be telling him?"

Diakos shook his head. "I haven't the slightest."

"That you're all suspects in her disappearance."

"You can't be serious. Me? A suspect?" Diakos laughed out loud, his head tilted back. "How did you come to that ridiculous conclusion, Mr. I'm-not-an-inspector?"

Samaras stepped away without answering him.

Diakos watched him meander through the final group of guests as Kallonis moved up to stand beside Diakos.

"How bold is that fuckin' guy?" Diakos mumbled to Kallonis. "Do you have everything under control?"

"Everything is fine. We've done as you requested. Everyone's information has been recorded."

Officer Samaras's voice filled the area as he addressed the remaining staff members.

"Everyone, please listen. Miss Dupont is still missing. We don't know if any crime has been committed at this time, but we have Inspector Petrakis on his way to look into the matter. Those of you who came on shift before the art show and are still here will need to make a statement as to your whereabouts throughout the evening. We're asking that you stay inside the hotel at this time. The rest of the guests are free to retire to their rooms. However, as I just requested, we want the hotel staff to wait for Inspector Petrakis. He will be along soon."

Diakos's staff didn't appear too happy with Samaras as mutterings rose throughout the room.

"What if our shift is over?" one of the room service guys asked. "Why do we have to stay?"

"Yeah," another from housekeeping said. "I don't feel safe here. I want to leave."

Things were falling apart. Diakos couldn't believe this was happening. He'd be out of a job when the media got wind of it.

"I can assure you that there is no danger," Samaras shouted, to be overheard by the staff's rising voices. "The police are here, and at this time, we suspect no foul play. I want to believe that Miss Dupont is in good health. Please feel free to go to your rooms if you're staying in the hotel. That means staff as well. We will be in touch by the morning."

"Mr. Diakos," someone shouted. "Sir!"

Diakos turned toward the reception area. His front desk clerk was holding up the phone.

"Call for you, sir."

"Tell them I'm busy."

"Sir, you're going to want to take this."

He turned to look at Samaras, nodded at the man, and then they both headed to the front desk. When he got there, he took the phone.

"This is the manager of the Lindos Palace Resort Hotel. How can I help you?"

"I'm General Constantine Doukas, Chief of Hellenic

Police in Athens. I'm calling to speak to one of your guests, Miss Roxanne Dupont."

Diakos stared at Samaras when he spoke into the phone. "I'm sorry, sir, but we do not know where she is at the moment. We have Rhodes police on site looking into the matter now."

"The Rhodes police? What?" The man gasped on the phone. "Put them on. I want to speak to them."

"Yes, sir." Diakos handed over the phone. "He wants to speak to you."

Samaras took the phone. "Officer Samaras here."

Diakos detected the tinny voice through the phone, shouting something at Samaras.

"Yes, sir. Inspector Petrakis will be here at any moment, sir." Samaras nodded. "I understand, sir. I'll tell him." Samaras wrote something down, then returned the phone to the clerk, who hung it up.

"What happened?" Diakos asked. "What's going on?"

"He hung up on me."

"What did he say? He sounded angry."

Samaras looked up at him. "He wanted inspector Petrakis to call him the minute he gets here. Gave me his personal cell number."

"How is Miss Dupont on the police radar in Athens?"

"Apparently, high-ranking authorities in the French government want Miss Dupont apprehended immediately. They're sending delegates to pick her up late tomorrow. Until then, they hold the Greek government accountable for whatever happens to her."

"What the hell?" Diakos mumbled to himself, taking a step backward. "Who is this woman?"

"I have no idea, but I'm sure we'll find out soon enough."

Samaras nodded toward the door. Inspector Petrakis was pulling in out front.

"I need a smoke." Samaras headed outside.

Chapter 5

INSPECTOR PETRAKIS PULLED UP to the front of the Lindos
Palace Resort Hotel in his rented car and found a spot close
to the lobby doors to park.

People in evening gowns and suits milled about. He took
in the scene as he exited his vehicle. Two security officers
stood at the entrance. It looked like they were checking the
ID of those coming and going.

Petrakis tucked in his shirt, adjusted his jacket, and then
made his way to the officers at the front doors.

"Who's in charge here?"

"Who's asking?"

"Inspector Petrakis." He pulled out his ID and flashed it
briefly.

The hotel security guys exchanged a glance. The name
Petrakis was well-known throughout Greece.

One of the officers raised a finger for him to wait, then

turned away and scanned the few people outside the hotel lobby. After a moment of studying the crowd, he pointed at a man leaning against the brick wall.

"He's in charge."

"Who is he?" Petrakis asked, losing an ounce of patience.

"Officer Samaras, sir."

Petrakis spied the man smoking off to the side. He nodded at the officers, then stepped away and strode toward the *man in charge*.

To his credit, Officer Samaras must have recognized Petrakis because he extinguished his half-smoked cigarette underfoot, sighed, adjusted his shoulders, and started toward Petrakis.

"Good evening, Inspector. We appreciate you pausing your vacation to come here so quickly." He extended his hand.

Petrakis clasped the man's hand but lacked the grip he expected from another police officer.

He'd recently made huge mistakes on a case that had left a stain on his name. He'd misread evidence, charged the wrong suspect, and had another man take over the case. Inspector Kokkinos had flown to Rhodes and, within one day, worked through Petrakis's errors and righted several wrongs.

The embarrassment was monumental.

There was even talk of Petrakis being suspended. So, jumping on this case, if, in fact, there was a person of influence missing, he had the potential to help restore his reputation to its original shine and luster.

"I understand something may have happened to a guest staying at this hotel."

Samaras nodded. "A woman named Miss Roxanne Dupont has gone missing."

"How long now?"

"How long, sir?" Samaras had a dumb look on his face.

Petrakis held his tongue, keeping his nasty rebuke at bay. "How long has she been missing?"

"Over two hours, sir." He checked his watch. "Actually, closer to three now."

"And what makes her a missing person at this early juncture?"

Samaras filled him in on the art show, her exit stage left to go to her room and change, the art critic waiting for her, and the empty hotel room. When he was done filling Petrakis in, he stepped back and scanned the lingering crowd.

Petrakis cleared his throat. "Are you staying on for a bit to pitch in?"

Samaras nodded. "I've been ordered to help for the remainder of my twelve-hour shift and to stay longer if needed."

"Good, so the first thing you need to do is notify the Coast Guard and have them move a vessel to this area near the hotel's beach. Email them Miss Dupont's photo and as much information as you can regarding her personal appearance, as well as any details of her actions you're aware of. And tell them to call my cell phone for updates before the sun rises." He moved closer to the entrance. "I'll wait inside while you do that, then you can take me to her room."

Samaras got on the phone. Within five minutes of typing like a madman and conferring with the front desk, he moved back to Petrakis by the reception area.

"It's done. The coast guard is on it. They'll have a vessel

in the area within the hour."

Petrakis nodded at him. "Now, take me to her room."

"Villa," Samaras said. "At this resort, the guests' rooms are often called villas as some come with a jacuzzi tub, too."

Petrakis eyed him suspiciously, wondering why that distinction was so important. Villa or room, it was the same thing to him. What if he had said suite?

"This way," Samaras said after an awkward moment of staring at each other.

Petrakis followed Samaras away from the lobby. The cop took him around the outside of the hotel, avoiding the main areas.

Miss Dupont's room was the last in a row. It was next to a fence made of thick bushes that bordered the back of the hotel. The outside walls had soft, discreet lighting. This allowed guests to locate their villas at night, especially after an evening of drinking.

Petrakis climbed the few steps to Dupont's door before stopping in front of an officer guarding it. The officer nodded at Samaras, then without a word, he turned and unlocked the room with an entry card before stepping aside.

Samaras took the access card and placed it in the recess in the wall to power up the villa's electricity.

Petrakis moved past the threshold, took out a pair of disposable gloves, and surveyed the room as he slipped them on.

Everything appeared normal. At first glance, there was no sign of a struggle. The woman's things were in order, just as in any other villa. He moved to the side and entered the bathroom. After examining the wet clothes, he turned back to Samaras.

The officer shrugged. "She got wet during the show. That's why she left to come here. The hotel manager understood that she would come to her room to change and then return. When she didn't return, they became concerned."

"It looks like she changed here, then left." Petrakis studied the makeup set next to the sink. He looked closer at the surface and saw traces of powder.

"It would appear that Miss Dupont changed out of her wet clothes, put on some makeup, and then exited her room." He reasoned all this out loud for Samaras's benefit.

The man stared on with admiration. Petrakis understood cops like Samaras. Career cops are officers who never excelled beyond their position and just simply remained there for too many years. Cops without ambition.

Petrakis glanced behind the bathroom door, saw nothing, and then moved back into the main section of the villa. After a cursory examination of the bed and the bedsheets, he determined nothing was amiss.

He searched through her personal things, but a cell phone and wallet were not among them.

The patio door was closed and locked from the inside. He opened it and stepped out onto the patio to have a closer look at the table and two chairs, which seemed to be pulled close to one another.

That left three possibilities. One, the hotel staff had placed them this way. Two, Roxanne used both chairs interchangeably. Or three, she recently had a visitor. Either way, this examination of her room was getting him nowhere fast.

Petrakis slipped back inside the room, closed and locked the patio door, then turned to address Samaras, who had remained at the main door to the room.

"Are there security cameras in this hotel?"

Samaras offered him a confused, perplexed expression.

"You didn't think to ask?"

Samaras shook his head. "I don't know if they have them or not." He spoke in a low voice, sounding embarrassed by his lack of skills.

Petrakis stared at the cop, his face slack. "How about we go to the hotel manager's office?"

Samaras nodded and stepped away from the door. Once outside, the officer watching Miss Dupont's room retrieved the card from the electricity slot, pocketed it, and then closed and locked the door behind him.

They strode around the hotel the same way they had gone to her room, then used the main entrance to access the lobby.

Samaras led him toward the manager's office at the end of the receptionist counter.

The door was open, and the manager was behind his desk.

Once they were settled in the office, introductions were dealt with, then Samaras eased back to allow Petrakis to take point.

"Mr. Diakos," Petrakis started. "What can you tell me about the missing woman?"

"Miss Roxanne Dupont, a resident of Paris, France, has been at the hotel for ten days. The purpose of her trip was part vacation and part presentation of her artwork. She had sent her invitations electronically several months ago. People from around the world came to see her." He paused to collect several papers on his desk. "We gathered all the names of the guests at the art show, along with contact information."

"Were you able to vet the contact information?"

"Vet it?"

Petrakis nodded. "Confirm the accuracy of the phone numbers and addresses offered to you by seeing ID and contact information on cell phones." Petrakis shrugged. "You know, things like that."

Diakos's face went blank, a vapid expression masking his features.

"I see," Petrakis said before Diakos spoke. "I understand you're a hotel manager, not a police officer or detective. Tell me, who handled this information gathering?"

"Hotel security, sir."

Petrakis glanced over at Samaras. "And when did you arrive on site?"

"I'm not sure. I didn't check the time. An hour ago, maybe more."

Petrakis turned back in his seat to stare at the hotel manager.

"So, at this point, we have nothing. No real information. And almost everyone has gone home."

"But we have names and phone numbers," Diakos protested.

"Mr. Diakos, what you have is a list of names and phone numbers of everyone *not* involved in what happened here tonight."

"How can you be so sure?"

Petrakis was surprised to see Mr. Diakos's eyes narrow in suspicion.

"Because, Mr. Hotel Manager, if someone was involved in a crime and was stopped to offer up their name and phone number, I assure you they would give fake information on both counts, especially after this particular person noticed that no one was verifying the data."

Diakos and Samaras exchanged a glance.

"Without verification," Petrakis continued, "what you did was an exercise in futility."

"I apologize, Mr. Petrakis—" Diakos started but stopped when Petrakis raised his hand.

"Let's just locate Miss Dupont, then we can go on our way without apologies."

Diakos nodded, his complexion a shade of red. "Do you think we'll be able to find her?"

"Mr. Diakos, can you recall at any time during Miss Dupont's stay where you saw something that you felt was strange to you? Something that stood out as odd?"

Diakos appeared to think about it for a moment, then shook his head. "No, nothing. She seemed quite excited about the art presentation and slightly stressed about it at the same time. I understand she intended to start an art career and was quite hopeful regarding this presentation."

Petrakis leaned back in his chair and regarded the hotel manager, caressing his chin. What sort of relationship would a hotel manager have to have with a guest for him to know that guest's future goals?

"Tell me something, Mr. Diakos, how well did you know Miss Dupont?" Petrakis kept his voice steady.

Diakos took a deep breath. "As much as any hotel manager would know one of their guests. Why?"

The manager's eyes skirted to the left to take in a photo of his wife on the desk.

"Mr. Diakos, your ethics or morals are not on trial here. You should feel free to become friends with whomever you choose."

Diakos blinked several times, adjusted his shirt, and nodded quickly.

Petrakis continued, "What I'm looking for is whether you knew her well enough that she might have entrusted you with certain things from her past. Little stories or something that may have to do with her disappearance this evening. Did she mention she knew another guest? That they arranged to meet? Anything of the sort could be helpful."

"Now that you mention it, she told me she was in an accident several years ago. Something about icy roads, a few cars involved, and her vehicle ended up in a ditch. She was trapped for several hours but alive. Her fiancé died at the scene, in the car, right beside her. I understand it was a terrible thing to experience. It took her months to restore the function of one of her legs. Do you think that could have anything to do with what happened here tonight?"

"We'll have to wait and see. I will need a list of all the hotel staff who worked this evening's shift and those who had come in close contact with her during her ten-day stay."

"That can be arranged."

They all stood, and Petrakis started toward the door but stopped in the middle of the large office. "Tell me something else, Mr. Diakos."

"Anything," Diakos said.

"The tables and chairs in each of the villas. Are they placed in specific areas on purpose? Or is it random?"

Diakos stared at him with that vapid look on his face again. "There is a specific way to set up each room, but I'm unsure of the exact methodology. Eleni Kouris, the head of housekeeping here, will be on her shift in the morning. She'd know better."

Petrakis made a note to search her out. "I understand you were the one who entered her room, Mr. Diakos, when you were searching for Miss Dupont. Is that correct?"

Diakos nodded.

"Who accompanied you to her room?"

"My head of security, Mr. Kallonis."

"Can you call him to your office? I'd like to have a word with him."

Diakos grabbed his phone. After speaking in whispers to someone on the other end of the line, he set it down gently and glanced up at Petrakis.

"I'm sorry, sir, but it seems no one can locate Mr. Kallonis. It appears he may have left the premises."

"He may have left the premises?" Petrakis lowered his gaze momentarily, then looked back up at Diakos. "Without your knowledge during such a situation? And this is your head of security?"

"He can't just leave." Diakos appeared flustered, color rising to his cheeks. "Of course, he'll be here somewhere. We'll locate him."

Petrakis frowned. "Mr. Diakos, let's not bullshit one another. You claim to have a missing guest, and after your head of security helps you inspect her room, he leaves the premises." Petrakis pushed back his shoulders. "Find him immediately before this falls apart at the expense of your hotel's reputation." Half of any patience Petrakis might have owned prior to entering the hotel's lobby was now gone. He wasn't about to be trifled with as if this was a joke. And if it were a joke, he'd rather be back in his own hotel room sleeping.

Samaras lowered his gaze and exited the manager's office in front of Petrakis.

Outside by the lobby doors again, Petrakis's cell phone rang.

"Inspector Petrakis."

"This is Nikos Regas with the Coast Guard. We've made it to the area of the sea you requested, but there has been no sign of a body in the water as of yet. We will continue to search with floodlights for several hours."

"Thank you. We appreciate your help."

He ended the call and then pocketed his phone. A boat would be the fastest way to leave the area, offering a dramatic end to her art presentation. Although, if no one knew about her boat exit, that wouldn't make sense.

Could this all just be part of her show? Especially since she had taken her cell phone and wallet with her.

If so, he would want to press charges. Something to teach people not to fuck around with law enforcement.

This sort of dalliance used up public resources and the police department's time, and Inspector Petrakis wouldn't stand for it.

Chapter 6

Darwin Kostas landed at the Rhodes International Airport wearing a disguise. He took a taxi to his hotel to wait for the rest of his team. Flying from Italy, he avoided heavy scrutiny at border control. This allowed him to stay under the radar as the ID he traveled with was less than foolproof as he commissioned it at the last minute.

Once he got settled in at the hotel—the rendezvous point for the team, not the hotel they were headed to—he messaged his man at the Lindos Palace Resort Hotel but did not get a reply.

Miller's lack of response worried him.

Darwin checked the time. He'd spoken to Miller earlier that afternoon when Miller was watching Dupont's room. What could've happened in such a short time?

At the hotel window, he watched planes take off from the airport as he dialed his wife on a secure line.

"Darwin?" Rosina answered. "You arrived safe?"

"I'm fine and checked into the rendezvous point, but I'm worried about our contact on the ground."

"One second, I'll bring him up on the screen."

Even though Darwin had a Greek last name, he couldn't speak the language other than the usual few pleasantries. But in his experience, most Greeks spoke great to passable English—especially in tourist spots. Rosina's heritage was Italian, and the funny thing was, they'd met in Toronto, Canada, many years ago.

Rosina cleared her throat. "Our contact's cell phone went dead about four hours ago. No signal since."

"Got a bead on his last location?"

"Just east of the hotel in question. If I'm triangulating it properly, it appears to be on a rocky outcropping."

"Nothing since? From any of his devices?"

"Give me a moment. I'll check everything we have on him."

Darwin detected a tinge of worry in her voice, and he commiserated silently by closing his eyes, hoping she would come back with something positive.

"I have nothing." She paused. "Absolutely nothing on him. No pings anywhere for four hours."

Darwin clenched his fist. He should've come sooner—or sent men to back up Miller sooner. He sat in the chair by the window and closed his eyes to think.

"That can't be good," Rosina added.

"I've got a dozen men meeting me here."

"Do not leave the rendezvous point without them."

Darwin opened his eyes. How did she do that? How did she read his mind and the idea that he'd head out now?

He wanted to go to the Lindos Palace Resort early, check-in, and act like a tourist. It wouldn't raise any alarms, but she was right. The plan was to wait for his men, then advance in pairs to two hotels in the area. These men were specifically waiting for their instructions from him, and without him, there was no job.

"I won't move until everyone arrives, honey."

"You promise?"

"I do."

"If something's happened to our contact, going now or going in two hours as a unit won't make a difference. What's done is done, and I know it sucks, but it is what it is. Just get there and make things right."

"I will, and I'll message to confirm we've vacated this place once the team arrives."

"I'm in the control room and won't move from here. Reach out when you need something, and I'll continue to monitor our contacts' devices in case one of them comes online."

"Make sure I know the second that happens."

"Absolutely."

He killed the call.

Was Brian Miller dead? Did the Russians get to him? The Greek police? Or was it Roxanne Dupont?

Darwin refused to believe Miller was the victim of some random event or an accident. The man was ex-military, honorably discharged, and one of the toughest men he'd hired for jobs in Europe over the past year. Some of his colleagues were arriving soon and would be disturbed if something happened to Miller.

There was no point in dwelling on it. They'd find out

soon enough.

He pushed up out of the chair and grabbed his suitcase.

While waiting for the others to fly in, he would review what caused the French government to pull their agent out of the field. Instead of calling her back in, they wanted Roxanne Dupont in custody. Whatever business brought her to Greece bothered the French. They had called Athens and put in an arrest request. That call came through to Rhodes and was being drawn up—if they could locate her, that is. Some inspector in Athens was being removed from active duty to fly to Rhodes tomorrow to escort Miss Roxanne Dupont back to France—but she wasn't aware of that yet.

And Darwin and his team couldn't let that happen.

Not with the information she had on her person.

The French did not want what she was selling to get into the hands of a buyer, namely the Russians. And Darwin couldn't allow any sort of sale to take place because what Roxanne was carrying would see him and his wife on the run, or worse—killed within a week.

But how did the French learn about it?

Darwin scratched his head. As far as he understood, only Roxanne and her boyfriend knew what they possessed. Once he dealt with Dupont at the hotel, he had to visit her boyfriend, and then this would end.

Although, for the Russians to be interested, they would have to know what the information was. Which meant Roxanne had reviewed it. This also meant Roxanne knew who Darwin was and why he couldn't allow that particular information to get into the wrong hands.

This led him to conclude that Brian Miller was an asset that may have been terminated.

He checked the time.

They'd learn more in a few hours as the rendezvous time approached.

If Miller had been removed, that would force Darwin's hand.

He'd have to kill a few of theirs to make amends and then the rest of them to make sure whatever Roxanne was selling didn't see the light of day.

And that led him down a scary road.

Having seen what she was trying to sell, Roxanne Dupont would have to be taken out as well. Knowing how sensitive that information was, she couldn't survive this ordeal, or Darwin's life was forfeit, and he'd worked too hard to stay off the grid.

It was the life of a mercenary, sure. But when the time came, could he kill a woman whose only transgression was selling sensitive data for a large payout?

A moral dilemma he'd face when the time came.

But if he did kill Miss Dupont, could he ever face Sarah Roberts again? Look her in the eye, tell her what he did. Sarah lived by a code, and killing a woman in such a way could be construed as going against that code. He'd worked with Sarah for many, many years and looked forward to seeing her and Parkman and the rest of them again soon.

But first, he had to deal with Dupont.

There had to be another way out, but he just couldn't see it.

Not yet, anyway.

Chapter 7

Inspector Petrakis got comfortable behind the hotel manager's desk. He'd spent the last hour scoping out the hotel, walking the grounds and the beach, and finding nothing out of the ordinary.

Now, coffee in hand, he surveyed his surroundings. To conduct several interviews, Mr. Diakos was kind enough to give him his office. Although, if he didn't have this missing woman to find, he would go for a swim and then take a nap as he didn't get enough sleep last night—meaning none at all.

Someone knocked on the door as he lifted his coffee to take a sip.

"Come in," he called.

One of the hotel's waiters stepped in, a sheepish look on his face. He moved closer, his hands thrust into his pocket.

Petrakis glanced down at his pad of paper. "Name?"

"Stelios Marinis."

Petrakis wrote the name down. "What is your role here at the Lindos Palace Resort?"

"I work in the kitchen and often perform room service duties for our guests."

Petrakis nodded. He asked several more questions regarding the man's age and address, then moved on to what he needed to know.

"What can you tell me about our missing woman, Miss Roxanne Dupont?"

Stelios shrugged. "I was called to deliver a meal to her two nights ago. When I took Miss Dupont's order to her room, no one answered immediately. I knocked several times and called out *room service*. Then I opened the door a crack with my master keycard."

Stelios stopped talking and stared down at Petrakis. After a moment, Petrakis gestured for him to keep going.

"The room was empty, so I left the tray just inside the door. I notified reception of what I had done and that the food was delivered, then I returned to work."

Petrakis made a few notes, then glanced back up at Stelios.

"Did you ever meet Miss Dupont personally?"

"Yes. There was another time when she'd placed an order."

Petrakis leaned on the desk with his elbows. "Do you remember when exactly? I'd need the day and time. Would you be able to recall what she ordered?"

Stelios glanced up at the side and tapped his chin. "It was five days ago, I think. She had ordered enough food for two people and asked for two sets of utensils. It was two main dishes, two salads, two desserts, and a bottle of wine. It was late, and our kitchen closed at eleven. She'd called right at eleven, too, that's why I remember it. The cook was upset. Anyway, I climbed the stairs, knocked on her door, and she opened it for me that time. I placed the tray with the trolley next to the small pool, said goodnight to her, and left."

"You said it was an order for two people. Did you see the second person?"

Stelios shook his head. "Her guest must've been in the bathroom."

"Male?"

"I would assume so, based on what I saw."

"What did you see?"

"A dark jacket was folded on the bed. It was definitely a man's jacket."

"Did you hear anyone talking? Any voices?"

Stelios shook his head. "No, I wasn't really paying that much attention. It was the last order of the day, and I just wanted to go home."

"Can you remember anything else that might stand out?"

Stelios glanced off to the side again, then looked back at Petrakis. "Not at the moment. Can I leave now?"

Petrakis studied the waiter for several seconds. The guy seemed frazzled to be a part of something like this—a criminal investigation.

Petrakis nodded at him. "You're free to go. Thank you for your help." He stood to walk him to the door. "If you think of anything else, no matter how small, contact me. A woman's life may hang in the balance."

Stelios muttered something, nodding to him. "I will," he whispered.

"I may be in touch again before this is over. Stick around

town." He always wanted to say shit like that.

When Petrakis opened the door, other hotel staff were outside waiting to be interviewed. They all looked tired, and he could tell that most of them wanted to be anywhere else but here.

"I'm looking for Ereni Stamou," the inspector said, a name Diakos gave him from the staff list.

All eyes fell on a girl with brown hair caught in a bun. She got up, adjusted her skirt, and entered the office while Petrakis held the door. She sat in the chair and waited for the inspector to sit, her foot tapping nervously on the carpet.

"Mrs. Ereni Stamou, right?"

"Correct," she replied, her tone clipped. She didn't want to be here, and it showed.

"When was the last time you saw Miss Dupont?"

"I don't remember. I must have seen her recently, but not today or yesterday."

"Did you see anything in the previous days that seemed odd, out of place?"

"Everything is odd as far as Miss Dupont is concerned. From the moment she arrived, the entire hotel dealt with her as if there were no other guests. We have important people who come every year, and we all want to satisfy them. Miss Dupont is no different."

"Your tone—do I detect some dissatisfaction with her?"

Ereni adjusted herself, sitting up straighter. "Not really," she said, a short, clipped laugh escaping her lips. "Just, I don't think anything's *happened* to her. She probably wanted the most attention she could get after her art show, and she has now accomplished that."

"You speak of her as if you know her well."

"I don't know the woman." Ereni shook her head. "It's just, I've heard things."

"What have you heard?"

"I know for a fact that she fought with the man who was looking for her."

"Who might that be?"

"That art critic guy, Mr. Whimsical."

"Cute." Petrakis leaned back, tapping his pen against his lips. "Were you able to watch the entire argument? Did it get physical?"

She shook her head. "Not me. I just do my job. I stay in the shadows. Out of sight, out of trouble."

"Probably a good strategy. So, did you see the argument?"

"Our van driver, the guy that transfers people to and from the airport, saw something. He recognized her at the airport when he was picking up other guests. She was meeting someone there herself. After Miss Dupont greeted the man with an embrace, they started fighting. Our driver's English isn't the best, so he couldn't understand everything. The man shouted at her. Something about how she would ruin his career and that she only cared about herself. She tried to calm him down, but then he stomped off angry. That's all I know."

"Did the driver tell you all that?"

"No, the porter did. The driver had told him the story."

"What are their names?" Petrakis picked up the employee list.

"The driver is Loukas Prasinos, and the porter is Makis Baros."

"Do you remember anything else you think might be useful to us?"

"I'm not sure what would be useful or not. I mean, I haven't *seen* anything suspicious. I only overheard a story about a heated argument at the airport." She adjusted herself in the seat again. "Can I go home, please?"

"Yes, Mrs. Stamou." He nodded for her to leave.

She got up and left without saying goodbye.

Petrakis didn't call anyone else. He needed to collect his thoughts. There wasn't much information to go on. Two nights ago, Dupont had a guest in her room. She fought with the art critic Nikolas Kovak and probably had other guests in her villa during her stay.

There was a slight possibility Dupont had a special *bond* with the hotel manager, a married man. When he'd asked Diakos how well he knew her, the man had glanced at the picture of his wife, which spoke volumes to Petrakis.

He'd never met the woman, but it looked like Miss Dupont was the type who enjoyed attention, so she could've just left the building. As a result, look at all the attention she was getting.

Or she was abducted. Perhaps she was dead.

Something told him this case wouldn't be as easy as he thought it would be.

Chapter 8

Faye Olympiou smacked open the door of her room in frustration. Nothing was going as planned. Booking a room next door to Roxanne Dupont's villa had worked out well, but she still wanted to get to know and meet her. They were the same age but didn't have the same lust for life.

She liked how Miss Dupont presented her exhibits and how she put her heart and soul into each piece of work she created.

Faye wished she could show her paintings, her *works of art*, as her father called them, which seemed so unskilled and empty compared to Roxanne's art.

Faye had accidentally discovered Roxanne Dupont online while looking for ideas to draw. Then she investigated further and followed her on all social media.

Approaching Miss Roxanne Dupont was something else altogether. She wouldn't know what to say to her. She'd be extremely anxious, wondering if Roxanne would respond politely. After all, Faye wasn't an important person like Miss Roxanne Dupont.

And now, the one time she actually got to speak to the one and only Miss Dupont to congratulate her like a normal person—without shame for her own self-worth—everything went wrong.

She couldn't grasp it, couldn't deal with what happened.

Was she cursed? Why did Dupont have to be so rude?

How come as soon as she wanted something, the universe conspired against her?

She said nothing to the police. Why would she?

This made her shudder, frustrating her further.

Her room was bordered on one side by Roxanne Dupont's and on the other side by one that was empty all day. At night, she'd often hear voices from Dupont's room, but it had been quiet today. However, someone was angry last night —like the artist was arguing with a man.

Faye was always quiet, keeping to the shadows. As the black sheep of the family, no one took her seriously. She'd become an expert in staying out of the way.

Although, many times, she felt like someone was watching her or that they could hear her thoughts. Other times, she woke from deep sleep because she thought someone was touching her, yet no one was in her room.

Her fear wasn't rational. It defeated logic.

She could try to sleep, but with so much anxiety, so much bothering her, there was no way she could go back under.

She changed into something more casual. Then she grabbed her cell phone and room key and returned to the art presentation room.

The authorities now seemed to be in all areas of the hotel. They held flashlights, peeked into dark corners, and circled the perimeter, guarding ingress and egress points. The lights of a ship resembling a Coast Guard vessel sat just offshore.

Two uniformed officers strode along the beach by the water, each wielding a flashlight. She didn't want to talk to them. They would ask her things she wouldn't want to answer. If attentive enough, they may deduce she was hiding something when, in fact, her only issue was being socially awkward.

After a short contemplation, Faye moved in the opposite direction and sat on a deck chair. She retrieved her cell phone from her pocket to look at some of the pictures she'd taken. Roxanne's work was amazing.

After several minutes of poring over last night's photos, Faye got up, took off her shoes, and left the phone on the bench.

She wanted to get her feet wet. The water made her feel at peace, as if it cleared her soul from all her fears.

Shoes in hand, she took several steps into the sea.

Did Roxanne do the same?

Did she enter the sea to get lost in some form of non-existence? Perhaps Faye should try that. At least the pain would cease. There would be nothing to scare her anymore.

The officers scouring the beach hadn't seen her. She was sure of it. Going in deeper and deeper, her pants got wet, and her room card, too.

She moved farther into the water until her neck was wet, then continued to her chin.

It seemed liberating, a sweet end to a life that caused her

pain.

Her head went under, and she kept walking.

Chapter 9

ONE OF THE POLICEMEN searching the beach had seen the fully dressed woman approaching the water. It seemed strange that she was going in without removing any of her clothes, but who was he to judge? When the woman was neck deep in the water and still moving out to sea, he shook his colleague's shoulder and pointed at her.

They ran to the water's edge when the woman disappeared from view.

After calling out twice, he jumped in to swim out to her.

When he caught up to her, the woman hadn't gone too deep yet, but she was already unconscious. He grabbed one of her arms, his feet barely touching the sandy bottom, and dragged her to shore.

Once on the sand, he immediately checked the woman's pulse, then lifted her chin. He opened her mouth and tilted her head to open an airway, then pinched her nose and blew into her mouth. The woman gagged and sputtered sea water from her lungs as the policeman turned her on her side.

"What's wrong with you?" he shouted, water dripping into his face from his own hair. "What were you thinking?" He lay down on the sand beside her, shivering now in his soaked uniform.

The woman coughed and tried to breathe on her own, and with each passing moment, she sounded better.

"Wait for us to call an ambulance."

"No," she choked out. "Don't." She stretched out her hand. "I'm fine. I thought—I thought I saw someone floating out there. I thought it might be the man you were looking for."

The policemen exchanged a glance.

"Did you really see something?"

"I don't know. I had a cramp, and then I went under." She cleared her throat.

The policeman, who was still dry, lifted his radio. He asked for a boat to come closer to shore to search the beach area. He told them that someone may have seen something, his eyes on the woman.

"Shit, my room card must've fallen out when I entered the water."

"Can you stand up?" the cop asked.

He wasn't sure he was doing the right thing by not calling an ambulance. He gave her his hand, and the woman got up without much difficulty.

"Thank you," she whispered. "I'm sorry if I startled you."

"Don't thank me, just be careful. You did scare me." He watched her face for a moment. "Are you sure you don't want to see a doctor?"

The woman nodded and turned away, starting up the sand toward a deck chair she had sat on earlier.

The policeman followed her for a bit, then stopped when his flashlight glinted off something shining in the sand. A mirror was partly submerged in the sand. He snatched it up and held it up for her to look at.

"Is this yours?" he called.

The woman turned back, squinted, and frowned, then started back to him.

The mirror had a bronze backing and a long handle. It looked like something crafted by a talented hand.

"Yes, it's mine," the woman muttered. "Thank you for finding it. I guess it had fallen out of my pocket earlier." Then, as if she thought of something else to say, she added. "It belonged to my grandmother." She took it from him. "Can I ask you a favor?"

"Of course."

"Because I lost my room keycard thing, can you ask for it at the reception? I don't want everyone to know what happened here."

"I understand. What's your name?"

"Faye Olympiou."

Walking slowly, they left the beach together. Behind them, a boat approached. The officer glanced back and saw it was the coast guard.

Not ten minutes later, he bid Faye farewell at her room door, having never told her that it was a woman they were looking for and not a man.

Some people had enough problems to deal with than involving them in a police investigation.

Chapter 10

"THIS NIGHT WILL NEVER end," Petrakis mumbled to himself. "And where is that Kallonis guy?" He picked up the phone to call Officer Samaras.

"Did you find the hotel's head of security yet?" he asked when the phone was answered by Samaras's voicemail, leaving a message. "And let me know if you find anything on the beach." He slammed the phone down.

He got up from his desk and went to the door. By the time he grabbed the knob, he had already forgotten the names of those he wanted to see next.

"I want to talk to the airport shuttle van driver," he said to the waiting crowd outside the office door.

A young man pushed off the wall and approached.

"Come on in." Petrakis motioned for him to enter, then went to Diakos's desk and glanced down at his papers for his name. "Tell me, Mr. Prasinos, when was the last time you saw the woman we're looking for?"

"Today, around noon, when I went to pick up other guests for the hotel."

"Where did you see her?"

"At the airport."

"Do you know what she was doing there?"

"As far as I could tell, she was there to pick up an acquaintance."

"I understand there was an incident." Petrakis's patience was thinning. If the van driver could just talk freely, it would save time.

"Everything seemed fine between the two of them, but then the man said something to her that triggered her. She got quite angry and rebuked him publicly."

"How could you tell she was angry? Were you able to overhear the words she used?"

Prasinos shook his head. "It was the look on her face. That man told her something that bothered her deeply."

"Can you tell me anything you may have overheard?"

"They spoke English, but I don't understand enough to know what they said. I only know some of the basics, like hello, good morning, good night, and you're welcome."

"Try to remember—it's important—is there anything you may have heard that'll help? Anything at all? Take your time."

The van driver stared back at him, saying nothing. After a moment, he shook his head. "It was a disagreement." Prasinos shrugged. "Nothing more, nothing less."

"This man could be a suspect. Give me an idea of their conversation. Were they just loud, or were they swearing at each other? What could you perceive from their fight?"

"I interpreted it as if he was telling her how she was hurting him, destroying him, that she only cared about herself. Something like that."

"How did she react to this?"

"At first, she laughed as if what he said had been funny, which appeared to irritate him even more. I saw him clench his fists, which made me wonder if I'd have to break up a fight. In fact, I was ready to intervene. I can't allow a man to hit a woman in front of me—especially a guest of the hotel I work for." Prasinos swiped a hand through his hair. "I took a few steps toward them, but Miss Dupont turned and walked away. The man followed her, and that was it."

"Would you say their misunderstanding was resolved?"

"I have no way of knowing that, but the guy seemed to be placating her until they were out of my sight."

Petrakis asked more questions like what the guy looked like, which direction he left in, whether he was carrying luggage, and so on.

After a few moments, he asked, "How often did you see her during her stay at the hotel?"

"Just once, the first day I transported her here. After that, I understand she rented a car."

"And you were able to remember Miss Dupont ten, eleven days later? That's impressive."

"I'm sorry, Officer, but have you seen Miss Dupont?"

"Meaning?" Petrakis ignored the contempt in the driver's tone—for now. But he noted it. Also, the use of *officer* rankled him, but he let that go as well.

"She's a stunning woman and a popular artist. A VIP guest here, sir. Although, my job doesn't revolve around the guests while they're staying here. Only when they're going to and from the airport. I don't often contact them during their stay here."

"Inspector." He decided to correct the driver. "Not officer. Now, you can go. Call in the porter on your way out the door."

The driver got up and left. Before the door closed, Petrakis overheard the driver say, "Hey, asshole, he wants to talk to you now."

The porter, seemingly agitated as if he'd done something wrong, entered the hotel manager's office, and Petrakis pointed at the chair.

Once the niceties were done and the porter had stated his name for the record, Petrakis got to it.

"Tell me, Mr. Baros, when did you last see Miss Dupont?"

"I saw her today when she arrived at the hotel around noon."

"Can you tell me about her demeanor? How was she?"

"She seemed relatively cheerful."

"Aren't you aware she had an argument at the airport?"

The man met his gaze without wavering for several moments, then nodded. "Yes, Prasinos told me. She fought with some guy at the airport but then seemed to calm down."

"What can you tell me about that fight?"

"Just what Prasinos told me. That the guy was angry with her. Apparently, he said she was destroying him."

"You seemed to want to get involved because you went on to talk to Mrs. Stamou about it. Why's that?"

"Because when the taxi brought the guy for Miss Dupont's presentation, he got out of the taxi before it even stopped completely. I ran to help, you know, to open the door for him, but he was distraught. He swore at the taxi driver and me. He stated his name at the reception, and based on what Prasinos told me, I understood he was the same guy. So, I told Ereni to pay attention to him. By that, I meant for her to steer clear."

"Have you ever seen this man before today?"

"No, never."

Petrakis set his pen down. "You're free to go, but I may be in touch."

The inspector watched him go, the door closing gently behind him.

The art critic, Nikolas Kovak, had to be involved somehow. And if not, he at least wanted to know what he fought about with Miss Dupont at the airport. What could Miss Dupont be doing that was ruining his life?

He grabbed the phone and called Samaras once more. When voicemail picked up again, he left him a message.

"Contact the hotel where Nikolas Kovak is staying and let me know how long he has the room. I need to speak with this art critic."

Petrakis sat back in his seat, a weariness overcoming him. He wasn't getting anywhere by sitting and talking with hotel staff. He was no closer to discovering what happened to Miss Dupont, and the trail was getting colder by the minute.

He picked up the phone again and called the front desk to order a double espresso. If Samaras ever found him, he still had to talk to at least three waiters, the maître d' and Kallonis. He took out his notes, got up again, and went to the door.

"The maître d'?" A man of medium height wearing a suit approached him. The inspector stepped aside.

"I don't think you're organized enough," the man said as he stepped past Petrakis. "If it were me, I wouldn't let anyone go. Everyone would stay inside until we learned what happened to Miss Dupont."

Petrakis was in no mood for a masterclass on how to do his job, especially from a maître d'.

"Mr. Tolis?"

"Yes."

"Mr. Tolis, how about I ask the questions, and you allow me to do my job as I see fit?" He glared at the man, his patience all but gone now. "When triggered, I don't usually have a lot of understanding for the position of others." His upper lip rose in a sneer. "My tolerance for shit is about zero. So please refrain from telling me how to do my job, and I won't school you on yours. Now, tell me when you last saw Miss Dupont."

The maître d' lowered his gaze for a moment, then looked him in the eye, properly chastised.

"It was when the show ended, and she told everyone she would change."

"How about during the other days when she was here? Did you notice anything strange? Did she come into the restaurant at all?"

"In the first few days, she came in, ordered, and left a generous tip, but then one of our other customers got annoyed. That's probably why she stopped coming." He glanced at his watch like he wanted to leave.

"Who was this other customer, and how could they get annoyed by Dupont placing an order and leaving a tip?" Petrakis rested his hands on the desk.

"A Russian man. When he saw her, he sent alcohol to her

table. I don't remember the number of his room. The first time, he even sat at her table. He wouldn't leave her alone."

"Could you tell if Miss Dupont knew him, or was this their first meeting?"

Tolis lifted one shoulder. "I have no idea."

"Did Miss Dupont seem bothered?"

"She was uncomfortable with the attention. She'd crossed her arms and wasn't smiling much."

"Was this Russian man at today's presentation?"

"Yes, he was. I saw him."

"When was the guest list for the art show distributed?" Petrakis leaned forward, wanting a copy of that guest list for himself.

"Today at noon. I needed to know how many would come and when. Miss Dupont and the hotel manager arranged the names on the list."

"Do you know who Mr. Kovak is?"

"Yes, Miss Dupont had informed us earlier that he was a VIP guest, and we had to pay special attention to him."

"How would you rate his behavior?"

"Sour," he replied.

Petrakis signaled him to continue, irritated with the one-word answer.

"As soon as the art critic entered, I located him and waved to a waiter to serve him. I eyed the man the entire time. He seemed to enjoy the presentation, and when it was over, Miss Dupont exited the building. He was angry, so he went outside for a smoke."

This admission aroused the inspector's interest. He leaned back and crossed his arms, not for the first time wondering where his espresso was.

"Did you see him smoke?"

Tolis seemed puzzled and scratched his head nervously. "Now that you mention it, I didn't see it with my own eyes."

"What made you guess he was smoking?"

"He was fishing in his pockets for something when he left. Since smoking is prohibited indoors and others went out to the specially designated area for the same reason, I thought he went out to smoke."

"How much time was he absent?"

"Five, ten minutes? I can't be sure. I was working, helping with the buffet, so my mind was elsewhere."

"Was the Russian there the whole time?"

"Yes, he was there." Tolis nodded.

"Did you see him talking to her?"

"She didn't talk to anyone. She just left at the end."

Petrakis leaned forward, placing his elbows on the desk. "If you remember anything else, let me know. You're free to go."

Tolis got up, straightened his chair, then walked out.

Petrakis called the waiters individually to get a statement confirming Tolis's comments on the Russian man.

If, at the end of Dupont's art show, many guests went out to smoke, then anyone could have the opportunity to harm her, assuming something bad did happen.

But so far, there was no corpse or phone call for money.

At this point, he had nothing.

He called Samaras again to see if the cop had any news but got his voicemail once more.

With no coffee delivered, he couldn't do a good job if he didn't have a clear mind, so he went to the front desk to see if a room was available for a few hours. Apparently, they had a bed in one of the staff rooms. He'd have to nap there as the hotel was full—except Dupont's room was vacant, but he couldn't sleep there.

The staff rooms were located near the offices, away from the guests, in a building at the edge of the property. He walked downhill to the villas just before the beach, where there was a road on his right-hand side. This road led to the staff rooms about fifty meters away.

The building looked older than the hotel. He entered through the main entrance, turned on the lights, and went up a set of stairs. Although it was only one floor, his feet felt heavy. Too much fatigue and tension for one day.

The room they assigned him was the last in a row. Holding a traditional skeleton key, he put it in the lock only to see the door open.

He entered slowly, only touching the wall.

He didn't expect to see what sat before him when he turned on the light inside the room.

Chapter 11

A BODY WAS LYING on the floor by the open patio door.

Petrakis identified himself, loud and clear, then took a slow step inside the room and ripped open the bathroom door—it was empty.

He jumped out of the bathroom and approached the terrace. Once he figured he was alone with the body, he kneeled by the man. Someone had struck him on the head. Petrakis checked for a pulse under the jaw but felt nothing—not even a slow heartbeat.

"What the hell is going on at the Lindos Palace Resort Hotel?" he muttered to himself.

He felt a square bulge on the man's inside jacket pocket. Petrakis eased out the wallet and flipped it open to the driver's license.

Mr. Christos Kallonis is head of security for Lindos Hotel. No wonder he couldn't get ahold of the man earlier.

He got to his feet and stepped back outside, retrieving his phone from his pocket. He called Samaras, who answered on the first ring this time.

Before Samaras could talk, Petrakis spouted, "I'm out at the staff rooms. There's been a murder here."

Samaras gasped. "What? A murder? Wait, you found Dupont?"

"No, it's the man in charge of the security for the hotel, Christos Kallonis. Inform the coroner. Call in a team. I want to lock down this entire area. If I could, I'd shut down the island, but we'll start with the hotel."

He hung up and rubbed his face. It didn't look like he'd be getting that nap.

He could sure use that coffee now.

Things had definitely ramped up a notch, and he had no idea what was going on, no idea at all.

Chapter 12

Faye woke, terrified and shaking. She flicked on the light beside the bed and took in her surroundings.

Exhaustion moored her to the bed, but she pushed herself into a sitting position, then stood and headed to the bathroom to splash water on her face. Something had happened earlier, but she couldn't remember what. She'd been losing her mind or her memory recently. It wasn't her fault. She couldn't be blamed for what she couldn't remember.

A handheld mirror lay on the counter in the bathroom, next to the sink. She lifted it to her face and felt its weight, examining it closely. The handle was thick and appeared to be hand-carved. On the back of the mirror, a three-dimensional representation of a woman had been rendered artistically. Under the form of the woman was one word: Hecate.

Hecate was the ancient goddess of magic and ghosts,

among a host of other things.

Then she recalled where she got the mirror. The cop on the beach had handed it to her. It had been Roxanne Dupont's mirror. She was sure of it.

When Faye turned it back around to examine herself in the mirror, she detected something. Agitated, her breathing stopped for a moment. She flipped the mirror upside down and set it on the sink.

Her pulse rang in her ears. She summoned the courage to hold the mirror up and dared herself to stare into the glass again.

"Did you just see that?" she asked herself before setting it back down.

There had been a shadow inside the viewing area of the mirror. Unless she was just seeing things, something was there. She forced herself to look back at it. When she did, the shadow took shape and formed the image of a corpse—a blonde girl in a red dress floating face down on the water.

Faye tried to avert her gaze, but then the mirror changed back to a regular mirror again.

Hands trembling, she set it down and looked away.

That dead woman—she knew who it was, but she couldn't do anything about it now. The dead had to remain dead. The last thing she wanted was to focus on dead people. It is much better to focus on the living.

She exited the bathroom, leaving the mirror behind, and moved to sit on the bed. There was no way she would be able to sleep again with the emotional state she was in now. In the past, she'd take a sedative, but she didn't have any with her.

"No more pharmaceuticals," she whispered out loud to feel like someone was giving her an order.

She rose again and stepped onto the terrace to get some fresh air. Once outside, she strode to the edge of the patio. People were scampering around in the distance.

"What the hell is going on over there now?"

She ran back in, changed her clothes, glanced at the overturned mirror on the bathroom counter, then went back outside.

Moving fast, she strode to where the people had gathered. Two police cars and an ambulance were parked on the side. People were gathered around the area, some crying, some staring blankly.

When she moved among them, Faye overheard that someone had been killed.

She stood on her tippy toes to see over people's heads.

A policeman wandering by bumped into her tripped, stumbled, and then caught himself. She frowned and gave him a disparaging look.

"Are you okay?" he asked. "Didn't you get any rest?"

She gawked at him, puzzled. Why was he asking about her state of rest?

"When someone's saved from drowning, they usually don't wander around outside. They go to bed and rest."

The cop stared at her in wonder. The policeman opened his mouth to talk again, but another cop signaled him. He shook his head and stepped away just as a car pulled up and stopped abruptly. The door opened, and a woman jumped out.

"My Christos, oh my Christos," she wailed as if in a state of delirium.

The woman ran to the ambulance as the paramedics were placing a stretcher in the back.

Someone raised a hand to halt them, then gestured for the woman to advance.

One of the paramedics lifted the sheet to reveal the corpse's head. When the woman's eyes focused on the face on the stretcher, she stumbled, then dropped to the concrete and bumped her head.

They released the stretcher and hurried to help the woman to her feet while the officers grabbed her arms.

Faye watched the inspector work and figured she should get to know him better.

After treating the fallen woman, the paramedics pushed the stretcher into the back of their ambulance, closed the doors, got inside, and then left the scene.

Faye observed everything from the side, watching and waiting for Petrakis to move her way. When he didn't, and growing weary of waiting, she returned to her room. She'd find him later. For now, the inspector could wait.

She walked around the hotel, staying in the well-lit areas. Normally, a woman walking alone with bodies piling up around a hotel would cause her to be frightened, but Faye felt nothing now—absolutely nothing.

Lost in her thoughts, she stumbled over something close to the path and almost fell over.

"What the—"

She turned back to see what had tripped her and gasped at the sight of a human leg protruding from the bush. Obviously, someone was too drunk to return to their room.

"Hey," she said, nudging the leg. "Wake up. Sleep it off in your own room."

Hesitantly, she pushed aside the bushes for a better look.

A rat jumped off the body and scurried deeper into the

bush.

Faye screamed before she could rein it back in. Dizziness overcame her as she got to her feet too fast.

After a moment, when no one came running along the path in answer to her scream, she moved away from the body and walked quickly to her villa.

Whatever happened to that person, man or woman, someone else could report it. This was getting ridiculous. What the hell was happening at the Lindos Palace Resort Hotel?

She got to her room and dropped onto her bed, wrapping herself in the covers. She curled into a ball to calm down, and out of the corner of her eye, she spied the mirror through the open bathroom door.

Even though she was afraid to hold it in her hands as she didn't want to see that blonde woman in the red dress, she grabbed it and kept the mirror's glass turned away from her.

After slipping the mirror under her pillow, she closed her eyes, concentrated on slowing her breathing, and eventually fell asleep.

She didn't dream.

Chapter 13

Darwin's team had arrived on separate planes. They'd met up at the rendezvous point, then drove to the Lindos Palace Resort Hotel, where half of them checked in, and the other half checked in at a neighboring hotel. The men had reservations under assumed names and had gone to their rooms intermittently, so it wasn't obvious they were together.

Darwin had laid out the plan. They were to stay in contact via mini earpieces that had a microphone. Maintain radio silence unless they bump into Roxanne Dupont. Once that happened, they were to apprise the team of her location and secure the asset at all costs.

Weapons had been delivered to the island the day before by a trusted Greek source, so now all of Darwin's mercenaries were armed to the teeth.

Upon arrival, Darwin had settled in, watched Roxanne's art show from the shadows, and then watched her walk off into the night. Stupidly, they would wait until her much-advertised show had ended, then approach her. She had to have suspected their presence and intentions because she disappeared, and with her, the location of the sensitive information she brought to Greece to sell.

Had she sold it yet? Is that why she bolted?

If so, Darwin was a dead man. Rosina was alone, back at their house in Italy. He had to make the call. Abort and run, or wait until Roxanne surfaced, then determine the extent of her knowledge, actions, and damage.

The hotel had called in the authorities and now had an inspector looking into things, with a cop helping him. Hotel security was a mess, too. One of their main camera guys, a man named Valentine, was off sick, and their head of security, Christos Kallonis, was just found dead by the staff sleeping quarters building.

Maybe Kallonis saw something he shouldn't have?

So much was happening at the hotel, yet no one knew what was going on. And, of course, Roxanne Dupont was still missing.

Darwin watched the crowd gathering while the inspector tried to ameliorate the situation.

He touched his earpiece and looked away so no one could detect his mouth moving.

"Any sign of the subject?" he asked.

All of his men signed in with negative answers.

He stared up at the Greek sky for a moment, lost in the stars, wondering what he would do.

One more day. He had to give it one more day.

Flashlight in hand, Darwin walked away from the Kallonis murder scene as the ambulance pulled out and made his way up the rocky incline east of the hotel.

Rosina could give him a rough idea of where Brian Miller was when his phone lost its signal. She'd even zoomed in and taken a photo with Google Earth.

Searching the area during the day was much better, but he didn't want to be seen in the sunlight. If something happened to Miller and Darwin was seen examining the spot, it wouldn't be a stretch to figure out they were connected.

Five minutes later, he stood in the general area Rosina had circled.

For reference, he kept glancing up at the hotel to stare at Roxanne's room. Her windows were in direct sight from this area. Miller knew what he was doing. There was no question. And this area was concealed pretty well from the general public. Sure, a guest in another room could look this way and see a man standing on the hillside, staring back at the hotel, but Miller would've been lying down like a sniper waiting for their kill to arrive. He would've made himself unobtrusive.

So Darwin got down on his hands and knees, with a tiny flashlight in his mouth, and crawled around the area. At first, he encountered nothing but rocks and dirt, but then he encountered tiny pieces of broken plastic.

He was sure it was the remains of Miller's cell phone. His cellphone's signal died because it was broken in this exact spot.

In a circular formation moving outward, Darwin searched the area around the broken phone pieces and stopped at a dark patch in the dirt. He understood what he was looking at as he drew near and sniffed it.

Blood—likely Brian Miller's blood.

And a lot of it—the kind of blood that a man doesn't walk away from.

Even without a body, Darwin could confirm his advance agent was dead.

He sat there for a moment, contemplating his next move.

The head of security was dead. Miller was likely dead. Dupont was missing.

And all that happened since the afternoon, which was just over twelve hours ago.

The operation was falling apart quickly, unraveling too fast for Darwin to grasp it.

He missed Sarah and Parkman. It had been a while since he'd joined them, but it wasn't time yet.

Someone had leaked information about him, and he couldn't get close to his friends until he secured and destroyed that information. Otherwise, he would put them at risk. He determined Roxanne Dupont and her boyfriend, Peter Singer, were the only ones who knew anything about it.

He called his wife to give her the bad news about Brian Miller while walking back to the hotel.

He and his men would lay low, gather information, watch everyone, and wait for the people who had the information he was looking for to raise their heads above ground.

Then he'd be there to cut it off.

In the meantime, he'd wait in the shadows and become unseen.

This operation just entered a new level—desperation mode.

Chapter 14

PETRAKIS REMAINED AT THE crime scene for some time after the ambulance took Kallonis's body to the coroner.

Studying the room, he found no trace of a struggle. There was no damage to the door, either.

Kallonis either came in alone and opened the door to his assailant, or someone was already inside and waiting for him, which made the most sense.

From Petrakis's cursory examination, he determined the killing blow came from behind. So, Kallonis had been jumped by an unknown assailant, or he knew the killer and felt safe turning his back.

Workers were roused by the noise of the emergency vehicles and the commotion outside. The inspector began the arduous task of interviewing them, one by one. After visiting seven rooms and chatting with the employees, he was getting nowhere fast—no one saw anything.

No one saw Kallonis enter the building. No one saw or heard anything strange around the presumed time of the incident. Each and every person seemed willing to cooperate but couldn't offer much as they'd mostly all just woken up.

The only information he gleaned that may help—although he had no idea how yet—was from the tenant in the room next to where Kallonis was killed. At some unspecified moment over the last few hours, they heard a repetitive squeaking sound for five minutes, and then it stopped.

Petrakis returned to the room where Kallonis's corpse was found and tried to replicate those sounds by shaking the furniture, but nothing worked. He stared at the adjoining wall for a moment, then sat on the bed and closed his eyes for a second.

People gathered outside despite his warnings to avoid the area. Even Kallonis's wife was outside. She was head of housekeeping, so he had to talk to her about the maids and which ones passed through Roxanne's room in the past few days. But with the crowd outside, gathering information right now would be impossible.

He called the front desk again, only to learn they still had no room for him unless someone wanted to share. Having no other choice and needing a rest, the waiter, who was sleeping in the next room, had an empty bed. He asked if he could borrow it and was soon accommodated.

It was almost dawn.

***

Petrakis's phone rang at seven in the morning, startling him awake. He didn't know where he was and what he was doing for several seconds. He answered in a heavy voice. It was Officer Samaras.

"The first shift of the hotel started at seven. Everyone's waiting for more information. Someone alerted the press, and the hotel owners want to know what's going on. They haven't decided what to say to the guests yet."

Petrakis had a headache, and only one response came to mind. "Coffee." He said the one word, then ended the call as he swung his legs off the bed. Minutes later, he approached the hotel and headed for the restaurant for that coffee.

Mr. Diakos came out of nowhere to stand beside him. The man looked sleepless and depressed, his eyes bloodshot.

"Inspector, we need to know what to do."

When Diakos spoke, he kept his volume low, probably afraid guests would overhear him.

Petrakis didn't respond. He just pointed at the coffeemakers.

"Yes, of course, have breakfast first, drink coffee. We'll serve you." Diakos pointed at the buffet.

Petrakis moved toward the coffee, filled his cup, then strolled to a small table and sat.

Officer Samaras came to sit next to him, holding a cup of his own. The inspector took a deep breath and drank some.

"Nikolas Kovak tried to leave the island last night," Samaras jumped in. "We picked him up. He's at the station waiting for you. There's been no trace of Roxanne Dupont and no idea who might have wanted to kill the security guard, Kallonis."

"Bring Kovak here."

Samaras frowned. "Why?"

"There was no official announcement banning Kovak

from leaving Rhodes. We mishandled this investigation. It'll leak to social media." Petrakis sipped from his cup. "Just tell them to bring him here."

Samaras seemed tightlipped for a moment, then he withdrew his phone and dialed out. Speaking in hushed tones, he had the officers at the station reroute Kovak back to the hotel.

When he spun back around, there was more redness in his cheeks. Was that embarrassment or anger? Did Samaras think Petrakis was doing a shit job? If so, he'd probably be right.

Samaras cleared his throat. "Also, the hotel owners want to be informed about everything. They're on their way here."

"I don't work for them. As soon as we have new developments, I'll inform the hotel manager, Mr. Diakos, and he can contact them."

"They were away, but now the family is coming. They are concerned about the safety of their current guests as they don't know if Roxanne's disappearance and what happened to Kallonis are isolated incidents or related to something more sinister. They're raving about the bad publicity."

Petrakis held his cup with both hands, already thinking about another cup. "Understandable, but while I'm here solving a case, that's what I'm here doing—solving a case. I'm not here to worry about their business or the future of their business."

Petrakis's phone rang, but he ignored it—not enough coffee yet.

Samaras went on about the impact on the island, the media, and the hotel as Petrakis studied the guests eating breakfast around their table. How happy were these people eating their eggs, their toast? The ignorance involved in maintaining that level of bliss astounded him. He could make them all run from the restaurant, pack their bags, and flee the hotel with one word. Something about this case made him feel that he shouldn't have been so forthcoming last night to volunteer. Perhaps this was one he should not have taken on.

A woman several tables over impressed him. Not only for her exotic beauty, gorgeous eyes, full lips, and short curly hair but because she watched him without regard. How bold of her.

Samaras was still on a tangent, talking about guests from last night and how they had questions about the murder.

Petrakis cut him off mid-sentence. "Let's go to the front desk." The inspector stood abruptly, knocking his chair back and making it scrape loudly on the floor.

There seemed to be some sort of panic at the reception counter. Outside the main entrance, several journalists appeared to be waiting for a statement while others were chatting off to the side with random guests.

From the sound of their accents, a group of Russians wanted to check in early and go into their rooms. The morning shift receptionist looked frazzled as another woman stepped in to help her process the guests.

When they looked up and saw Petrakis staring at them, they froze. The woman closest to the side of the counter whispered something to her colleague, then came around the side and strode toward him.

"Good morning, Inspector. I'm Evelyn Diakos."

"The manager's wife, I presume?" He studied her face as they shook hands, waiting for her to continue. She was familiar, as he'd studied the family photos in Mr. Diakos's office the night before.

"Can I talk to you somewhere private?" she asked in a low voice while gesturing to the side of the reception area.

The inspector nodded and motioned for Samaras to wait for him.

Once they were hidden away in the manager's office, far from eavesdroppers, Mrs. Diakos met his gaze, her face deadpan now.

"Tell me how close you are to finding Roxanne Dupont."

Petrakis held up his hands. "Mrs. Diakos, I can't discuss an ongoing investigation with you. Unless you have something to tell me?"

Evelyn took a deep breath as if she was about to say something she'd regret, then thought better of it with a subtle shake of her head.

"If she isn't found immediately, our hotel's reputation will be damaged for years to come. We may find ourselves without a job, and we employ a lot of people. Are you aware of how many people are dependent upon their livelihood from this company?"

Perturbed and tired of the oh-my-poor-business attitude, Petrakis took a step back. "Mrs. Diakos, a colleague of yours, was killed yesterday."

Evelyn nodded.

Petrakis continued, "There's a murderer somewhere in this hotel or near the hotel, and yet you're worried about the hotel's reputation?"

As soon as the words were out, he regretted their harshness. He didn't have to offer an opinion about her questions. She had a right to want to keep a lid on developments. He endeavored to stick to the facts and work on the investigation—as was his job—and leave *reputations* to other people.

"Yes, you're right. Forgive me. So much has happened since last night that I find it difficult to process." Now, it was her turn to stare at him with a puzzled expression.

"Do you know if Kallonis had any enemies?" Petrakis asked. "Anyone who would hate him enough to want the man dead?"

Evelyn hesitated for a moment, then shook her head.

Something about this woman gave Petrakis the feeling she was hiding something from him.

A colleague called her name from the main hallway.

"Forgive me, I must go."

"We should talk soon." He nodded, then followed her out of the office, almost bumping into Samaras.

"I don't know what's going on at this hotel," Petrakis said. "I need more coffee, then I have to speak with Mr. Diakos. Tell him I'll meet him in his office."

He stepped away from Samaras and headed back to the restaurant.

While passing through the lobby, he caught a glimpse of Evelyn Diakos. She appeared visibly upset, hands tapping her reddened cheeks.

Petrakis continued through the lobby until he got back to the coffeepot in the restaurant. As he poured, he considered Evelyn's connection to the security man, Kallonis.

Why pull me somewhere private to talk?

Did she expect him to reveal some truth he'd discovered? Did she think he'd be more willing to speak his mind if no one was listening? And if she felt she needed that level of privacy, was she projecting her own integrity—meaning *she* couldn't be trusted?

Petrakis arrived back at Diakos's office, his mind still racing.

"What the hell is going on in this hotel?" he whispered to himself as he sat behind Diakos's desk.

When his cell phone rang again, he checked the number this time. It was from police headquarters.

"Good morning," he said into it.

"Why did I get a call from the French Directorate General about a woman named Roxanne Dupont while nothing has been announced yet regarding her disappearance?"

Petrakis was lost for words. Was Dupont that important?

"Deputy Chief, I have no idea."

"Are you the right one for this case? I mean, should I be sending in someone else?"

"I don't know that either, sir."

"What the hell do you know?"

If he sent someone else, it would probably be Inspector Alexander Kokkinos. The name alone upset him. They disliked each other immensely. Kokkinos was the most egocentric and ambitious man who ever made it in the police force. And he was the same man who almost ruined Petrakis's career a few months back.

"Sir, I can handle things here."

"Yet you don't have any updates."

Petrakis paused. If he told him the hotel's security guard was murdered, the chief would definitely send that asshole. If he didn't tell him, he'd hear about it later, get demoted for lying by omission, and still, that Kokkinos asshole would show up.

He decided honesty was the best course, but as his mouth opened to speak the truth, all that came out was, "No, no updates."

"Look, the last thing I need is another shitstorm, especially now that the French authorities are involved. You have twenty-four hours to get me something, anything. Is that clear?"

"Yes, sir," he said, but the line was already dead.

Someone knocked on the door before Petrakis had a chance to hang up.

The door opened, and Samaras entered, Diakos right behind him.

"We need a statement for the media," Samaras said. "It can't wait. Terrible things are already being written about the hotel. We think"—he gestured between him and the hotel manager—"that we need to take the lead on the information before it's too late."

Petrakis eyed them both. "And what will happen to those guests who remain in the hotel? Panic? Would everyone just check out?" He waited, but neither man responded. "How about we say nothing about Kallonis at this point?"

Diakos nodded. "That can work."

Petrakis rubbed his face, then his eyes. After taking a sip from his surprisingly cold coffee, he stared at the wall momentarily.

"One thing at a time. I agree. First, we will talk to the press about Roxanne Dupont. The French already know about her disappearance, so there's no use trying to keep it a secret." He spun around to face the men who were staring at him. He addressed Samaras when he spoke this time. "As for the investigation into the murder of Kallonis, it must be kept under wraps as long as possible. After speaking to the press, I want all the names of the people staying at the hotel from yesterday and today. Samaras, take care of this." He turned to the hotel manager. "Mr. Diakos, I want you to find the maids who cleaned Dupont's room for the past week. I need to speak with them while we wait for the art critic, Kovak, to arrive back at the hotel."

He got to his feet, adjusted his suit, and started for the door.

"Let's go, gentlemen. We have a case to solve, and I need some real fucking coffee."

Chapter 15

Faye Olympiou hadn't slept well. She got up and went to the restaurant early for coffee.

She noticed the hotel manager pacing in the lobby, glancing repeatedly at his watch. Could he know the truth? Was he waiting for the cops to come and make arrests?

By the time she was on her second cup of coffee, the manager greeted the inspector, and then he stepped into the restaurant and grabbed a coffee. She watched that cop from last night sit with the inspector. They spoke in hushed tones, too low for her to hear. The inspector's eyes were puffy from lack of sleep, and the other policeman seemed to be talking non-stop.

She leaned closer as their voices rose a notch, staring at the inspector. It would seem that no one had discovered the body she'd tripped over yet. She'd wait a little longer and then go there again. It couldn't have been her imagination like that shit she was seeing in the mirror.

She'd seen the body in the bush after stumbling over that protruding human leg.

Yet, there was something in that mirror, too, something haunting her now. She hadn't dared to look at it again.

As soon as the inspector left the restaurant, she left. Her curiosity wouldn't let her have peace of mind. She had to see that body in the bush in the light of day.

Strolling along the same path she had taken the night before, Faye scanned the ground carefully, looking for the foot that tripped her.

Not looking where she was going, she bumped into a young blond man in a swimsuit with a towel dangling off his shoulder.

Too early for a swim, she thought and apologized for her carelessness.

Over ten minutes later, after having walked the length of the path, she didn't find the body anywhere.

Either she was imagining that, too, or someone came back and moved the body.

The only thing that could prove there was even a body there in the first place would be to find some residue of its presence, some bodily fluids that soaked into the ground. Disgusted by the thought, she didn't know what was worse— losing her mind and imagining things or finding proof that a dead body had spilled blood and pus into the dirt recently.

The path wasn't long, and after scanning the edge of the bushes carefully, she found an area where the shrubs were matted down. When she leaned in, the smell hit her first. The ground looked wet in two spots, the color of the thick sludge-like goo a dark reddish brown.

"So it *was* here," she said in a hushed whisper. "And they moved it."

But who moved the body? The people who put it there? Or the authorities, and they just didn't announce the discovery of another body yet?

She moved the bushes aside in search of anything else, but all she found were crumpled branches.

Perhaps someone fainted and fell into the bush, and that's all there was to it. That could've happened, but something told her that the body was dead and not sleeping. Besides, how could anyone account for the spilled blood on the ground?

She took the walkway back to her villa to lounge or nap to get her mind off things and relieve some stress. All this shit was getting to her.

Once inside her room, she laid on her freshly made bed, then jumped back up, startled. What if someone took the mirror? She should have hidden it. Leaving it out in the open like that was stupid.

But where had she left the damn thing? It wasn't next to the table or in the bathroom. She closed her eyes and concentrated on her breathing. In the silence of the room, she heard someone whispering. Her heart pounded as she rummaged through the entire room, even looking under the bed.

Then she found it. The mirror was on the carpet under the bed.

How did it get there?

Hesitantly, she grabbed it by the handle and held it away from her face. Those whispers grew louder once she had it out and was sitting on the bed.

Were they *real* whispers or just the voices in her head?

With a deep breath, she angled the mirror to her face and glanced at it.

At first, she saw nothing but her own reflection.

But then a black shadow ran across the screen.

A short yip escaped her throat, and the mirror dropped from her hands.

"Fuck you," she shouted at the stupid thing.

After picking it back up and facing it away from her, she dropped it in the trash bin and left the room.

Chapter 16

Inspector Petrakis hated being in the spotlight. It made him uncomfortable and clumsy.

But in this case—literally and figuratively—he had no choice. Officer Samaras had stayed on as a courtesy despite nearing exhaustion. His shift had ended hours ago, and he wasn't an inspector, but the local police detachment felt they needed one of theirs planted beside Petrakis, and they hadn't been able to replace Samaras yet.

And now, Petrakis had to stand in front of cameras and talk to the press. Donning a serious, unwavering facial expression, he exited the front of the hotel and stepped into the foray of cameras and journalists to face what he took great measures to avoid at all times.

The journalists jockeyed for position, forming a semi-circle around him, questions spewing forth in a torrent.

Exemplifying the very definition of F.I.N.E., which stood

for, Fucked Interior, Nice Exterior, he waved for silence, knowing that the deputy chief would be watching.

"Ladies and gentlemen of the press, I am in the awkward position of announcing to you the disappearance of a French citizen. As of late last night, the artist known as Roxanne Dupont went missing. If anyone knows her or may have any idea where she might be, please contact the Rhodes police. That's all I have to report now, thank you."

He stepped away with his head down to avoid eye contact as a barrage of questions rose in a wave of voices.

At the hotel entrance, Samaras caught up with him. "That art critic Kovak is waiting in the manager's office."

Petrakis nodded and followed Samaras toward the lobby. To his right, he caught sight of that exotic woman from earlier in the restaurant. She seemed to be watching him, looking away quickly when he glanced at her.

"Who is that woman?" he asked Samaras under his breath.

"Which woman?"

"The woman over there. The one walking away from us."

Samaras glanced toward her, but it was too late—she'd disappeared around a corner.

"I don't know who you're talking about."

"It doesn't matter."

They continued across the lobby, the din from the media at the front of the building decreasing with each step.

A police officer stood outside the manager's door, his hands clasped in front of his abdomen. Nikolas Kovak sat in a chair inside the office, looking visibly upset. When Kovak saw them enter, he spun around and shouted in English. Petrakis spoke English well, so it wasn't an issue to continue speaking that language.

"Mr. Kovak, I understand you're upset." Petrakis sat behind the desk, his eyes not leaving the art critic.

"You have no idea how upset I am. I'm annoyed and waiting for a good explanation as to why you disgraced me at the airport as if I were a common criminal. Tell me, why was I not free to board my flight? Am I being detained for some unknown reason?"

Veins protruded at his neck while he spoke, and his face reddened further.

Petrakis glanced at Samaras, who had fucked this all up by grabbing him at the airport and taking him to the police station when he wasn't a person of interest.

"I am Inspector Petrakis. You spoke with my colleague yesterday before more information became available to us. And so now that you're here, I want you to describe your day from the moment you arrived at the airport in Rhodes."

"You want more details? What exactly are you looking for? Someone to pin this on? Did you find her body?"

"Mr. Kovak, please, just tell me about yesterday."

Kovak glanced around the room, a disgusted look on his face. His upper lip rose to form a sneer.

"Mr. Nikolas Kovak," Petrakis said, his voice louder, tone hard. "Do not forget where you are. This is a room filled with members of law enforcement. We are investigating a missing persons case. Something happened last night, and we are determined to get to the bottom of it. Whether you offer us your help or not is up to you. Whether we want to hold you for quite some time is up to us. Choose your next words wisely." He cleared his throat. "Now, I'll ask once more. Tell us about your itinerary yesterday."

Kovak seemed to come to terms with something that had been bothering him—perhaps his pride or huge ego—because he nodded, then opened his mouth and started talking.

"My plane landed on time yesterday, and Miss Dupont was waiting for me at the airport. She picked me up and then dropped me off at my hotel. Later that evening, I arrived here and watched her art presentation. Afterward, I waited for her to discuss it, to talk about the details. While waiting an exorbitant amount of time, and because it was late in the evening, I asked the front desk where she was, and we discovered that she had disappeared. I remained according to the instructions given to me by hotel security. Then, as I grew weary, I stated my contact information as your officers requested and left the premises."

"How well do you know Miss Dupont?" the inspector asked, crossing his arms over his chest.

Samaras stood awkwardly next to him, writing furiously in a notebook. Petrakis found it quite distracting.

"I met her a year ago in London at an exhibition of our mutual friend."

"And who is this mutual friend?"

"How that is relevant is beyond me, but his name is George Walls. At that exhibition, Miss Dupont persuaded me to view her own artwork, which she had in her studio. After one look, I saw her talent and agreed to an exclusivity deal for my gallery. She agreed to make a presentation for publicity sake, and then I would transfer her works to my gallery."

"Were you happy with your collaboration?"

"Yes." He frowned. "Of course. She's extremely

talented."

"Yesterday, at the event, did you have any acquaintances other than Miss Dupont? Or rather, did you recognize anyone else?"

He shook his head, glanced at the floor, then back up. "No, no one. We had agreed that I would invite my acquaintances to the gallery where her permanent exhibition would be displayed. They could view it all then. The art presentation was to garner new viewers, not those who would see it when it reached its resting place."

"Do you know why she was anxious about your presence?"

"Anxious about my presence? Roxanne?" He guffawed. "That's ridiculous. That woman was never anxious about anything. She always did what she liked, when she liked. Roxanne was a bold woman."

"How do you mean, 'bold'?"

"It was a general impression I have of her. Who knows? She's a strong-willed woman. Determined to do things her way and only her way. I've never seen her entire collection, so maybe her exit thing is her wanting me to be satisfied that I chose her for my gallery. This is certainly garnering a hell of a lot of attention."

"Do you smoke?"

"What has that got to do with anything?"

"Please, just answer my question."

"No, I do not smoke, Inspector." Kovak's tone breached on disrespect.

"What did you do when you stepped outside last night?"

"I wanted to talk on my phone in private."

"How long was the call?"

"I didn't time it. Ten minutes, maybe fifteen. Why?"

"Can we see the call you made?" Samaras spoke up, probably to feel useful.

"Of course." Kovak took out his cell phone and tapped a few keys as Samaras moved over to stand beside the man. Then Kovak tapped a few more. "That's strange. I remember talking to my assistant in London last night."

Petrakis looked at Samaras and then back to Kovak. He caught a slight tremble in the man's hand. This interview was making Kovak nervous.

"Can your assistant confirm this call you made?"

"Yes, of course. I can call her now."

"Do you have anything else you'd like to add? Anything you feel might help us in locating Miss Dupont?"

Kovak shook his head. "I can't think of anything except I hope you find her. That woman's paintings cost a fortune."

Petrakis shook his head and stared down at his hands. "Mr. Kovak." He looked up and met the man's gaze. "I had hoped you would tell me yourself. Witnesses saw you fighting at the airport with Miss Dupont."

Kovak reddened further again. He hesitated, glancing around the room, then stared back at the inspector. "I've known Roxanne for a long time. So, we had an intense conversation. I didn't consider it important as such incidents are private and often disgraceful."

"Yet, you told her she was destroying you, and you don't consider it relevant to mention something like this when it happened in such a public place?" Kovak sighed, and Petrakis continued. "What did she do to you? How was she *destroying* you?"

Kovak inhaled deeply like he was pausing to find the

courage to speak. Petrakis studied the man's face, waiting for him to speak. Would he tell the truth or lie—and if he lied, could Petrakis see that lie on the man's face?

"As I told you, Roxanne only cared about herself. She had already sold some of her best work without telling me. Logically, I'd be upset as I had photographed it previously, and now it wasn't coming to my gallery. Not to mention, she'd sold it to one of my best customers. As you can likely tell, this wasn't good for me and would hurt our relationship going forward. It hurt our trust."

"In the art world, would this be considered a betrayal? And did you hate her for that?"

"The word *hate* seems a bit harsh. It clearly irritated me, and I had to reconsider doing business with her. I mean, could I trust her?"

"Then why did you come to this art presentation in Rhodes?"

"I wanted to have the chance to convince her of the damage she'd caused us both."

Petrakis grabbed a pen off the desk and tapped it against his bottom lip, frustration warming his collar. "Did you end up finding her after the art presentation? Did you try to *convince* her of her misdeeds? And when you failed to succeed, you killed her? Then you got rid of the corpse? Is that how it happened, Mr. Kovak?"

Kovak rolled his eyes and blew air out of his mouth. "This is a disgusting farce of an investigation. You're all absurd. Like I would waste time and my life on a slut who couldn't keep her word. Like she was the only artist in the world." Kovak shook his head. "Please, Inspector, offer a man a slight amount of dignity in such interrogative procedures." He took in the men around him, one by one. "You are looking for a murderer without a corpse. You're all a bunch of fucking clowns. Please find something better to work on. Any jury would laugh this out of any courtroom."

"Be careful how you see this funhouse show, Mr. Kovak. You could end up on the ride of your life without a safety bar." Petrakis got to his feet. "May I remind you, most murderers would declare their innocence. Many dare to commit a crime, big or small, but few dare to accept the consequences. Another outburst like that, and I'll have to assume the worst. Wasn't it Shakespeare who once said, 'methinks thou doth protest too much.'"

"C'mon, Inspector, you don't even know if a crime has been committed. Either lay out the charges you will accuse me of or let me return to the airport. Otherwise, I will be forced to contact the British Embassy and my lawyer." Kovak also got to his feet.

The inspector watched him briefly, then nodded at the officers by the door. The policemen stepped aside.

"Don't leave Rhodes until we tell you to," Samaras said. "It's a lovely Greek island. Stick around for a few days. Enjoy the food and the weather. We'll be in touch."

Kovak glared at them, cursed the Greeks under his breath, and then exited the office.

Diakos jumped in through the open office door the second Kovak exited.

"You can all leave," the inspector told the police officers standing around Samaras.

"Inspector," Diakos said. "I just discovered the hotel's owners will be here at noon. I brought you the list of all the hotel staff, permanent and seasonal. I have put an asterisk next to each name so you can understand who worked during the days Roxanne stayed here and a second one for those who may have come into contact with her."

"Samaras," Petrakis called as the door was about to shut.

The man stuck his head back in.

"Go through this list. Start the interviews."

"Yes, sir." He took the papers and left.

"Sit with me for a minute." The inspector gestured at a chair.

The hotel manager nodded and took a seat.

"Did Kallonis have any enemies?"

Diakos bowed his head and wiped his wet eyes before the tears were visible.

"Not that I'm aware of. He was a wonderful man who kept a low profile. He did his job well and never created any problems for us. He was well-loved."

"Can you tell me anything about his marriage? Have you ever heard anything negative? Anything at all? I mean, it's one thing to be looking for a missing woman, but something else entirely to be investigating a murder. Let's not kid ourselves here. With Kallonis's dead body showing up, it's likely Miss Dupont is dead, too. In fact, I'm moving forward with the presumption that they're both connected somehow."

Diakos swallowed audibly. "Inspector, all marriages have their ups and downs. But if I knew anything specific, I'd certainly tell you."

The inspector tapped his fingers on the table, heat rising near his collar. He was getting nowhere with this investigation and could use more coffee.

Mr. Diakos opened his mouth, closed it, then started talking.

"Kallonis's wife had an affair." He'd lowered his voice for that sentence. "She eventually came to her senses and returned home. That was hard for him, but he never said anything to me. There was a long period where he avoided me. He wouldn't look me in the eyes, but then he got better over time. Although, I'm not sure how that could help. His wife would never want him dead."

"Did you find out who she slept with? Is that something you were privy to?"

"No."

"Who might know this mystery man other than Kallonis's wife?"

"My wife might. At that time, they had become close. In fact, Evelyn helped their marriage. She helped them bond again, so I think Kallonis's wife might have confided in Evelyn."

"Where were you at the time of Kallonis's death?"

"Heading home to go to bed with my wife."

"Okay, Mr. Diakos, you can leave. Can you notify your wife I'd like to speak with her?"

Diakos got up hesitantly and stared at him.

"Is there something you'd like to add?" Petrakis asked.

"Do you have any news on Roxanne?"

"No, unfortunately, we have nothing."

Diakos turned away and lumbered from the office, the weight of the past twenty-four hours drawing his shoulders toward the floor.

Petrakis stared at his empty coffee cup, understanding Diakos's dejected appearance.

He was feeling it, too.

Chapter 17

Faye was heading to the front reception desk when she saw that inspector again.

She wanted to tell him that she had heard voices at night in the villa next door—Dupont's room—and that she had heard Roxanne arguing with a man the night before her disappearance.

Then she reconsidered. Telling the inspector all that might cause him to want to question her. She'd have to keep her mouth shut unless she could find a way to say it to him anonymously.

"Good morning," the girl at the reception desk said. "How can I help you?"

The other employee behind the counter looked confused and nervous as she rearranged paperwork, her fingers letting papers slip and fall to the floor.

"I would like to stay a few more days if possible." Faye

showed her room key. "I'm Faye Olympiou."

"Stay?" the receptionist asked, doubt in her voice. She immediately realized her error and tried to correct it. "Of course, stay more days." She tapped on her screen.

Faye nodded. "Yes, please."

"If you'll give me half a minute while I call the person in charge of bookings."

Faye leaned on the counter and waited. She noticed the young blond man she'd bumped into on his way to the beach. This time, he was dressed in jeans and a white T-shirt. She smiled awkwardly, lowered her gaze, and watched him walk toward the lobby doors.

He glanced back at her over his shoulder, smiled once, fiddled with his keys, and then stepped outside.

The receptionist set down the phone. "It looks like our booking manager is away from their desk. I can set you up. Just tell me how much longer you would like to stay?"

"Four more days."

"Perfect. Let me see if the villa you're already in is available for the extended stay." The girl typed on her computer again.

A man whispering something to himself strode through the lobby, swearing in English. Two police officers followed him at a distance.

She knew the guy from somewhere. Had she seen him on Roxanne's social media? Or was it in the art presentation? Could he be a suspect in her disappearance?

Faye turned back to the receptionist, who looked confused.

"Is there a problem?"

"It appears your villa has another reservation for

tomorrow after your departure. I was looking to see if the dates fit so I could put the other guests elsewhere, but it doesn't look like I can. Apologies for the wait." At least the girl was polite.

Faye now watched the other woman at the front desk. Her name tag read Evelyn. Even with a pile of papers next to her, she ignored them and did something on the side. It looked like she was rapidly texting on her cell phone.

Someone moved in from the side, and Faye recognized him as the hotel manager.

When Evelyn saw him, a cold smile formed on her lips, and she slipped her mobile phone into her skirt before he saw what she was doing.

Evelyn stood. "My love, are you all right?"

"The inspector wants to see you."

"Excuse me?" The receptionist said, pulling Faye's attention back to her. "Would you mind if we moved you to the other side of the hotel?" The receptionist had broken her concentration. She'd been so focused on Evelyn and the manager that she forgot what she was standing there for.

"No problem at all. When?" Faye watched Evelyn walk away with the manager, adjusting her skirt.

"After 14:00. We will call and send someone to take your things."

"That works. Thanks!" She smiled and glanced over at the manager, who happened to be looking at her and reciprocated the smile in the context of good hospitality.

"Do you know if there is any news about Miss Dupont?" Faye asked the girl.

"Unfortunately, no." She shook her head, glancing around. "It's as if the earth opened up and swallowed her whole."

"I can't believe it." Faye kept her voice low.

"Neither can I." The girl rubbed her forehead.

"You look exhausted. You should get some rest."

"Thank you." The girl frowned, then stared at her computer screen.

Faye turned and watched everyone in the lobby. She saw the police, the guests, and the security officers.

It all made her wonder if they'd ever figured out what had happened or were ready for what was about to happen.

Chapter 18

Someone knocked on the office door just as Petrakis took his first sip of an extra-large coffee.

"Come in," he said, loud enough to be heard.

Evelyn Diakos entered hesitantly.

"Sit down, please." He nodded at the chairs.

Mrs. Diakos sat across from him. He didn't talk to her for a few seconds, so he just watched her, assessing how uncomfortable she was becoming. There was something about this woman, something she was hiding from him. How could she be so involved with the hotel's inner workings, to be the manager's wife, that she hadn't asked about Kallonis's death? People were attracted to darkness, like rubberneckers on a highway, trying to catch a glimpse of the accident. Movies and books were written about it, and people paid good money to watch murder on the big screen. So when it happened in real life, as tragic as that was, everyone wanted to know the details—especially if it happened to someone they knew or cared about.

So what was Evelyn up to? Why hadn't she asked about Kallonis? And what about their guest, Roxanne Dupont?

"Will you be asking me questions?" she started. "Is that how this works?" She fidgeted, fixing the hem of her skirt.

"Tell me about your job here at the hotel," Petrakis said. "I understand you're the one responsible for the spa."

"Yes." She nodded, her eyes staying on his. "However, since I've worked reception for many years, I pitch in when they get busy and when I can leave the spa for a bit."

"Like today?"

"Yes, there are many arrivals and departures, not to mention those journalists and worried staff. These are difficult times for all of us at the moment." She adjusted her legs, then crossed and uncrossed her arms.

"Have you ever spoken with Miss Dupont?"

"I've served her at both the reception and the spa. She was—sorry—*is* one of our best customers. She was always polite, without many demands, and always left big tips. We're all very sorry about her disappearance and hope she turns up safe."

"When was the last time you saw her?"

"The day before the presentation. She came to the spa to get done up, not that she needed much, of course—she shone on her own."

"What did you talk about?"

"We just talked about women's things. I don't think any of our conversations would be connected to the case."

Petrakis stared at her for an extended moment. "Let me be the judge of what may or may not pertain to the case." He cleared his throat and leaned forward. "Did you suspect she would just up and run?"

He'd unsettled her further. She adjusted herself again and glanced away, averting her eyes now.

"She'd prepared a speech for her guests *after* the presentation. She had every intention of being here throughout the evening. Roxanne was quite excited about this step in her career." Evelyn's eyes moved back and forth, then settled on Petrakis's gaze once more. "Something has happened to her. I'm sure of it."

"Then tell me something, Mrs. Diakos." Petrakis leaned back in his chair to appear less threatening.

"Of course, if I can." She nodded at him to proceed.

"What was your relationship with the security officer, Christos Kallonis?"

"Relationship? How do you mean?"

"Did you have one?"

Rattled now, Petrakis caught a glimpse of her lower lip trembling.

"I'm the hotel manager's wife. I have a relationship with all the employees, Inspector, which we maintain at a professional level. If you're implying otherwise, then you'd be wrong in that—"

"What about Kallonis's wife?"

"Eleni? We've been friends for years since we've worked in the same field for so long."

"And you worked with her husband, but you had no connection, no working relationship? Nothing at all?"

"Well, I avoided him when I could, so yeah, no connection at all. He wasn't good for her."

"What makes you say that?"

"She told me. They were only staying together because of money—it is too hard to make it on your own nowadays. She planned to leave him at some point."

"Had something specific happened? Or did they just fall out of love?"

Evelyn glanced down at her lap, where she fiddled with an errant nail. "She just wasn't happy."

"Let's change this up now. Where were you last night?"

"I was at home." She looked up. "I went to bed early."

He wasn't going to get the truth from this woman. She was wasting his time, and now his forgotten coffee was cold.

"Mrs. Diakos, if you remember anything you feel might help us with Roxanne's disappearance and Kallonis's murder, please contact me at any time."

"I can leave?"

"Of course."

Mrs. Diakos rose from her seat and strode out of the office, leaving the door ajar.

Why was she lying? Or could the claims of a relationship just be a case of wild imagination, word of mouth, or hotel gossip?

With these thoughts in mind, he called Officer Samaras and had him come to the office.

"Anything happening?" Petrakis asked when Samaras stepped inside. "Any developments?"

"Not much, Inspector, other than preliminary reports from the medical examiner that Kallonis was likely killed from a blow to the head by a blunt force object. And we have a few guys from forensics in Miss Dupont's villa right now, but they aren't getting much as it's a hotel room. Multiple fingerprints and hair samples will probably appear registered to previous guests."

The inspector listened carefully, feeling the clock ticking. He had yet to come to a single conclusion other than Roxanne had a guest over the night before she disappeared. He didn't have any persons of interest in both cases and guessing—grasping at straws—wouldn't help. He couldn't even tell if the two cases were connected or not.

He rubbed his temples and sighed.

Then, he realized that he hadn't watched the surveillance cameras yet. He'd been waiting for Kallonis, and then the man was found dead.

Samaras was still talking about waitresses and how the couches and chairs were set up in each villa when he raised a hand for silence.

Samaras closed his mouth.

Petrakis grabbed the phone and dialed the front desk to find out where the camera feed was located.

He learned it was all one level below them, where the staff offices were located. He didn't know how to get down there, but it was time to find out.

"Follow me, Samaras."

Petrakis exited the office and moved toward the elevators. Once he boarded with Samaras behind, they dropped one level, and when the doors opened, he stepped out into a long corridor.

Office doors lined both sides of the hall. He passed the night auditor's door, two other unlabeled wooden doors, the hotel kitchen, and a lunchroom for the staff before he reached the security door.

He knocked, Samaras standing at his shoulder.

"Enter," a voice shouted from within after a moment.

Petrakis opened the door and eased inside, holding it for Samaras.

A long desk lined the right wall, and above it, mounted on the wall, were four large TVs. Each was split into four small windows on each screen where the feed of quad cameras displayed real-time action throughout the hotel. That amounted to sixteen cameras monitoring everything.

The man at the desk grabbed a half-eaten sandwich and took a bite.

"We haven't been introduced," Petrakis said, stepping forward.

"I know who you are," the man said, his mouth full. He pointed at the screens, still chewing what looked like a ham and cheese. "Saw you on the TV." He smiled at his own humor, then swallowed. "I'm Gregory Valentine. What can I do for you?"

"I'm Inspector Petrakis, and this is my colleague, Officer Samaras. I need you to walk me through the cameras, the areas they record, how long they store their feed on the cloud or the server, and then I need you to show me footage from yesterday."

Valentine wiped his hands on his pants and got to his feet. There was a mess on the floor where cables were strewn about. He was out of uniform, but that was probably because he seemed to be working on changing out some of the electronics.

"Without a warrant, I'll have to get permission from Mr. Diakos, which I don't think'll be a problem. Then I have a form you'll have to sign to make it all official and shit. You understand, I'm sure."

The man's accent was off somehow like he was from

Crete or a village up north. Petrakis was about to ask him where he was from when he decided against it. Better not to waste time on trivial questions.

"Absolutely. Please, get the permissions you need, then show me what you've got."

"I'll need a few minutes." The man leaned over the counter, grabbed a rectangular black unit the size of an average PC, slipped it under his arm, and then moved to the door. "I'll be right back. Please wait in here."

Petrakis nodded. "Do what you have to do. We'll wait here—just hurry."

Valentine slipped past Samaras, leaving the door to the hallway open.

Petrakis watched the cameras on the wall, the lobby with people standing at the reception desk, the front of the hotel where valets were taking the keys to park a car, and three cameras covering the parking lot, which he understood was off-premises about a block away. Everything happening on camera is being recorded, stored, and saved.

This was perfect.

What happened to Roxanne, or even who killed Kallonis, may be right here in this room, stored on a server or wherever the hell these IT guys stored shit.

The answers to everything could be right here, and he'd been upstairs conducting interviews like an idiot.

No wonder he was shown up on the last case by Inspector Kokkinos.

He stared at the cluttered desk and read some of the names on the drawers. Then he opened the one closest to him. After rifling through several papers, he found nothing that would help.

Under the desk, cables were strewn about as if several items were disconnected at once. He looked closer and saw that some cables had been cut with something sharp. They weren't just unplugged. They were sliced clean off.

After more than five minutes had passed, Petrakis stepped out of the security office. Samaras was uncharacteristically quiet as he stood in the far corner, tapping at something on his phone.

It gave Petrakis time to think and process what he knew. The hotel owners would be there soon, too, and he had to decide what to say to them. He'd prefer if they closed the hotel, but he also knew that probably wouldn't happen.

Contacting Kallonis's widow was high on his list of priorities. There was a lot to do, and with each minute that passed, he felt no closer to figuring anything out. Samaras was willing to help, but he had to be managed and directed. The man wasn't a detective or an inspector.

Petrakis checked his watch. They were nearing the ten-minute mark.

"Where the hell did he go?" he asked out loud.

Samaras exited the office and shook his head, slipping his phone into his back pocket.

"No idea."

Petrakis strode down the corridor, knocked on the next door to his right, and then pushed it open. Three people were working with stacks of papers piled next to them. They all stopped what they were doing and glanced up at the intrusion.

"I'm Inspector Petrakis. Can any of you tell me where your security employee, Mr. Valentine, would go if seeking permission for us to view security footage? Or can one of you call the manager and get him down here?"

The three of them exchanged glances, with two of them shrugging.

The woman sitting closest to the door said, "As far as we know, Valentine is out sick today. He didn't come in yesterday either."

Petrakis spun around so fast he lost his balance and bumped into the doorframe. Then he was back in the hallway and running for the exit, knowing every step was futile.

"Who the hell was in the security office then?" he shouted to no one in particular. Beyond the exit door, the stairs were empty.

Whoever that man was, he was long gone.

Petrakis ran back to the room with the three employees. They were all still sitting there, staring at Samaras, who hadn't moved an inch.

"Is there anyone else on staff named Valentine?"

"We have only one Valentine working here," the same woman said. "He works across the hall."

Petrakis didn't speak—couldn't speak.

"I need all the logs from the surveillance cameras."

The woman who'd been answering him got to her feet and adjusted her skirt. "We have no idea where that would be. Security handles all that. Valentine was off for a few days, and Kallonis"—she paused to catch her breath, then swallowed—"Kallonis was working extra shifts to manage all that—"

"We should call the manager," her colleague piped up.

Petrakis glanced her way. "Call whomever you want, Diakos, Valentine, doesn't matter to me, but make sure it's someone who knows that camera system." He shot a hand back to point across the hall and bumped into Samaras's chest.

Why was he standing so fucking close?

"I'll call Valentine." She held the phone to her ear while staring at Petrakis, then shook her head. "He didn't pick it up. I'm on the fourth ring."

"Call Diakos. I want him here immediately."

The woman nodded frantically, tapped buttons on the phone, and stood back up to listen, her face a darker shade of red.

She held the wireless phone out from her ear and looked at it. "That's strange. I have no dial tone—"

It rang in her hand. She pressed a button.

"Hello?" A pause, then, "Valentine, thank goodness you're okay. Right, I understand." She moved forward, stepped past the inspector and Samaras, then moved out into the hallway. "We need your help with the security cameras."

Petrakis followed her into the security office.

"Right, but where is it?" she asked. "What? Could you be wrong, Valentine? There's no computer there. Just a bunch of wires." She leaned down and touched one of the frayed cords. "They've been cut," she said, almost to herself.

"Valentine, could the computer be somewhere else?" Her face hardened, and she slowly spun to face Petrakis. "Sir, it's possible that all the security digital storage has been stolen."

Petrakis clenched his fists, and his jaw tightened. Things were getting worse for him by the second. Worse and more complicated. He should've grabbed that guy who claimed to be Valentine before he left with the damn storage unit under his arm. How stupid could he be?

"Is there any other place this information is stored?"

"Valentine, the inspector is asking if this data exists elsewhere. Yes, yes, okay, I'll call you back."

The woman set down the phone and moved over to several black boxes.

Petrakis approached from behind, although he really didn't know what he was looking for. Everything was just cables and lights.

The woman turned back to him. "It would seem the cables that connect the monitoring system are all cut. The system is completely broken. Even the cloud was erased. Nothing appears to be recording, and nothing has been stored anywhere."

Petrakis stared at her for a long moment, then said, "Thank you." Then he turned to Samaras. "Call everyone and tell them to come to the manager's office."

"Everyone?"

"Yes," Petrakis snapped, running down the hall to the elevators. "Every damn person in law enforcement and Diakos and everyone else who works here and is trying to help with this investigation." He slapped the elevator button. "A man was murdered, and a woman is missing, and someone infiltrated the hotel security office to steal the camera footage. Something is going on at this hotel, and I intend to get to the bottom of it immediately. Now make the fucking calls." The last few words came out louder than he expected. It wasn't Samaras's fault the investigation was falling apart around him. The man just happened to be an easy target.

On the next floor, while Samaras moved off to the side to make his calls, Petrakis jogged to the restaurant. He wanted a large coffee that was hot before he lost his shit on everyone in Diakos's office.

Near the coffee machine, he overheard two waitresses chatting a few feet away behind the wall that led to the kitchen.

"I feel so sorry for him," one woman said, her voice gravelly like she was a heavy smoker.

"Come on," the other woman said, her voice higher pitched like she was in her late teens. "He wanted her bad. The whole hotel knew it. His wife must have known, too."

"Do you think she really cares?" Gravelly asked.

"No," the younger one said, a small giggle escaping her. "But being the laughingstock of the workplace isn't doing her any favors. Especially if you hold such a prestige position with the hotel."

Petrakis held his coffee cup in his hands and waited. One would drop a name, and then he could get to the bottom of what the hell was happening at this hotel.

"Do you think they were fucking?"

There was a pause, then, "I don't think so, but you never know. Not that he didn't want to—she didn't want to."

"How can you know something like that?"

"Thanos told me he'd seen him trying to kiss her, and she pushed him away."

"Rejection sucks. As a married man, what was he expecting? That's why he's always in a shitty mood. Wasn't getting any."

They laughed at the same time as their voices moved closer.

Both of them were about to exit the kitchen.

The inspector held his cup to his mouth and sipped from it, then moved toward the lobby. He heard the women exit the kitchen behind him, still chatting in hushed tones, oblivious that he overheard them.

He'd interview them later about who this married man was and who it was that he supposedly fell in love with. That sort of thing happened often in the workplace, and it certainly wasn't illegal, but if one of them held an important position and the other felt coerced, and if maybe one was blackmailing the other …

But first, he wanted to speak to a man named Thanos. Apparently, he was in the know.

It could be irrelevant information, but it could also be connected to what was happening. He'd know more than he needed to know soon enough.

He took a deep breath at the manager's door and pushed it open.

"Inspector," Samaras said as he got to his feet.

Petrakis moved to the desk and set down his coffee. He took a moment to recite some of the physical details of the man they'd met in the security office to Samaras, who noted them in his small book.

"Find a sketch artist. We need hotel staff looking for this man, but add a warning not to approach him. Also, mention his accent."

"He sounded like he was from a village, sir."

Petrakis stared at Samaras. "You heard that, too?"

Diakos barged in, the office door slamming into the wall. "What happened, Inspector?" he asked, his volume too high in the enclosed space.

"Someone pretending to work for hotel security stole the unit that stores your camera footage and cut all the cables." Petrakis pursed his lips as he watched Diakos narrow his eyes.

"That's impossible." Diakos stared off to the side as if in a daze.

"It would seem, Mr. Diakos, that someone quite powerful is among us. Someone is motivated to kill for whatever reason, and they are not afraid of the authorities. We saw the man ourselves and can identify him."

Diakos glanced between the two of them. "And you didn't apprehend him?" His voice was rising again.

"He posed as your security man, Mr. Valentine."

"But Valentine is at home sick."

"We know that now."

"Sir," Samaras jumped in. "The man spoke a dialect of Greek. That mean anything to you?"

Diakos looked like he had swallowed something distasteful. His entire expression changed briefly, and then he was back, looking like a bored hotel manager.

"No, that means nothing to me."

Petrakis saw many tells on Diakos's face. The man was clearly lying as the color drained from his cheeks.

Why would the hotel manager lie bold-faced when he wasn't good at it?

What the hell was the manager hiding now?

"Do you have a Thanos on staff here, Mr. Diakos?"

Diakos blinked and refocused on Petrakis's face. "We do."

"How many employees are named Thanos?"

"Just one."

"Make sure I see him as soon as humanly possible."

"What's he got to do with all this?"

Petrakis stared at Diakos for several heartbeats. "He may

be the key that unlocks this mystery." He waved his hand. "Get him, sir. A woman is missing, and a man was murdered. Let's expedite this investigation. Hurry along now."

Diakos spun away and stormed out of his own office, obviously fuming at being talked down to in such a way.

Maybe next time, he'd consider not lying to the investigating inspector.

Chapter 19

FAYE NEEDED OUT OF the hotel. A walk along the beach, to breathe the sea's salty air, would replenish her and calm the voices in her head. However, only when she did something radical did the voices quiet for a time.

The heat soaked through her shirt, making her regret not wearing her swimsuit so she could get her feet wet at least.

The path took her by a rocky beach area, and then farther along, she made it to the hotel beach. Once on the sand, she took off her shoes and waded in the water up to her ankles, the sea cooling the soles of her feet after walking on the hot sand.

She glanced around to see if she was alone. The idea to strip naked and take a dip overwhelmed her. This area was private and reserved for the guests of the Lindos Palace Hotel. Since there was so much shit happening back at the hotel, the beach was empty today.

She disrobed and piled her clothes neatly at the side, concealed by a large outcropping of rock. This was something radical. This might help calm her.

Naked now, she ran for the water and jumped in, the sun high and warm overhead.

She swam for several minutes, enjoying the freedom, the peace, and quiet until it was interrupted by voices moving closer.

No longer alone, she had to go back and get dressed. She swam back to shore quickly and slipped into her clothes while still dripping wet, just as the others arrived.

Within ten minutes, she returned to her room and got out of her soaked clothes. A quick shower later to remove the salt from her skin, she lay naked on her bed, staring at the ceiling.

Maybe it was a mistake to book those extra days. She shouldn't be here, messing in other people's business.

And that mirror—it still spoke to her, whispering shit in her ear from across the room, getting louder and louder.

Angry now, she pushed up off the bed, grabbed the mirror, and held it away from her face.

Why did it have such a hold over her? The cursed thing wasn't just a reflection of what stood in front of it. The mirror was a reflection of one's soul, one's misdeeds. Staring into it spoke volumes of darkness and depravity.

Yet, she had to look in the mirror again. A person had to face their fears.

Almost against her will, the mirror turned slowly in her hand, the screen black.

Then, an image of a man carrying what looked like a corpse appeared. She gasped and dropped the mirror on the bed.

Her arms wrapped around her legs as she brought them to her chest. While taking deep breaths, she wondered if the damn thing was some kind of small TV and not a mirror at all.

A hundred thoughts raced through her mind. Who was the corpse in the image? Who was the man carrying the corpse, and better yet, why was that image revealed to her? Was this all related to the body parts she discovered in the bushes, or was it all an illusion?

Or the simpler explanation raised questions about her own sanity.

The more she thought about it, the more she couldn't find the nerve to calm down. She slipped under the bedsheets and tried to concentrate on her breathing while keeping her eyes closed. After a few minutes, she almost succeeded.

Then she thought about Roxanne and how she wanted to be a part of the solution, not the problem. She had to inform the inspector about the male voices she heard the night before Roxanne's disappearance.

In the bathroom, she splashed cold water on her face. Knowing she would change rooms as soon as she requested at the front desk, Faye started packing her things.

When she was ready, she grabbed the pad of paper the hotel supplied by the bed, then picked up the pen.

She wrote: One day before Roxanne's disappearance, she argued with a man in her room. She folded the note and tapped it in her hand.

Now, how would she get it into the inspector's hands?

An idea hit her. Jotting his name down on one side of the paper, she exited her room with the note in her pocket.

Not wanting to be seen carrying all her bags, she walked

along the row of rooms until she came to one of the cleaner's carts parked outside a propped open door. Through the crack in the door, she saw a woman making the bed in the room, humming to herself.

There was only a slight breeze, so she felt it was safe enough to leave her handwritten note on the cart just outside the room. The maid would see it and turn it into her boss, and it would make it into the hands of the inspector. It would not help much, but at least it would be off her chest. She would've done her part.

After setting the note down on a small group of tiny soap bars, Faye turned around and headed toward the back of the hotel, where the staff entrance was, right beside a row of large dumpsters.

No one was outside on a break, smoke or otherwise. The back area was empty, but it stank badly.

"What the hell is that smell?" she whispered.

It had to be the dumpsters.

She approached one and sniffed the air around it. It was rank but no worse than where she'd been standing moments before.

The second dumpster was a bit worse, but the third smelled of death.

Whatever was reeking up the area was in the third dumpster.

She moved ten feet away, inhaled cleaner air, held her breath, and then ran back to the third dumpster and opened it.

A cat had somehow gotten trapped inside. When the lid rose, the cat jumped out inches from her face, making her yip a short, high-pitched wail of surprise and release the lid in a panic. Her hands flailed at the cat that had already bolted behind the garbage bin. The short air intake from within the dumpster was so dense and rank that she gagged. The scent of whatever the hell was inside it was so heavy around her that she could taste it, swallow it.

She should have left the hotel yesterday.

It was only a matter of time before someone came out to investigate what all the noise was about, so she eased back against the far wall, hidden from the rear door of the building, a hand pressed to her chest.

Seconds later, a dark-haired man opened the back door and headed toward the villas with a covered tray. He wasn't at all interested in the smell or trying to see what was causing it.

The back door opened again just before she moved from her concealed spot against the wall.

This time, it was the inspector. He stepped out and looked around, holding the door. Did someone tell him they heard a scream out back?

He seemed to survey the area from the limited vantage point of the door, then stepped back inside, the door closing firmly behind him.

What the hell was going on? Why didn't he smell that rank odor?

Before the back door opened again, Faye ran from her spot at the wall, grabbed the garbage bin's lid, lifted it, and glanced inside. Several black bags were about halfway down, with one broken open, ripped—more likely torn open by that disgusting cat. Part of a human head peeked out, the eye dried up and sinking into the skull, the hair wavy and messy.

That dead eye stared up at her, accusing her of wrongdoing. She abruptly closed the bin, letting the lid slam down hard, then walked away at a fast clip. Her stomach churned at the vision, and her knees trembled, the air cleaner with each step.

Something spun in her head, making her dizzy, and she dropped to the pavement not twenty steps from the dumpsters.

When she opened her eyes, one of the cleaning staff hovered over her, a water bottle in one hand, a wet cloth in the other.

"Are you okay?" the woman asked.

Faye tried to sit up.

"Easy, don't rush. Go slowly." The woman set the cloth down and held Faye's arm.

"Thank you," Faye muttered. "The sun must've gotten to me."

From the corner of her eye, she saw the note she'd written protruding from the maid's pocket.

"What room are you staying in?" the woman asked. "Can I help you get somewhere?"

"No, thank you. I appreciate your help. I'll just go and lie down in my room. I'll be fine—"

A huge bang from the back of the restaurant cut her off.

A loud, piercing scream followed it.

The maid seemed rattled as she got to her feet.

Faye edged away, preferring to go to her room. Better to disappear now, as she could only imagine what had just happened at the back of the hotel.

The body wrapped in black garbage bags had just been discovered.

Chapter 20

Petrakis surveyed everyone in the manager's office. Samaras had done a great job collecting them all for this impromptu meeting.

The time had come to find out who was sleeping with whom. Someone was killing people behind the scenes and then attempting to cover it up, and Petrakis needed to put an end to it. The staff were uniquely positioned to paint a picture of the hotel and the guests therein.

He raised his hands as he surveyed the fifteen to twenty faces.

"Good morning. I know you all have jobs to do, but what we have to discuss can't wait." He walked out from behind the desk and leaned back on it, crossing his arms.

Something was happening out in the lobby as he heard voices rising.

"What now?" he whispered under his breath as he pushed

up off the desk.

The voices drew closer to the door, and then it banged open, nearly smacking Samaras, who stood beside it.

"Inspector, we need you. It's urgent." The man wore a stained white apron. "I'm one of the cooks from the kitchen. Sir, you have to see what we just found."

Petrakis glanced around the room at the surprised looks on the faces of the other staff, huffed out a heavy sigh at the interruption, and then strode from the room.

"Everyone, get back to work," he shouted over his shoulder. "We'll meet again in a few hours."

The cook signaled the inspector to follow him even though he was two steps behind.

Samaras and Diakos followed close behind him.

"What the hell's going on?" Petrakis asked the man in the apron. "What made you break up our meeting?"

The cook didn't answer him, and Petrakis had to take the stairs two at a time to keep up with the man.

The man led him to a side exit door, then outside. The cook held the door open until all three men stepped out into the sun.

Petrakis looked around but saw nothing wrong.

A woman sat on the grass at the edge of the pavement while someone helped her drink from a water bottle.

A garbage truck was parked off to the side, and two city workers sat on the grass by their truck, shirts open. They appeared to be lounging in the sun, but Petrakis guessed they were trying to calm down after something bad happened.

"Will someone please tell me what the hell is going on?"

The cook who dragged them all outside pointed at a black garbage bag on the concrete by one of the dumpsters.

No one spoke a word.

His temper rising at their evasiveness, the inspector approached the bag.

Something stuck out of the side of it. From a distance, he couldn't tell what it was, but as he drew closer, the side of a human head became visible.

He'd seen a lot over the years, but human heads in garbage bags were rare for Greece.

Samaras had followed, but when he saw what stuck out of the bag, he slowed and moved away. The man was gagging, fighting off the urge to vomit.

When he'd decided to become a cop, to work for the Greek authorities, he saw it as a secure job, a secure salary, and the shit he had to deal with on the island wasn't as big as being a cop in Athens.

"Get me some gloves," he shouted at Samaras without looking back at him.

Petrakis moved closer until he stood directly over the bag with the semi-exposed human head.

It didn't take Samaras long to obtain disposable gloves. He rushed up to Petrakis, averting his eyes from the bag at their feet.

The inspector slipped them on and then dropped to his knees in front of the bag. The smell was unbearable, which he expected. Humans stank. That's all there was to it. While alive, we covered up our smell with deodorants and colognes. But when we die, our true nature comes out of our disgusting vessels.

Petrakis lifted the edge of the bag and peeled it back, careful not to touch the rotting flesh of the head.

From the little he could determine, the head once

belonged to a young blond man. The neck had been severed clean. This looked like the work of a coroner or doctor, someone who knew what they were doing.

It wasn't Roxanne Dupont, and it wasn't Kallonis, as his body had already been removed from the premises.

Which meant he had *another* body on his hands.

Petrakis got to his feet and swore to himself. After a moment, he yanked off the gloves and tossed them toward the open garbage bin.

"Samaras, call the ambulance and explain that we have another body at the Lindos Palace Resort Hotel. We need this bag and any other bags in these bins taken to the medical examiner for possible identification. Secure the site and keep everyone away from the bins. Got it?"

Samaras nodded, the phone already going to his ear.

Petrakis strode away and returned inside, where the hotel manager awaited him.

"Is it another body?" the manager asked, his face white.

"Unfortunately." Petrakis moved past the man, leaving Diakos behind.

When the inspector turned back, Mr. Diakos was looking outside.

"Guys, none of us can help with anything," Diakos shouted. "Maria, go home for the rest of the day. We'll talk on the phone."

Petrakis waited for Diakos to finish talking to his staff, then followed him back into the hotel.

Once they reached the main floor again, Diakos's cell phone rang. He slowed, read the screen, and then picked up the call.

"What happened?" he asked, staring at nothing in

particular. "Please tell Mr. Boslov that if he wants extra drinks in his room, that can be arranged." Diakos nodded. "Right, well, he can go to the beach bar or wait for the main bar to open at seven." Another pause. "Wait, you told him that, and he still doesn't understand? Okay, I'm coming up." Diakos covered the mouthpiece. "I'll see you in my office after I deal with this."

Then Diakos turned and headed the other way, talking animatedly on the phone about alcoholics and guests.

Petrakis got to the manager's office and began to write up some of his findings. He would have huge reports to write later when this was all over, but he didn't want to miss some of the smaller bits of details.

He tapped the pen on the top of the desk twice before he fumbled it, and it flipped out of his hand.

"Fucking shit," he mumbled, bending down to pick it up.

Something caught his eye under the desk. A small folder was taped to the underside of the desktop.

He frowned. What's the hotel manager hiding? Taking his time, he peeled off the folder. He'd tape it back in a few moments as this was snooping more than it was investigating. But what would it hurt to see what he'd hidden?

He flipped open the top of the folder with a glance at the door. Inside were photos of a couple from afar. The woman was elegantly dressed, and the man wore a suit.

Why would Mr. Diakos have these photos hidden under his desk?

Petrakis retrieved his cell phone and photographed them. Once they were secured back in place under the desk, he gathered his papers and headed for the door. Out in the main lobby, he caught sight of Diakos talking to a tall man while a woman from housekeeping stood patiently next to him. As soon as the woman saw him, she hurried over to where he stood.

"Excuse me, sir, but aren't you the inspector?"

"I am." He nodded, and she handed him a folded piece of paper.

"I thought I'd give this to you. Someone left it on my cleaning cart about an hour ago."

He unfolded the paper and read it.

One day before her disappearance, she was arguing with a man in her room

"Who gave this to you? Did you see who left it?"

The woman seemed flustered. "No one, sir. I simply found it on my cart."

"Can you remember anything unusual that happened today? Anything at all?" After asking the question, he realized how stupid that was. The whole place was unusual lately. "What I mean is, in the usual course of doing your duties. And I'm not talking about the incident at the back of the restaurant."

The woman frowned and stared off to the side briefly as if trying to remember her movements.

She refocused on him. "Nothing else happened. At least not that I can remember, except for that poor woman who had a dizzy spell from the sun."

"Did you have the note before the woman who was dizzy or after?"

"Before."

"Okay, I'll need your name in case I want to talk to you again?"

She nodded. "It's no issue. I'm Barbara Wilmer."

"You don't have a Greek name."

"I'm from the UK. I came for a vacation a few years back and never left."

He nodded as if he understood that and said, "Thank you, Miss Wilmer. If anything else comes to your attention, please contact me directly."

She smiled at him and left.

Diakos had finished his conversation with the client and was walking over to him.

"Sometimes customers don't know what they want, and it's our job to help them find it."

"Are the owners of this hotel here yet? It's almost noon."

"Follow me," he said. "We're meeting them in one of the conference rooms."

Petrakis followed the manager, looking more haggard by the minute, down a couple of corridors until he opened a set of double doors to a large room with a conference table and chairs that could seat at least fifteen people.

"Take a seat wherever you want," Diakos said. "I'll have coffee and tea and small snacks brought in. The owners will be here shortly."

Diakos disappeared down a hallway, and Petrakis pulled his phone out to call Samaras, who was still out back waiting for the ambulance to take the body parts to the coroner. Nothing had changed back there—he was still waiting.

Petrakis called the Coast Guard next, only to learn they'd found nothing and abandoned their efforts in the sea near the beach by the hotel.

With time on his hands, he contacted the medical examiner handling Kallonis's body to confirm what he already knew. The man died from a blow to the back of the head by a blunt object.

After hanging up, he went to the whiteboard on the wall and grabbed a marker. He wrote down the names *Roxanne* and *Kallonis* and then added *a white male*. Could all these incidents be connected in some way?

Someone knocked on the door, and before he could react, it opened, and Diakos entered with an older couple.

"Mr. and Mrs. Markakis, I'd like you to meet Inspector Petrakis."

Diakos raised both hands in a dramatic manner when only one hand would do. He seemed uncomfortable in the presence of the owners, so Petrakis ignored Diakos and stepped up to the couple.

They all shook hands, and then Mr. Markakis signaled for Diakos to leave them.

Petrakis recognized the owner. Mr. Markakis was in those photos taped under Diakos's desktop. In those pictures, the woman he was with was not the woman in front of him. It was not his wife.

What the hell was Diakos doing? Was he blackmailing the owner? Holding something against him? Or should he wait to use those photos later if he needs them?

"What misfortune has befallen us with all these evil deeds?" Mr. Markakis said when the three of them were alone. "So many things have happened when a hotel should be a destination, a vacation spot where good times are had by all." He glanced at his wife as they took a seat opposite Petrakis. "We don't know how to react to all this, Inspector. Should we close? Isolate a wing? Should we make announcements?"

Petrakis watched the couple for a moment, gathering his

thoughts. They were both dressed well. It was obvious the couple were used to money. The woman, however, despite being indoors, wore dark sunglasses. Eccentric? Migraine? Or was she hiding bruises and tears?

"Let me start with some basic facts. Then we can decide what to do next. One of your guests, Miss Roxanne Dupont, went missing last night. No one has seen her since. Your head of security, Christos Kallonis, was found dead earlier this morning, and within the past hour, we found a human head in the dumpsters out back by the rear of the kitchen. I don't have a clue what's happening in your hotel yet, but I can tell you there are many secrets, and we've definitely got a murderer lurking somewhere in the shadows."

Markakis glanced at his wife again, then back to Petrakis. "For the sake of the hotel's reputation, how much of this can we keep sealed." His hands opened in front of him, pleading with Petrakis. "You must understand, sir, this will serve as a devastating blow to our reputation. It could completely ruin us, and then what? No one would buy the place. We'd never be able to sell it, and we still owe a considerable amount of money for it." Markakis's tone was tight, his voice monotone. "Please, all I'm saying is none of this is our fault. Why should we have to pay for it? Otherwise, my staff will cooperate fully, as will we, during the entire investigation. And when the perpetrators are located, we can all go back to our regular lives." He leaned back and clasped his hands together on the table. "That about sums up our concerns, Inspector."

"I'll be talking to the chief of police today, who is my immediate superior. I can't control what makes it to the media as everyone is on social media nowadays, but I can certainly conceal most of the brutal details, which I'll discuss with my bosses."

"We'd be eternally grateful for anything you can do, and my family would be willing to make a large donation to the Rhodes Police Department for their full cooperation."

The implication that they could be bought annoyed Petrakis, but he didn't let it show.

"Everything can be done if there's the right amount of motivation," Markakis continued.

His wife touched his elbow as if to calm his slide into hell with those good intentions.

Petrakis was about to lose his temper. He'd been called dozens of names in his career, but one of them was never corrupt.

"Mr. Markakis, if you're implying that you can sway how we investigate a murder at your hotel by offering us cash, you'd be sorely mistaken and dangerously close to breaking the law—"

"Please forgive me, Inspector, as I meant no disrespect. I'm desperate and simply wanted to express my gratitude for anything you can do to help protect my hotel." The man lowered his head slightly, which was all part of the show.

Something was wrong with this man and this couple, and Petrakis suspected Diakos knew all about it.

"I will need to continue to use your hotel as a base," the inspector said, hoping to close this pointless conversation. "If you want to keep as much information in-house, then allow me full reign here until the case is concluded."

"Yes, of course," Markakis replied. "I'll instruct the manager to give you anything you need."

"Perfect, then I think we're done here." Petrakis got up,

hoping the owners did the same. When he opened the door, he almost bumped into Diakos, who was sitting just outside, perhaps listening to the entire exchange.

"I was just about to knock," Diakos said. "We have a problem."

"What sort of problem?"

"The media are uncontrollable at the front of the hotel. They're suggesting all sorts of theories. What should we do? Will you be able to make an announcement?"

Petrakis stared. He almost laughed at the absurdity of it all. Bodies were piling up at this hotel, and everyone had a secret.

"You, Mr. Diakos, or the hotel owners are welcome to address the media. Right now, I am investigating several murders and a missing person. I need you to collect and bring me all the keys to every conference and meeting room in the hotel. I don't want anyone to have access to any area without my knowledge for the next few days."

The Markakises exited the room and stood beside him.

"What are you looking at me for?" Mr. Markakis asked Diakos. "Bring the inspector anything he needs and cooperate fully going forward. Consider him your new boss until he finishes his investigation here."

Mr. Diakos blinked twice, then nodded. "Please allow me half a minute to get to my office and gather what you're requesting. I'll also include the schedule for the few companies that want to rent out our conference rooms this week."

Diakos stepped away and strode down the corridor. The owners went after him, following Diakos down the hallway.

Petrakis closed the door behind him and made sure it was

locked. Then he meandered through the large expanse of the hotel until he made it to the restaurant and exited out the back to where Samaras was still waiting.

Petrakis didn't want to talk to the chief and couldn't talk to the press. There was nothing to say yet.

As the lead inspector on a missing persons case, and now a multiple murder case, he had no leads, no idea where things were headed, and bodies were starting to pile up.

This was a clusterfuck, and a disaster rolled into one failed career choice that would end him long before the Markakises lost their precious hotel.

And if the chief threatened to take him off the case, he'd stay in the hotel as a guest, free of any charge.

Mr. Markakis would see to that.

Or Inspector Petrakis would tell the world about the man's affair and all the terrible murders that took place at the resort known as the Lindos Palace Resort Hotel.

If this case ruined him, he'd take down as many lying, no-good fucks with him as possible.

That was something they could count on.

Chapter 21

FAYE SAT ON HER bed and stared outside her room's patio door, waiting for someone from the hotel to arrive. They'd notified her that someone would soon take her to her other room.

The mirror hadn't stopped its incessant whispering. She'd placed it face down on the bed beside her, wondering what she should do—leave it behind, throw it in the trash, or bring it with her.

The urge to examine the mirror's surface overwhelmed her when she glanced at it.

Quickly, she picked it up and held it at arm's length.

The mirror itself was covered in black.

She took a deep breath, turned it away from her, unable and unwilling to stare at it any longer, and then stashed it in her suitcase.

The moment she zipped her suitcase closed, someone

knocked on the door.

"Half a minute," she called out.

In the bathroom, she splashed water on her face. Then she applied a fake smile that showed teeth, exited the bathroom, and opened the room's door.

The clerk had come with a trolley. He introduced himself, smiled back, and grabbed her suitcase to place it on the trolley.

"Can I ask you a question?" Faye used her innocent little girl voice, making sure she sounded shy and nervous. "What's going on at this hotel?"

The boy, no more than eighteen, shook his head in a short burst. "They don't tell us much."

"Is there anything you know about that missing woman? I mean, she stayed in the room next to mine." Faye shivered to display a level of fear for his benefit.

"No one says anything." The young man swiped at an errant hair that slipped off his forehead. "They'll do their searches and hopefully locate her. Otherwise, she's probably just flown home or found some guy to shack up with."

"Didn't they find something in the garbage that belonged to her?"

The boy glanced at Faye. Then his eyes darted away. "Well, it wasn't hers as far as I know." He picked up his pace. "They'll keep looking and likely find more pieces."

Faye slowed her pace. "Pieces?"

The boy slowed and glanced back at her. "Yeah, they found someone's head in the trash."

"A head?" She clutched at her chest.

He scanned the area to ensure no one was looking at them, then leaned in conspiratorially. "Don't tell them I told you."

Faye shook her head to show she was in collusion with the boy. "Do they have a suspect yet?" She kept her voice low.

The boy shook his head. "Not that I'm aware of. It's just scary, you know."

She nodded.

After body parts turn up at a hotel, along with other dead people and guests who are missing, many of the other guests would usually deem that a reason to get the fuck out of there as soon as possible.

This hotel resort spot on the beach in Rhodes was about to get tarnished with a terrible reputation.

While following the boy to the other side of the hotel, he stopped in front of an older couple who seemed to be arguing. The woman whispered something intensely, and the man spoke louder, but it was still hard to pick up what they were saying.

The older man noticed them approaching and stopped talking mid-sentence.

"Good morning, sir," the boy said as he passed them.

"Guests of the hotel?" Faye asked when they were out of earshot.

"No, they're the owners of this place."

Faye stopped and turned to stare at them as the owners walked in the opposite direction.

The owners were called in. Of course, they were.

As soon as they arrived at her new villa, the clerk opened the door, put her things inside the room, and left without waiting for a tip.

Faye opened the porch door and stepped outside. The

view was magical, and the small pool seemed to invite her.

She dragged the deck chair into the shade and sat there to appreciate the calm, peaceful view.

But it was quickly disrupted when her neighbor stepped out onto his patio and spoke in an angry accent to someone—it sounded Russian. When she didn't hear any responses, she figured the guy was on the phone.

She couldn't understand a single word. It was just a bunch of random consonants and vowels that made no sense. Every now and then, she caught an English insult.

Annoyed at the disturbance but curious about what the man could be saying, Faye pulled out her cell phone and hit the record button on her voice memo app. Later, she'd find an app to translate it.

A second voice stepped out onto the patio less than a minute later. They debated something. Then she heard the distinctive sound of a slap—a hand smacking into flesh—and a deep grunt.

A thick bush separated the patios, but that was it. Neither side could see the other patio, but hearing them wasn't an issue.

Faye moved quietly to the bushes and separated them to peek through. She could see one of the men—she'd seen earlier at the reception desk.

Then he turned toward her.

She jumped back so hard that she lost her balance and stumbled onto her butt. She quickly left her cell phone on the ground and crawled into her room.

The front-desk Russian guy had responded quickly. He ran around the bushes to see who was watching them from next door.

Faye dove toward the inner side wall, obscuring herself from view from the outside. He wouldn't see her if he were willing to enter her room using the open patio door.

After waiting several minutes without seeing the man, she peeked around the corner.

Her patio was empty.

She couldn't hear anyone outside anymore, either.

She crawled onto her patio and snatched up her phone, happy it was still there.

Heart racing in her chest, she found an application that would translate Russian into English, connected headphones, and clicked for it to start.

A robotic voice only recognized slightly less than half of the Russian words. The English translation was garbled and didn't make a lot of sense. She wrote down some of the words she'd managed to translate with a piece of paper and pen.

You are an idiot ... that is, USB, garbage ... a job ... they will come ... we're fucked. There will be a massacre ... mark my words.

Faye stared at the paper.

"My fuck," she mumbled to herself. "A massacre?"

It's too bad she hadn't recorded the entire conversation. Could these guys have anything to do with the body parts she'd found in the bushes? Did they change their minds and wrap the pieces in garbage bags only to dump them in the back dumpsters, and now they're pissed because those bags were discovered?

Who were these guys? Who was the person they chopped up, assuming it was them who did the killing?

An idea hit her. She opened her suitcase and tossed her

clothes out of the way until she found the mirror.

Easing it out slowly so as not to aim it at her face until she was ready to stare at it, Faye lifted the cursed thing.

When she turned it around, a black shadow passed over the glass screen, and she understood what had happened.

Her heart raced in her chest at the realization.

The voices she'd heard arguing in Roxanne's room were that of a Russian man arguing with another Russian, not Roxanne.

Perhaps Miss Roxanne Dupont didn't understand what they were saying, or better yet, did Roxanne know how to speak Russian?

How many Russians were staying in the hotel?

What were they doing here?

Did they do something to Roxanne? Was anyone else in danger?

There will be a massacre ... mark my words.

What the hell did that mean?

Maybe Faye needed to speak with the inspector after all.

Or would that get her killed—like Roxanne?

Chapter 22

PETRAKIS WIPED HIS BROW in the heat as he stood beside
Samaras, waiting twenty feet from the garbage bin. The smell
of the bin's contents was too rancid to be that close to it.

"Did you call the ambulance again?" he asked.

"Like, a hundred times."

"And?"

"They don't answer. At least not after the first call went
through when I summoned them to come to pick up another
body."

Just as he finished talking, a police car rounded the
corner, followed by an ambulance.

"Where's forensics?"

Samaras shrugged. "Beats me."

Petrakis approached the ambulance as it stopped, and the
driver rolled down his window.

"Inspector Petrakis," he said as a greeting. "You guys'll

have to wait until forensics gets here. In the meantime, don't let anyone near the dumpsters."

Two policemen had approached after having parked their cruiser.

They exchanged a look—no one wanted garbage bin duty, especially if that bin had chopped up body parts.

The officers silently approached the bin—Petrakis let them, knowing they'd pay for their curiosity. The taller one opened the lid, peeked in, and then jumped back, slamming the lid hard. He gagged twice and wandered off to the side.

They wouldn't be touching it again anytime soon.

Samaras's phone rang.

He answered it. "What? Really? Which part?" When he paused, he glanced over at Petrakis. "Don't let anyone touch anything. I'll be right there." He smacked his phone, then slipped it away.

"They found a foot."

"What? Where?" Petrakis shook his head to clear it. This can't *actually* be happening. "Who found a fucking foot?"

"It's in the hotel's dumpster next to this one."

"You're kidding."

Samaras shook his head.

The inspector spun around and headed for the hotel parking lot, with Samaras following close behind him. They got into Samaras's car, and less than half a kilometer later, they parked at the back of the neighboring hotel.

Their staff had gathered around the garbage bin, just like at the Lindos Palace Resort. It's just this bin was green.

"Who found the item?" he asked when he stepped from the car.

The crowd parted to reveal a young man drinking water

on a concrete ledge.

Petrakis approached him, observing the pale boy. He looked sick and was probably drinking water to be rid of the vomit stench in his mouth.

"Tell me what happened."

"I came to throw away the garbage." He pointed. "I noticed a bag that was left out of the bin. So I went to get it and threw it out. There were holes where it looked like animals had tried to get into it. The side was torn, and it smelled terrible. When I touched it, I saw what looked like the bottom of an amputated leg. I dropped it and ran inside to call the cops."

Petrakis tapped the boy's shoulder once, then stepped away to head over to the bag. Samaras popped up beside him with a pair of gloves in his hand.

Where did he get all the gloves?

Petrakis slipped them on, then bent down and opened the bag. He shook his head and closed it. Samaras had stepped back, a hand over his mouth.

Petrakis glanced at him. "Forensics will be working overtime on this island, I presume."

"We'll need to know the identity of this man," Samaras said, his hand muffling his voice.

"No shit." Petrakis glared. "Call forensics so they can come here when they finish with the first bin." Petrakis moved away to approach the hotel staff. "I need to speak with the hotel manager."

"He'll be here in about—" The woman talking got cut off as the door behind her smacked open abruptly, and Mr. Diakos emerged from the inside.

Petrakis frowned in confusion. Diakos wasn't the

manager he expected to see.

"What brings you here?" Petrakis asked him.

Diakos approached him. "We have common staff. Sometimes they need help, and we send someone over, and vice versa."

Now, that was annoying. If the problem at the first hotel couldn't be contained to that hotel, then it would widen his investigation parameters even further. All this, and he didn't have a single suspect yet.

The chief was going to lose his shit on him, and there was nothing he could do about that.

What the hell was he thinking when he decided to get involved?

"Samaras, we'll need a list of this hotel's staff now, too. Diakos, I'll need a detailed list of the staff commonly working between both hotels."

"Yes, sir," Diakos said and stepped away.

Petrakis recalled that conversation he'd overheard between those two waitresses several hours ago in the restaurant.

He turned to Samaras. "Hey, did you ever manage to locate that Thanos Spyros guy for me?"

"No, I lost track of time with all that has been happening."

"Okay, I'll do it. You've got a lot more work now." Petrakis stepped away and approached Diakos, who was explaining to the hotel staff that everything needed to remain confidential while the authorities investigated what had happened.

Most of the staff stared back at him in shocked silence. These sorts of events were rare for this area—for any area, really. Usually, only big cities had such things taking place, and even then, it was still rare.

"As the manager just told you," Petrakis cut in, "don't say a word to anyone as this is all under investigation and cannot be stated publicly yet. If it's leaked to the press, then I'd be forced to close the hotel, and you'd all be out of a job for a short while, and no one wants that. Now, contact us directly if you notice anything suspicious or something that seems strange to you, no matter how insignificant it may be." The inspector nodded at that group, patted Diakos on the shoulder, and then walked back over to Samaras.

"Stay here until the team arrives," he told him, then returned to the Lindos Hotel. He wanted to walk back on his own and clear his head.

The temperature was blazing hot as it was early afternoon, but Petrakis took his time, watching the sides of the road as he walked. Midway, he stopped and stared at the distance between the hotels. No one would carry body parts in garbage bags from one to the other. Whoever did this drove the bags to area garbage bins.

And where was the crime scene? Where did the murder take place?

To dismember a corpse, it would have to be done in a controlled environment. Otherwise, the perpetrators risked discovery. This space wasn't likely to be inside either hotel as rooms had registered guests, and unless they were going to bleach the room, they'd leave evidence behind. So, was it done off-site somewhere, and the body parts were driven here from miles away? If so, the likelihood of him solving this case was almost zero.

Standing in the sweltering heat, he watched a buzzard

approach something on the ground. He remained silent and still until it landed, then ran at it, shouting to scare it off.

The bird shot back into the sky. Petrakis visually marked the spot on the ground where it had landed.

When he got there, panting for air in the heat, he found no more body parts, but he found something interesting.

A man's ring, made of some sort of unidentifiable material he'd never seen before, depicted a spider. He snatched up the ring, pocketed it, and returned to the Lindos Hotel.

Not ten minutes later, he strode by two reporters looking for a story, entered the air-conditioned lobby, and stopped at the reception desk. He asked reception to contact Thanos Spyros and then headed to the manager's office.

Just before he entered, he caught sight of a man watching him from around the corner at the end of the hallway.

Petrakis paused and looked away as he registered who it was, and he did not believe his eyes for a second. He wanted to confront the man but decided to move inside the office as if he hadn't seen the man. If he'd given chase, the man would be long gone. As far as Petrakis could recall, that particular hallway had an exit at the end leading to the outside, where cars were parked.

But he couldn't let the asshole get away this time, and Samaras was busy at the other hotel.

He grabbed his cell phone, turned on the camera, and set it to video, then ripped open the office door and recorded out in front of himself as he ran toward the corner where he'd seen the man watching him.

The man had come out of hiding and didn't expect to be chased. Even though Petrakis was running, the man's face was filmed from a distance before he turned around and ran in the opposite direction. The man made the corner in seconds flat, rounded it, and was gone.

Petrakis pumped his arms, but when he got to the corner and looked the length of the hallway, the exit door at the end was just closing.

He'd never catch the bastard now.

Staring down the end of the hallway would do him no good. He leaned against the wall to catch his breath and then turned and walked toward the reception desk. When he got there, Evelyn Diakos, the manager's wife, was working. He nodded at her, raised his phone, and pressed the button to play the video back.

"Can you tell me if you recognize this man?" He held it up for her to see.

"What man?" Evelyn asked as she stretched forward to watch the inspector's video.

"Do you know him?" Petrakis asked again.

"The image is grainy. Let me try to improve the resolution."

Petrakis handed over his phone. He watched as Evelyn played the video and paused it twice, staring at the screen.

Then she looked up and met Petrakis's gaze. "I know him. He's usually a guest at the hotel next door but prefers our facilities."

"Can you tell me if he's staying at the other hotel right now?"

Evelyn looked doubtful. "I'm not sure. I mean, that's what he told us."

"When was the last time you saw him?"

"I can't be sure. I'm not always here. I work mostly in

the spa." She shrugged. "Probably yesterday."

"Can you be more specific? Morning, afternoon, evening?"

"Morning." Evelyn scratched at her temple. "He's been here for a week at least. He asked if he could use our facilities while staying next door, which works for both hotels. We always share clients."

"And he pays for this privilege?"

She nodded. "Of course, he always pays on the spot. Otherwise, our charges would go to the other hotel, which can be a nightmare."

Evelyn stopped talking as a man moved up to the counter beside Petrakis.

"Someone asked to speak to me. I'm Thanos."

"Yeah, me. Just a second," he said, raising a finger. He turned back to Evelyn. "Get me this guy's name and room number in the other hotel. I have to speak with him today."

She nodded. "That won't be a problem, provided he hasn't checked out yet."

Petrakis motioned for Thanos to follow him. He hurried inside the manager's office, took a seat, and gestured for Thanos to sit across from him.

"Thanos, tell me who this man is. Have you ever seen him?" He handed over his cell phone.

Thanos watched the video and then handed back the phone.

"Yeah, I've seen him around. What of it?"

Petrakis stared at him for a heartbeat. "Tell me about your beloved manager. Who was it that he made a pass at?"

Petrakis hit the record button on his phone.

Thanos shook his head, fiddled with something on his

pants, then started talking.

"It was no big deal, really."

"Great, so telling me everything won't be an issue."

Thanos crossed his legs, then uncrossed them. He took a big breath. "One night, as I returned to the staff rooms, I heard our manager's voice. I took another route to come around behind them. He was talking with a woman."

Thanos stopped and looked away as if studying the pictures on the wall.

"And?"

Thanos jumped and looked back at Petrakis. "Well, he grabbed this woman, then pushed himself up against her body. She tried to push him away, and I bolted before they saw me. The last thing I wanted was to get involved in some love affair and end up losing my job over it. I mean, this is the manager we're talking about."

"Did Mr. Diakos see you?"

"No, if he had, he would've definitely spoken to me to keep my mouth shut."

"Do you suspect others know about his behavior with this female?"

Thanos shook his head.

"Who was the woman? Did you recognize her?"

Thanos nodded. "It was Roxanne Dupont. Everyone knows he wants her, but she always rebuffs him."

Was a spurned lover a motive for someone to commit murder? Had we fallen so far as a race?

"Have you told anyone what you saw that night?"

Thanos shook his head. "No one, Inspector," he replied without looking him in the eye.

Why would he lie to him? What could he gain from it?

The waitresses knew all about it.

"Thanos?"

He stared back at Petrakis. "Yes?"

"You're lying. You told someone. Why lie about it?"

Thanos took a deep breath, most likely afraid for his job.

"After telling a few of the girls in the kitchen, I realized I was wrong to say anything. In this place, you keep your mouth shut. You keep your job. It's that simple. I shouldn't have said a word. If Mr. Diakos hears what I said, then I'm in big trouble." He fumbled in his pockets for something. "Can I smoke?" He pulled out a pack and snatched up a lighter.

"We're done here. Smoke outside."

Thanos got up and left. He wasn't gone more than a few seconds before someone knocked on the door.

"Come in," he called.

Mr. Diakos opened the door, slipped inside, and closed it behind him.

"I understand you have video footage of a person of interest," Mr. Diakos said.

Petrakis gestured for him to come closer. "Come, sit, we should talk."

Diakos seemed anxious, but he obeyed without protest.

Once the manager was seated, Petrakis leaned forward and showed him the footage on his camera.

"Do you recognize him?"

Diakos looked carefully at the phone. "Should I?"

Petrakis leaned back in his chair and put his phone away.

"It would seem your wife knows this man's face."

Diakos lifted one shoulder. "She would have a better eye for our guests than I would. I'm more into the managerial side of things. Sure, I deal with the guests when there are problems, but day-to-day dealings aren't something I'm involved in much."

Someone knocked again.

"Come in," Petrakis called out.

Samaras stepped inside. "We have a team of men to help us investigate. The chief felt you needed more help." Samaras sat next to the manager. Mr. Diakos nodded at him.

"Okay, gentlemen, it would seem we aren't getting anywhere too fast with this investigation, so now it's time to ask the hard questions."

"The hard questions?" Diakos said, his tone higher than normal, his brows raised.

"Well, for example, Diakos, tell us about your feelings for Miss Roxanne Dupont. In fact, tell us why you hid the fact that you had feelings for her in the first place."

Petrakis stared at him until Diakos couldn't bear it and looked away.

After what felt like a minute, Diakos said, "Our relationship was purely professional." He spoke slowly and clearly.

"I have a witness that claims you threw yourself at her, trying to kiss her, but she resisted."

Diakos smiled.

"Did I say something funny?" Petrakis asked.

"No, it's just that you asked about my feelings for her. I don't have any. I just wanted to fuck her like everyone else at this hotel."

The inspector glared at him while Samaras gawked at that answer.

"Look, Mr. Manager, you can fuck around and joke with us all you want, but I assure you it won't end well. We have dead bodies piling up, and we're still looking for Miss Dupont. I don't see anything funny about this situation, nor do I like the fact that you weren't more forthcoming. If you don't want any suspicion falling on you in any way, then you had better be more forthcoming going forward before we find out about things after the fact."

Diakos didn't lose the half-smile on his lips. That humble manager who cared about the hotel and his clients whom Petrakis had met yesterday had disappeared.

"Our relationship was purely professional, not because I wanted it that way, but because she didn't want anything more. On her second night here, we were in the restaurant late, having drinks and discussing the art show. She was all laughter and hints, you know, sexual innuendos, so I made my move when I was escorting her back to her room, and she rejected me. Life goes on. No big deal. I didn't want a *relation*ship, nor did I have feelings for her. As I said, I just wanted to fuck her, which is something I enjoy with certain guests from time to time. Anyone in my position would do the same if he had such a piece next to him."

"Mr. Diakos, not just anyone—you. Does the institution of marriage mean anything anymore?"

"Look, not that it's a crime to fuck who you want, Inspector, but I have an open relationship with my wife. I just regret that I wasn't more careful and someone saw me. Otherwise, who really belongs to anybody anymore? Every marriage has infidelity. The rare few may not, but we weren't born to be married. Men and women alike seek variety."

"Interesting, but it doesn't justify the fact that you hid it from us when we were looking for the woman who spurned your advances."

"I didn't speak up because this information isn't useful and would only serve to have you delve into me and my life unnecessarily. Why waste your investigative efforts? I flirted, and she said no, it was over. The issue is to locate our missing guest, nothing else."

Petrakis stared at Diakos. He should've paid more attention to this man. There was something about the man that he didn't like. And what was he doing with blackmail photos taped up under the desk Petrakis sat at now?

"You know what, we aren't getting anywhere with this, are we?" Petrakis got to his feet. "I'll continue to investigate, along with the help of my team. If you still withhold information, Mr. Diakos, I'll ensure it doesn't go well for you."

"What, you'll throw the book at me?" Diakos said as he got up from his chair, seemingly annoyed.

"I'm not that cliché." Petrakis watched as Diakos headed for the door.

They exchanged a look, and then the manager was gone.

"Something is going on with that man," Petrakis said when the door shut behind Diakos. "Watch him, tail him, find out everything you can about him and his wife. They're up to something. I can feel it."

Samaras nodded quickly. "Do you think they're directly involved in all of this shit? Involved, as in they killed someone?"

"I wouldn't put it past him. Did you see how he smiled and talked about how he just wanted to fuck her?"

"I saw that." Samaras stepped back, his thumbs hooked in his belt line.

"The odds are, he's not involved, but I don't like the

bastard. And sometimes, you just never know."

"True, Inspector, you just never know."

"Now go, find me a suspect. We need to arrest someone soon."

"On it."

Samaras strode from the room, and Petrakiș considered calling the owners back for a meeting.

He wondered what they would think about the man they left in charge of their beloved hotel.

Chapter 23

IF FAYE WAS GOING to stay several more days, she needed to leave her room and enjoy the sunshine. She had changed into her bikini and sat on a lounge by the sea, a sunhat shading her eyes.

The waiter who served her area hadn't come to take her order as he seemed involved in a client dispute.

It had been over fifteen minutes. She'd waited long enough.

She got up quickly, stepped onto the hot sand, stumbled on her feet, and bumped into a man walking by.

"Oh, I'm so sorry."

The man tripped over the chair beside hers and smacked into the ground, losing the juice he'd been carrying in the sand.

"I am so sorry." Faye had retaken her seat and was slipping her flip-flops on. The sand was too hot for bare feet.

"Please, let me get you another drink."

"No need," the man said, getting back to his feet and brushing himself off. "It was an accident. Forget about it."

"I'm so embarrassed. The sand burned my feet, and I stumbled. At least let me buy you another drink."

"It's fine, you don't have to."

The man waved her off, grabbed his empty cup, and walked three rows of chairs away, where he plopped down and rummaged through his bag in search of something.

When she saw where he was sitting—and that he was alone—she went to the bar and ordered a replacement drink for him and one for herself, then charged it to her room.

Moments later, his drink in hand, she headed his way. As she drew near, she noticed that his attention was elsewhere. He was watching a small group of men. Close enough now to hear their voices, she detected the Russian language from the men staying in the room next to her.

"A thousand apologies," she said, startling him.

He grunted and looked up at her, distaste on his face. Then he nodded, took the drink she was handing him, and looked away.

"Thanks," he muttered, his attention back on the group of Russians, even though his face was angled out toward the sea.

She dropped onto the empty seat beside him and sipped from her mojito.

"You don't mind me sitting here, right?" When he didn't respond, she added, "I'm Faye."

"I'm George," he said, still staring out at the sea, his eyes diverting occasionally toward the Russians.

"Are you staying here for a few days?" she asked.

"A few days, yes," he said, then sipped his drink.

"Vacation or work?" she asked.

Not looking at her yet, George said, "I'm just here for fun."

"For fun? You?" For some reason, this man was annoying her. Why was he watching the Russians so intently? Were they bothering him somehow?

"I also came for fun. Rhodes is lovely, isn't it?" She stopped talking as she'd already lost his attention.

One of the Russian men shouted something at another one and got up to leave.

George rose from his chair and looked directly at her, leaving his drink on the small table beside him.

"Nice meeting you, but I have to leave now. Thanks for the drink." He strode off, meandering around lounges, walking in the general direction of the Russian male leaving the beach.

Faye leaned back and watched, sipping her beverage. She got up and followed him as soon as he was a dozen meters away. She doubted he'd notice her with his attention on the Russian, which could be fun. They were up to something that would offer her a sense of adventure.

One after the other, the trio walked along the beach, gradually moving away from the Lindos Hotel toward the one next door. Faye moved onto the grassy area to follow them less conspicuously while George stayed on the sand.

Minutes later, the Russian man entered the other hotel through the beach access door, and George followed him.

Faye ran for the lobby doors, which were closer to her position up near the road now, and entered a full minute after George had done so.

When she entered the front, both men had made it up one level to traverse the lobby. From where she stood, she had a full view of the elevators—the Russian was stepping on, and George was already inside.

Both men were on the same elevator now.

The doors slid closed, and it began to ascend.

She ran closer to see which floor they would stop on.

The dial had paused on the second floor.

Having no idea what intrigued her about this, other than the whole adventure of it all on an otherwise boring holiday, she ran for the stairs on the side. By the time she made it up a couple of steps, she almost bumped into a group of men speaking Russian as they descended.

Something was off somehow. Why were there so many Russians on vacation at the same time? And how come they all looked ready to fight, with their bulging muscles, crew cuts, or bald heads?

She made it to the second floor, where the elevator doors were already closed, and turned back around to head to the lobby. What the hell was she doing? This was reckless and foolish but exhilarating at the same time.

Maybe she should talk to the inspector. Her new friend, George, may be in trouble.

Back in the lobby, which was empty except for a young couple checking in who was clearly speaking in an American accent, she ran to the side counter to speak with a clerk who was shuffling papers.

"I need to use your phone to call the inspector at the other hotel."

"Of course, ma'am." The clerk didn't offer any facial expressions of concern. He just nodded, responded to her, and kept filing his papers. "Just press the number three. It'll dial their reception." He handed her the phone.

Faye dialed out, put the phone to her ear, and then turned around to watch the lobby in case any of the Russians were close enough to listen to her.

When the line was answered at the Lindos Palace, she cut them off and said, "You must notify the inspector. I heard noises on the second floor of the neighboring hotel. I think someone's in trouble. I heard screams—" Then she killed the line.

She set the phone down gently, thanked the clerk, who had stopped shuffling papers and was staring at her now, and then exited the building in a half run.

She couldn't understand why George was so interested in the Russians. Were law enforcement and the Russian men under surveillance? That might be the most likely scenario.

Fifteen minutes later, with no one interrupting her progress, she reached her room and closed the door behind her, locking it firmly.

She dropped onto the bed right beside that horrible handheld mirror.

After a few seconds of staring at the back of it, she grabbed it and spun it around.

The corpse of a woman lying face down materialized in the small glass. There was blood on her head.

Like watching a TV screen, a man stepped into view on the mirror's surface, a rolling pin in his hand.

Faye tossed the mirror onto the bed. Shaking now, she opened the minibar for a drink.

It was only a fucking mirror. How was it possible she was seeing images inside it?

She was either crazy, or that mirror was a mini TV thing.

She stopped what she was doing, the small bottle of whiskey in her hand.

Was she crazy? Or was she being enlightened? There was no way she was losing her mind … right?

She drank the small bottle of whiskey in one go, sure that it was her mind that was gone now.

"Russians and spies and people following each other throughout multiple hotels in Rhodes," she whispered to herself. "Yes, I've completely lost my shit."

She scavenged in the minibar fridge for another bottle of whiskey, not forgetting what the Russians next door had said about a massacre coming.

Maybe she wasn't crazy after all.

Chapter 24

THE PHONE RANG, STARTLING him out of his sleep. Petrakis jerked upward so hard he almost slipped off the bed.

They'd given him a fold-out cot in one of the conference rooms so he could take a power nap as Samaras brought a few of the new investigative team members up to speed. He needed the team to interview people, gather camera footage from the other hotel, and call guests who had already checked out—basically knocking on doors as if these crimes had happened in a residential area. There had to be a witness to something. If they kept knocking, they'd find them.

In the meantime, he'd needed a one-hour power nap, which just abruptly ended.

He grabbed the phone. "What?"

"There's more trouble at the resort besides this one." It was Samaras.

"What sort of trouble?" he asked, his mouth dry and in

need of a toothbrush.

"Sir, we need you. Now. I'm in the lobby."

"I'm coming," he said, hung up, then cursed twice.

Less than four minutes later, he met Samaras in the lobby, still trying to blink away the sleepiness. Samaras led him to his car, and they started across the short distance to the other hotel.

"What's this all about?" Petrakis tried to keep his eyes open, but the bright sunshine had other plans. He'd be happy when he was back inside a building.

"Someone called the Lindos asking for you. Apparently, they heard noises and that someone was in trouble or screaming or something like that."

Petrakis looked sidelong at him. "You aren't sure why we're going over to this hotel?"

Samaras snapped a look at him. "I didn't take the call, sir. The girl at the front desk did, then she called me, and I woke you up."

"Why me?"

Samaras pulled into the front of the neighboring hotel and stopped the car. "What do you mean, why you? I'm confused now."

"Aren't noise complaints usually handled by hotel security? Why wake me up unless you found another body or someone confessed to all this fuckery?"

Samaras stared at him. "Sir," he said, "the caller asked for you specifically. I would think that if it were a noise complaint, the hotel would've handled it, and no one would've called looking for the inspector." He lifted one shoulder. "I figured it had to do with the case we're working on as you were called for specifically."

Petrakis stared back at him a moment longer, his eyes almost adjusted to the light, then nodded. "Fine, let's go check on this noise complaint." *Then I'll go back to sleep for an hour*, he didn't add out loud.

The receptionist pointed at the stairwell inside the lobby and said, "It's on the second floor."

The inspector hit the stairs, running with Samaras following close behind. He reached the floor and slowed to look left and right down the corridor. Two cleaning carts were in the hallway, and a guest was strolling to his room, key card in hand.

Everything seemed calm and normal.

The inspector gestured for Samaras to head down the corridor, working one side of the hallway and placing their ears close to the room doors.

Samaras nodded his understanding and moved to the first door on the left as Petrakis got to the one on the right.

Walking room by room, they neared a member of the hotel cleaning staff as she gathered towels over her arm.

She was about to knock on a door ahead of Petrakis when she saw him and stopped, her hand suspended above her head.

He flashed his badge, then signaled her to step back and wait. Confused, the middle-aged woman slowly eased back.

Petrakis slipped in front of her and put his ear to the door. People whispered harshly inside the room in a language he didn't understand.

It sounded Russian.

Behind him, the cleaner's cart was a meter away. He grabbed several towels like the maid had done, draped them over his arm, and knocked on the door.

Samaras stood to the side and then shooed the woman away.

After a moment, when the small peephole in the door darkened, he said, "Housekeeping."

"Nyet," a man yelled through the door.

"Housekeeping," he said. "Someone ordered towels."

More footsteps moved close to the door. The peephole darkened, lightened, then darkened again.

The lock snicked out of place, and the door handle turned.

When the door drew inward, a tall, blond bear of a man eased out the small opening. The angry look on the guy's face wasn't just because of the intrusion by the hotel staff—something else was going on in this room.

Petrakis saw several dark red spots on the man's shirt.

Recently, someone had bled on him.

"I brought your towels," Petrakis said in Greek.

The man gawked at him—if such a huge man could be guilty of gawking with his mouth open, eyes wide, large brow furrowed—it was more of a dumb look like the guy was just plain dumber than a bag of wing nuts.

Without waiting for a reply, the inspector thrust the towels toward the man, which made him jump and try to block the inspector's arm. They smacked into each other, knocking the towels from Petrakis's hands.

He bent over to pick up the towels. "Hey, there's no need to be so mean about it—" Petrakis pretended to stumble and fall forward, diving between the man's thick thighs and the doorframe.

He landed hard on the floor, spun around, and had hands on him before he could take in the whole room.

What he did see in that second was three other men standing around a fourth unfortunate soul who had been tied to a chair, his face a bloody mess.

Then the guy who'd answered the door had grabbed the back of Petrakis's shirt and pants and lifted him off the floor, manhandling him toward the door.

Someone stepped in—Petrakis hoped it was Samaras—and did something to the burly man. The hands holding Petrakis vibrated abruptly, then released him.

Petrakis dropped back to the floor, which was only a few inches, with the big man landing beside him, clutching his neck below the chin.

"Everyone, calm the *fuck* down," Samaras shouted above Petrakis's head.

The inspector pushed up to his feet and adjusted his clothes.

All three men in the room had reached for a weapon, with two training their guns on Samaras and the third man aiming at Petrakis.

"Gentlemen," Petrakis said in English, raising his hands slightly, the man still gasping for breath at his feet. "We're Greek, and I'm pretty sure you're all Russian, but isn't that funny?"

Two of them frowned at him, their weapons unwavering.

"Okay, I'll tell you what's funny." He stepped closer to the man in the chair, who looked unconscious, blood mixed with mucus oozing off his chin. "What's hilarious is that this is a Mexican Standoff." The man aiming his weapon at Petrakis frowned. "Do you guys understand Greek or English?"

Petrakis didn't want to get shot, so he kept his hands

chest high. When none of them responded, he moved even closer to the man holding the weapon on him and forced a smile.

"I'm Inspector Petrakis, and this here is Officer Samaras. Killing a member of law enforcement won't be in your best interest." He jerked his head toward the man in the chair. "So, how about we take this guy to get some medical treatment, and you fellows run along? Playtime's over."

He lowered his hands and turned to face the man in the chair. Why was he familiar?

Then it dawned on him.

This was the man in the video on his phone, the man he chased.

The one he was looking for.

One of the Russians eased backward and opened the sliding door onto the balcony. Then he slipped outside, put away his weapon, and hopped over the railing.

It was only about an eight-foot drop—no issue for a man in top shape.

Another man lowered his weapon and followed suit.

The guy who opened the door slowly got to his feet, breathing better now, and eased around Samaras, making his way for the corridor.

Samaras lowered his weapon, and they both stared at the last Russian who hadn't taken his eyes off Petrakis.

All guns were aimed at the floor now.

The man moved closer to Petrakis. "You shouldn't interfere in things that do not concern you. Stay out of our affairs."

"Is that a warning? Like one of those sentences that end with an, *or else*?"

The weapon clicked in the man's hand, and he moved a few feet closer, his jaw clenching.

Petrakis detected Samaras raising his weapon.

"I don't threaten pigs. I mutilate them. Come near me or my men again, and you will be torn into pieces. None of my men will hesitate next time. I will give them the kill order if either of you two interferes with my business."

From the look in the man's eye, Petrakis had no doubt he wasn't bluffing. In fact, he felt the man's urge to pull the trigger and started to wonder why he hadn't yet. Was it because he was alone in a room with two law enforcement officers now or because his men had fled in fear?

"Are you saying the men who ran are loyal?" Petrakis didn't wait for an answer when he said, "They didn't look too loyal to me."

The Russian sneered. "You question the loyalty of my men from one moment in time, one example." The man shook his head and tsked a couple of times. "You are a very stupid man. Very stupid."

"Uhm, sir," Samaras whispered behind him.

He detected Samaras shuffling behind him but had to keep his eyes on the armed man in the room. That man was scaring the shit out of him.

"Yes, I would question their loyalty. I didn't even draw my weapon, and they ran from your side like little girls—"

"They didn't run, *svin'ya.*" He nodded behind Petrakis.

"Uhm, sir," Samaras said again.

Doubt filled the inspector. What the hell was happening behind him?

He eased around and glanced over his shoulder.

At least ten men filled the opening of the hotel room

door, all armed with weapons trained on Samaras's face, with a few aimed at him for good measure.

He eased back to stare at the man in front of him, surprised his nerves hadn't made his knees give out.

"You see?" the man in charge of the Russians said. "My men didn't run. They went to tell the others we were about to have a pig roast." The man nodded once, his gaze over Petrakis's shoulder. "Let them go this once." He glared at Petrakis. "Pry into my affairs again, and you do not walk away. I hope for your sake this is understood."

Petrakis waited a moment, then nodded slowly.

The man spit on the carpeted floor of the room. "Now, get out of my sight, you irrelevant *svin'ya*."

The men parted to make a pathway for Petrakis to walk.

No one touched him as he followed Samaras out the door and down the hallway.

He didn't start breathing again until they were on the stairs.

"Inspector, are you okay, sir?" Samaras slowed at the lobby and turned back. "That was scary."

"Good work"—he swallowed—"on subduing that brute at the door. What did you do to him?"

"A quick jab to the throat. Works on any man, any size."

"Thank you."

"Inspector," the receptionist called before they reached the front doors. "Please, sir. One of our clients has fallen. He's hurt."

Petrakis started that way as it gave him something to do, something to take his mind off what had just happened.

It looked like he figured out who was dropping bodies around the hotels. But how could he prove anything, arrest anyone? These sorts of men were above his pay grade.

He wanted out of this hotel and into the fresh air. His heart was beating in his throat, and he needed to call this in and let the chief know everything.

The chief could make the tough decisions.

To feel useful, though, he could help the front desk clerk deal with this issue first. Then he'd go outside, call the chief, and hand this cursed case over to someone else.

Fuck it, I'm out.

That Russian man scared the shit out of him. He wasn't afraid to admit it and didn't want to see him again.

Outside the access door to the pool, a man lay sideways on the grass just off the raised path. He must've tripped and twisted his ankle because it was already twice the size.

"Have you called an ambulance?" he asked the clerk.

"He refused treatment, sir. Told us no ambulance. Apparently, his friends will come to get him."

Petrakis bent down and looked into the man's face.

He was one of the Russians from the room. The one who had jumped from the balcony.

And there it was, handed to him on a silver Russian platter, his one-way ticket into their little gang. All he had to do was hand this asshole off to the chief and then be done with the case.

"Well, hello there. I think we need to have a long chat."

The Russian tried to get up but cried out with the pain in his ankle. By Petrakis's guesstimate, the man had dragged himself through the lobby and out toward the back pool area without much trouble. Still, now that his lower leg was blowing up like a pufferfish's body, every movement was met with violent currents of pain.

"Samaras, call an ambulance. Don't listen to this man. He needs that ankle taken care of, and then we can chat with him."

Samaras quickly dialed out while Petrakis took a peek back inside the lobby.

None of his comrades were loitering in the area. They had precious moments to get this man offsite without his friends knowing, and they needed to do it fast.

He glanced back at Samaras. "Did they say how long?"

He nodded. "A few minutes. They were close, still dealing with those body parts at the back of the Lindos Hotel. They'd gladly take this call and come back later for the other."

"This man is in custody now. Consider him dangerous. While we wait, watch out as his friends may come."

"You take me nowhere," the Russian spat. "I don't go nowhere with pig. Fuck you, whore cop."

"We're trying to help," Petrakis said in a high-pitched voice. "Your ankle is in bad shape, asshole. We fix it *real* good."

"Fuck you, whore *svin'ya*."

"Nice, but no thanks. Perhaps some other time, cocksucker." Petrakis whispered the last word.

The man lunged at Petrakis's leg but came up short, clenching his eyes shut and pursing his lips at the pain.

"Hurts like a bitch, don't it?" Petrakis was enjoying himself. A little payback to how scared he was in that hotel room not five minutes ago didn't hurt one bit.

The ambulance pulled up a minute later, and two paramedics hopped out, grabbed a stretcher, and wheeled in through the front doors of the lobby.

Petrakis waved them over, then looked at Samaras. "Once he's loaded in the back, you'll need to go with him to the hospital. Secure him there with your cuffs. I'll speak with him in a few hours once that ankle's treated."

Samaras nodded, probably happy he got to leave the premises. Handling one injured Russian was something he could manage. Staying here and handling a dozen armed Russians and an unknown purpose was much more daunting.

"I can do that," Samaras muttered.

The paramedics lowered the stretcher and removed a backboard, which they set on the ground beside the man.

He seemed to acquiesce because he let them load him onto the backboard without protest. On the count of three, the paramedics lifted him gently onto the wheeled stretcher and secured the man.

"Gentlemen," Petrakis said to the paramedics. "This man is in custody. Officer Samaras will accompany you to the hospital and stay with this man until I arrive. Understood?"

Both paramedics nodded, with one shrugging. None of this mattered to them. They were just transporting an injured man to the hospital.

"Okay, let's go."

Petrakis followed them to the waiting ambulance, where the Russian was loaded without incident.

Samaras jumped up into the back and turned to toss the car keys to him.

"Take my car back to the Lindos Hotel. When you're ready, come get me at the hospital."

Petrakis nodded. "Will do. Be safe." Then, as an afterthought, he added, "And thanks."

The cop was growing on him. He'd backed him up quite

well with the Russian brute at the hotel room door, and he was quick on his feet. He'd have to remember this man when he was done with the investigation at these hotels. He deserved a case of beer or a few good bottles of wine.

Samaras closed the ambulance doors, and seconds later, it pulled away from the front of the hotel.

Petrakis watched it leave, then glanced up at the balconies to see if anyone was watching him.

The balconies were all empty.

"Score one for the good guys," he whispered, then started toward Samaras's car.

It was time to return to the Lindos Palace Resort and get the owners of both hotels to close down while he called the chief and updated him on everything.

He was almost done with this place, this case. Yet, something told him it would get worse before it got better.

Chapter 25

Darwin Kostas had listened to the entire exchange in the hotel room with the Russians and the inspector. How Petrakis walked out of that room was impressive, but now the man had interfered with the Russians. Viktor, the man in charge, had specifically said not to fuck with him, not to interfere with his business, and Petrakis went and did exactly that—he took one of theirs away in an ambulance.

Not a smart move on the inspector's part.

That was the problem with everyone—they always underestimated people like Viktor. His men, the Russian mafia, belonged to the *bratva*, the brotherhood.

Darwin watched the ambulance leave, then saw Petrakis driving back to the Lindos Hotel.

With no sign of Roxanne Dupont yet, he had to keep the inspector close, so he started the trek back to the hotel, leaving four of his men behind to keep an eye on the

Russians. They had orders to extract the Greek agent—alive —from the Russians if at all possible.

The listening devices that had been planted gave Darwin everything and nothing.

He knew Dupont was still missing, and no one knew what she was selling. What he wanted was the location of the items she had planned to sell to the Russians.

But this gave him a reprieve—for now.

He had just started back to the Lindos when his phone rang. Rosina.

"Talk to me. Got anything new?"

"A body was discovered on the other side of Rhodes."

"Another body?" he asked, his voice rising. "What the hell's happening?"

"It was in a private residence."

"How is it relevant?"

"They just ID'd the body."

"And?"

"His name is Peter Singer. A British man. He was Roxanne's—"

"Boyfriend," Darwin finished for her.

"Well, ex-boyfriend now."

Darwin stopped walking to look out at the sea. "Is Roxanne their only person of interest?"

"She is, but they're still examining the residence, collecting forensics. According to a news source, policemen are canvassing the area right now. One witness claimed Singer's girlfriend was over several nights ago, then she left alone. Although, at this point, I don't think they knew Roxanne was his girlfriend. I figured that out, but catching up will take them a few days."

"Good, so there's still time." Darwin started walking again. "With Singer gone, our focus is Roxanne and the information she's carrying. Remove her and destroy that information, and we're golden. Hit me up when you have something or anything, and stay safe. We're not out of the woods yet."

He ended the call without telling her about the Russians, Petrakis, and their suspect in the ambulance with Samaras.

It would only worry her unnecessarily.

He was worried enough for the both of them.

Chapter 26

FAYE WAS IN OVER her head, but that's how she liked it—no, she *loved* it. Curiosity governed her every thought, her every motive. Money wasn't something she ever needed to worry about. Her parents had plenty, so she killed them and reaped the rewards.

Now on a permanent vacation and bored, meddling in others' affairs gave her a rush.

And logically, she had concluded that if the Russian men were busy at the other hotel with George and probably that inspector now as she'd called him away from the Lindos, that would mean the room the Russians occupied next to hers would be empty.

At least, she hoped so.

She couldn't sit still. She had to check.

When the sliding door was moved aside enough, Faye stepped onto her patio. She moved around the lounge chairs and out onto the grass to the end of the bushes separating the two patios, then stopped.

To appear casual, she yawned, stretched, and glanced over her shoulder at the sliding door of her neighbor's room.

As far as she could tell, no one was inside, or at least no one was visible from the outside.

She stepped back inside her room, secured the patio door, ran to her main door, and exited. When she saw no one lingering anywhere, she moved down the pathway to the next room's door and placed her ear to it.

She couldn't hear a thing.

When she tried to open the door, it was locked.

"That would be too easy," she whispered as she returned to her room.

She decided to check the patio door by walking up to it. Maybe they hadn't locked it.

Outside again, she skirted the bushes and strode up to their glass door with no preplanned story if they were to stop her.

Maybe she could get away with pretending to be drunk and coming home to the wrong room. Maybe she could claim to be a call girl who was given the incorrect address.

Either way, she was determined to get inside their room, even only for a few minutes.

At the glass, she cupped her hands to the side of her face and looked inside. The room was in poor condition, but it was empty.

Gently, she pushed on the glass, and the door slid open, to her surprise. Heart pounding, she slipped inside her neighbor's room.

What a complete mess. Chairs were toppled over, the

sofa sat out from the wall, pillows were on the floor beside the unmade bed, and a vase of flowers was knocked over on the table.

This room was double the size of hers, with an added bedroom to the left. Papers were strewn about across the double bed of the second room.

She moved closer and examined the papers. It was mostly photos of men and women with names below them and a code written in Cyrillic letters.

Looking closer, all she could determine was some of the names were in French, and some were in Italian as they had Latin-based characters.

She opened a folder and saw a face she recognized.

Miss Roxanne Dupont covered the vast majority of these photos, several with a lot of writing about her, all in Russian letters.

What was their interest in Roxanne? How could gangster Russians be looking to buy art from her?

Faye frowned. That seemed odd. Something else was up at the Lindos Palace Resort Hotel and didn't have to do with art.

The door to the room snapped open, and two men entered.

Luckily, neither man looked into the bedroom as they moved inside the main part of the room.

Afraid of being caught, she leaned against the wall by the door, hoping the men would step outside to the patio so she could just leave through the door.

Her heart raced, and she breathed through her mouth to keep it quiet.

Why the hell did I have to come in here?

The thump and scrape of furniture legs on the floor told her they were cleaning the place up.

"I let you use this space for your men, and this is how you repay me? You let it go to shit?"

The movement of furniture stopped. The man was speaking English.

"Watch your mouth." This man had a Russian accent, but it wasn't too harsh. "You didn't *let* us use anything. Nadia ordered it this way, and you obeyed like a good little boy."

"This was supposed to be a simple transaction. Five minutes tops, and look at the mess your men made. Not to mention the corpses piling up and that *fucking* inspector asking questions. I'm surprised the cops haven't told me to lock the place down yet."

"We will get what we've come for and then leave. Until we do, you will close nothing. Some things are more valuable than your hotel. Cross Nadia and she'll burn this place to the ground without hesitation."

The other man gasped, and then furniture noises picked up again as the men returned to work tidying up the place.

"Keep your mouth shut," the Russian said. "I call her now. She wants to tell you something."

A phone rang from inside the room, sounding tinny like it was on a speakerphone. Then, a female voice came through. "We have to take measures to protect ourselves, Mr. Markakis."

"What sort of measures?" the English man—Markakis—said.

"We will meet now. This can be put off no longer."

The line died. A long pause followed.

"Fuck," Markakis said.

"Give me a location for her to meet with you," the Russian said.

"I have no idea," Markakis replied, anger tingeing his voice. "Tell her to come here," he said after a few seconds.

"Here? In this room?"

"Bring her here. She'll be safe. Our rooms are private. Your men will offer security. No one can enter a room without paying for it or producing a warrant."

"Okay," the Russian said.

Faye could hear him dial out, then he spoke Russian and hung up.

"I am leaving," Markakis said. "I can't be seen in this room until she arrives. If you need something, leave a message at reception. They'll get it to me. Just tell them you're calling from the Russian Embassy and that it's urgent."

"You know what happens to you and your family if you run, yes?"

There was a pause while Faye held her breath, and then a door closed. The man must've answered him with a nod or something physical.

Did they both leave? Or just the English one?

She held her breath as long as she could, then breathed slowly through her mouth until she detected footsteps approaching the room.

She was out of time. The man was still in the room.

She had nowhere to hide.

Then she saw the closet.

That was her only hope.

Faye dove for the open door and slipped inside, easing it closed behind her.

When she peered through the slats in the door, the man entered the bedroom, his eyes glued to the phone in his hand as he typed something.

She had made it with less than a second to spare, and now her heart was racing.

The Russian man eased down to sit on the bed.

Undetected was great, but now she was trapped in the closet.

Okay, this is stupid—and dangerous.

How long could she remain in a closet?

Probably as long as she wanted to live. Exiting the closet while any Russians were in the room wouldn't bode well for her.

She leaned against the back wall, figuring she'd be in for a long stay.

Unless someone wanted one of the jackets dangling off several hangers beside her head. Then, her stay would be shortened and probably painful.

Wouldn't it be hilarious to be killed because someone needed to change their clothes?

She didn't think so.

Chapter 27

PETRAKIS PARKED IN FRONT of the Lindos Palace Resort Hotel, killed the engine, and stared out the windshield. If he'd known how bad things would get, there was a good chance he would've just continued his vacation. A missing guest was something he could look into. But the French government was looking for Roxanne now, and wasn't she just an artist?

Now, bodies were piling up around the hotel. What appeared to be the Russian mafia were in two hotels, and they had just abducted Petrakis's only suspect and were beating the shit out of him while he was tied to a chair. The man was likely dead now, but what could he do to help him? Petrakis simply didn't have the resources on the island to launch any sort of attack on that hotel room.

They threatened the inspector's life as if what he did for a living meant nothing to them. And everyone at the Lindos Palace Resort was either fucking each other or trying to fuck each other—and their guests. This is what he would call a clusterfuck of epic proportions. And he was quite aware that he didn't even know the half of it. There was much more going on than it seemed.

He took a deep breath to calm his frazzled nerves and then stepped out of the vehicle.

A man walking by slowed in front of his car glanced at him and then continued into the hotel.

What's his problem?

He'd seen that man around the hotel before but hadn't spoken with him yet. The man did not look Russian, but he had the hardened features of a man who had done horrific things.

Petrakis got out and headed for the lobby doors to catch up to the man. He'd ask his name, at least.

When he got inside, the lobby was empty. Petrakis frowned and moved toward the reception desk.

The hotels had to be closed. There was no other way around it. He hadn't even spoken to Kallonis's widow yet, hadn't had a chance to search the area outside the hotel, hadn't sent the man's ring he'd found to forensics either. He still had to go to the hospital to talk to the Russian once the man's leg was tended to—and now he had strange men staring him down, then disappearing once they entered the lobby.

Samaras briefed the assembled cops and reassigned them to specific tasks. They'd have to meet in the mornings and evenings to compare notes and start to piece everything together. Sure, it was only midafternoon on the day after Roxanne Dupont disappeared, but things were moving fast, and it was all slipping through his fingers just as quickly.

The receptionist must've changed shifts, as it was afternoon now, and he didn't recognize this woman.

"Excuse me."

She glanced up at him. "How may I help you, sir?"

"There was a man who just entered the lobby. Did you see which way he went?"

She frowned, glanced over Petrakis's shoulder, then tilted her head. "A man? I'm sorry, who are you?"

This new receptionist wasn't paying attention to anything.

Petrakis brushed it off. He'd find that man another time.

"I need to speak with Mr. Markakis?" he told the girl, doing what he could to have an even tone, one that didn't reflect his rising temper.

"You're a guest here?" she asked, moving away to pick up the phone. "What room are you staying in, sir? I can call the manager, Mr. Diakos."

"I am Inspector Petrakis." He had trouble keeping the volume out of his voice now. The girl stared back at him, dumbfounded. "Find Markakis, not Diakos, and tell him to meet me here."

"Uh, yes, sir," she said, a hesitancy in her voice. Or was that annoyance?

She dialed out, mumbled into the phone, dialed again, then set the receiver down.

"I'm sorry, it would seem no one has seen him."

Have we lost him, too?

He was about to get her to call Mr. Diakos when someone thundered down the stairs from the second floor and stepped into the lobby.

"Speak of the Devil," Petrakis said, moving away from

the counter to meet Markakis. "I was looking for you. We need to talk."

"Has something happened? Any new developments?"

The hotel owner's face was flushed as if he'd been exerting himself. A muscle twitched under his eye. He looked quite stressed and anxious.

Who wouldn't be stressed with everything that's happening at his hotel?

"Follow me." Petrakis led him to the conference room where he'd tried to sneak in a nap over an hour before. Once inside, Petrakis moved to the counter to pour himself a glass of cold water, then sat at the table.

Markakis sat across from him.

Petrakis sipped from his cup while the hotel owner stared on expectantly.

"Can we hurry this impromptu meeting along, Inspector? I have things to tend to."

"Well, things are only getting worse, and I fear for the safety of your guests."

"Would you recommend I hire a few more security personnel until these matters can be concluded? If so, I can have them here within the hour."

Petrakis shook his head. "Unfortunately, you must lock down both hotels immediately. There are people with weapons walking among your guests. Powerful people from other countries, and until we learn why they're here, they're unpredictable. The entire situation is volatile."

"What?" Markakis looked shocked. "What people? How is this possible?"

"They have already abducted a suspect of mine. It's impossible to do our job without risking the lives of your innocent guests."

Markakis stared back at him, appearing to be in deep thought. "They have abducted a suspect …" he trailed off and shook his head. "No," he said calmly, his tone firm. "Just no."

"What do you mean, *no*?"

"I will not shut down anything. However you want to do your job is up to you, but don't come in here and tell me how to do mine. I refuse to allow my hotel's reputation to suffer for the misdeeds of others."

Petrakis took a moment to respond by sipping from his water glass. "You're dangerously close to obstruction charges."

"How's that?" Markakis asked, raising his voice. "Because I'm running a business here?" He leaned closer to Petrakis. "Do you know how many guests are in these two hotels at the moment and the transient nature of these guests? For example, I've got tourists flocking in tomorrow from the airport to check-in. Where will they go when the hotel is closed? Then how about the day after?" Markakis shook his head. "The hotel is full of staff who need paychecks, Mr. Petrakis. No sir. I refuse to close my hotel because you may *perceive* that it's impeding your investigation. Find a judge who'll sign some form of injunction to shut me down temporarily, and I'll have no choice but to comply. But I will not shut down this hotel voluntarily."

The inspector rose to his feet.

Markakis got up, too.

"Mr. Markakis, closing the hotel voluntarily for a few days so we can get a grip on things will benefit your reputation. Find alternatives for your current and incoming guests. Lose a little money to allow us a chance to figure out what's going on, and I'll speak to the press about how amazing you've handled yourself in the face of such calamity."

Markakis shook his head and looked away. "I owe too much money to close for even one day." He fixed his attention back on Petrakis. "It would damage me and the hotel irreparably if even one day is missed. Please, just do your job as best as you can whether guests are in their rooms or not, and I'll speak to the press."

"So you won't close down? Even for a day?"

Markakis headed for the conference room door, opened it, and turned back. "The hotels stay open. Do whatever you need to do, Mr. Inspector, but I'll fight to keep these buildings open and available to my guests until my last breath. Good day."

Markakis moved away from the door, and it closed slowly, the latch loud in the empty room.

Petrakis grunted under his breath and punched the table beside him.

His phone rang. He slumped back in his chair. Samaras was calling.

"What's up?"

"Inspector." The voice cracked, and then he heard a moan. "They took him."

"Samaras?" Petrakis sprung forward in his chair.

Something like a gunshot rang out on the other end of the line, then the connection died. "Samaras!" he shouted.

He immediately dialed Samaras back, but it went to voicemail. Then he called the police department, got to his feet, and ran for the front of the hotel.

When the line was answered, he explained to the officer on duty that Officer Samaras had been traveling with a suspect in an ambulance that was en route to the local hospital. That ambulance may have been ambushed. Samaras just told him that someone abducted his suspect.

He made it to Samaras's car in minutes and exited the parking area seconds later. The route to the hospital was direct—there was only one way from this part of the island. He had little doubt he'd miss the ambulance if it got ambushed en route, but he'd be too late.

He tried Samaras's phone again but got voicemail once more.

Less than two kilometers from the hotel, he came upon several cars in the ditch, with the ambulance parked on the side of the road, steam rising from under the smashed front end.

He jumped from the car. "Police! Step back." He pushed his way through the crowd of onlookers staring at the wreckage.

The back doors of the ambulance were open.

He drew his weapon and approached. When he had a clear view of the inside, he slipped his weapon away.

"Oh no," he mumbled, seeing Samaras on the floor, his breathing labored. The Russian with the wounded leg was dead, with a large hole in the middle of his forehead, his eyes wide and unmoving.

Samaras's abdomen was covered in blood. Petrakis was still able to see three holes punched in the man's shirt, one near the base of his ribcage. Blood bubbled out of his mouth from damaged lungs.

People died in ambulances, but who gets killed in one?

Petrakis scrambled inside the ambulance. He wrapped an arm around Samaras's shoulder.

"I tried—" Samaras muttered, then coughed.

"You'll be fine. You're going to make it, my friend. Just hang in there." Then, after a moment, he asked, "How many were there?"

"Too many, sir. They came from all sides." He coughed, but this one wasn't as violent. "It was the Russians. Too many of them, sir."

Samaras's breath was catching now like he was choking.

"Come on, man, you'll be fine." Petrakis fought to stave off tears. "Just stay alive, stay awake."

"Tell my Anna"—he coughed—"tell her I love her, and I wouldn't change a thing. Tell her she was the last"—he inhaled a short burst of air—"the last thing on my mind. I smiled on with last breath—"

Samaras exhaled and slumped in Petrakis's arms.

"No," Petrakis whispered, looking down into Samaras's face. Then he shouted, "Don't you fucking die on me."

Petrakis twisted around bodily to press on Samaras's chest. He wept, even though he only knew the man for less than a day.

Samaras had been a fellow officer.

He had done his job, worked overtime, and hadn't complained about a thing. Petrakis had used him like he was expendable, ordered him around, and was annoyed by him. All that was Petrakis's own attitude.

And now the man was gone.

"No," he whispered, sniffling, fighting back tears. "You can't fucking die."

Knowing the man was dead and not coming back didn't

stop Petrakis from smacking Samaras's ribcage on the wild chance that the man's heart would restart and the approaching paramedics would patch him up and send him home to his Anna.

But nothing worked. Petrakis failed him in death as in life.

He cradled Samaras's head and wanted to let all the pressure and anxiety go, let it all out, and cry, but then he'd lose his mind in a fit of rage, and the Russians would win.

No, the right thing to do was leave the ambulance. Let the professionals handle Samaras's body properly, process it, and give the man's fiancée a chance to grieve. And while all that was happening, Petrakis would find those responsible and either kill them if they happened to resist arrest or arrest them and arrange some form of payback once they were on the inside.

Someone had to pay for this, and the law wasn't strong enough to exact a decent comeuppance.

He rocked back and forth with Samaras's head in his lap, not wanting to leave him yet, fighting the fury that threatened to rise within him.

"Inspector?" A uniformed policeman stepped into view at the back of the ambulance. "Please exit the vehicle and come with me. Another ambulance will be here shortly. This is a crime scene now, sir. You have to get out."

His phone rang.

Petrakis blinked away the tears and eased out his phone on the third ring. Call display said it was the deputy chief.

He answered it without saying a word, Samaras's head still in his lap.

"Inspector Alexander Kokkinos will be there at midnight

to take the lead on the murders," the chief said. "Pick him up at the airport. Fill him in and brief him on everything. Also, you can't close the hotels, for fuck's sake. Who do you think you are?"

Without waiting for an answer, the chief hung up.

Petrakis took a deep breath and slipped his phone back into his pocket, completely crushed that he just lost Samaras and the case all in the same minute.

"Sir?" the persistent policeman said from the back of the ambulance.

"This man—" Petrakis started, then stopped to swallow as his throat threatened to close. "This man was a good cop."

"No issue there, sir. We just need you to exit the ambulance—"

"I will," he snapped. "This man's name was Samaras. Call who you need to at the station, but get me his fiancée's address."

"Her address, sir?"

Petrakis lowered Samaras's head to the floor of the ambulance, took a deep breath, then got to his feet and exited the vehicle.

"I don't want her to hear what happened from anyone but me. I owe that to Samaras."

The policeman watched him for a long moment as Petrakis stared back inside at Samaras, wondering how things got so fucked up.

"Half a minute," the cop said, stepping away to get on his phone.

A few minutes later, as other emergency personnel arrived on site, the policeman approached him with a white piece of paper. An address was on it.

Petrakis stepped away from the carnage, got in his car, and headed toward the city. He put the address on the GPS and drove on autopilot.

As soon as he calmed down, he called the hotel. He needed the address for Kallonis's widow, too.

Later this evening, he'd have Inspector Kokkinos at his feet. Everything would change from then on, so he wanted to offer condolences to both women before he had that asshole pissing him off.

It was the least he could do.

***

He parked within walking distance from Samaras's apartment building so his fiancée wouldn't see her man's car. When he arrived at the lobby, he found Samaras's last name and rang the apartment.

After waiting several minutes and ringing the buzzer a few times, no one responded.

He should've called first, but he couldn't bear to go back to the hotel yet.

He lumbered back to the car with more weight in his step.

Once Kallonis's address was programmed on the GPS, he saw it was a fifteen-minute walk. It would be good for him to walk, to get some fresh air.

He stopped at a mini market that he happened upon and got a small bottle of water and a sandwich.

What would happen if he died? There was no message to leave for anyone. He didn't even have a pet. Always alone, his only relationships were occasional affairs. His life was his job.

While chewing the dry ham and cheese sandwich as he walked down the street, he recalled how proud he felt the first time he wore his uniform—yet, now, it all felt so useless.

Samaras was dead. Some of his blood was still on Petrakis's hands, literally and figuratively.

The image of Samaras taking his last breath made him want to scream. It made him dedicate himself to catching the fuckers who killed him, too.

He tossed the rest of the uneaten sandwich in a bush when Kallonis's house came up on the left.

It was a small, detached house with a cute garden out front. The front door opened as he approached, and a woman stepped out.

He slowed down, then eased behind a tree to watch.

He was close enough to see the woman was quite happy, with a huge smile on her face. Someone behind her had their hands on her ass, playfully shoving her out the door.

"What the hell?" Petrakis mumbled and started forward again.

Then he recognized the woman and stopped in his tracks.

Mrs. Evelyn Diakos, the Lindos Palace Resort Hotel's manager's wife.

Was she having an affair—with Kallonis's *wife*? Was this what Diakos was talking about earlier?

These women certainly weren't friends. They were acting too intimate to be just friends.

He held back, waiting for Evelyn to leave.

Several minutes later, once she had cleared the area, Petrakis approached the door and rang the bell.

Footsteps approached on the inside.

A female started talking as she unlocked the door. "What happened, baby? What did you forget—?" She stopped when she saw the inspector on her stoop, her smile freezing in place. "Can I help you?"

He withdrew his badge to display it as they hadn't officially met yet—but what an actress. From the playful expression she wore for Evelyn to the mask of mourning and loss for her dead security officer husband, the change was an exercise in liquidity.

"Please, come in." She directed him to the living room.

On the way in, she picked up a pack of tissues.

"I'm sorry for your loss," he whispered, feeling more emotional than usual after having just had Samaras die in his arms. He considered his sanity for having come here in the first place after such a nerve-wracking event. "It's tragic what happened," he added.

While talking, he watched everything she did. He decided not to mention Evelyn until he had a better picture of what was going on here.

"I haven't been able to manage what happened," she whispered, barely loud enough for him to hear. "It seems so unreal. I can't go back to work yet. I see him everywhere I turn." Tears rolled down her cheeks.

If he'd come at any other time, he would be convinced those tears were genuine—she did just lose her husband in a senseless murder—but he'd seen her happiness and pleasure with Evelyn moments before, making him question how real her tears were.

"I can't even imagine your pain, but I have a few questions I need to ask."

She nodded and dabbed at her eyes.

"Do you know if your husband had any enemies? Someone who hated him enough to want to hurt him?" He tried to keep his tone gentle, but watching her fake sorrow tested his limits.

She shook her head and stared down at her lap. "No one that I can think of. My husband was a peaceful man. He wouldn't hurt a fly." She wiped at her tears again, and he held himself back from knocking the tissue from her hand.

"The last time you spoke to him, did he say anything weird or comment on something different about his day?"

"Nothing out of the ordinary."

"Did he usually spend all day at the hotel?"

"During the busy season, he rarely came home on time. So, yes, it was his full-time job, and he loved what he did."

"How were you able to handle him being away so much?"

"I'm used to seasonal work. We work hard for about eight months, and then we do almost nothing."

Petrakis decided not to say anything about the relationship with Evelyn Diakos. He would think about how best to broach that topic and deal with it later.

"Do you remember anything unusual, anything at all that might help with the investigation?"

She seemed to contemplate his question momentarily, then shook her head. "I can't think of anything at the moment." She met his gaze. "Please find out who did this. How am I supposed to move on?" She blew her nose.

Petrakis placed a hand on his stomach, feeling physically sick watching her.

"I'm sorry this happened," he said and stood, needing to extricate himself from her living room.

He pulled a business card from his pocket and handed it to her.

"If you remember anything that you feel may help us, anything at all, please call me."

He headed for the door.

In her front hallway, tears wetting her cheeks, she tried to speak, but nothing came out, so she nodded at him, opened the door, and let him out.

Petrakis headed back toward Anna's house.

He needed to speak to Mrs. Diakos now. Mr. Diakos wasn't what he seemed, either. Then, there were the Russians roaming freely through the hotels. He should leave them to Inspector Kokkinos—of course, with a warning about their intention of having a pig roast if another cop gets in their way. He hated Inspector Kokkinos, but he didn't want the man dead.

When he returned to Anna's house, he decided to buzz her apartment again. The apartment bell rang, but he got no answer. She was still out. He'd have to return another time.

Back in the car, he called the station for an update on Samaras's body. Maybe they'd already called next of kin, and he missed Anna because she was on her way to the station.

When he got through to the officer on the scene, he identified himself and asked, "Where are they taking Officer Samaras's body?"

"Half a minute," the officer said. After a moment, he came back on. "He's been taken to the city morgue."

"Okay, thanks."

He hung up and thought he'd call before heading to the morgue. Maybe they could tell him if Anna was already there.

He found the number and dialed. When it was answered, he said, "Put me through to the morgue."

There was a pause, then a man answered, his tone subdued, like he was eternally bored.

"City morgue."

"This is Inspector Petrakis. The body of Officer Samaras was just brought in. Who's in charge over there? I need to speak with them."

"Please hold."

While on hold, the line to the morgue offered soft piano music. He laid his head back, stared at the car's roof, and then closed his eyes.

Almost a minute later, another man answered the phone.

"Hello, can I help you?"

"A colleague of mine, Officer Samaras, was recently brought in."

"Okay, what can I do for you?"

"Has anyone called his family his fiancée?"

"No, no one has called anybody."

"Why's that?"

"Because we don't know who he is."

Petrakis opened his eyes and stared out his windshield. "What do you mean you don't know who he is?"

"Sir, I don't even know who you are."

Petrakis gripped the phone tighter. "I am Inspector Petrakis." He used every ounce of control to keep his tone even. "I was in the back of the ambulance when Officer Samaras took his last breath. I just want to make sure I get to explain what happened to Anna, his fiancée."

"Well, we did just have a gunshot victim come in. This guy was shot in an ambulance, but we're still trying to identify him."

"Identify him? Just open his wallet, use his ID, his police badge."

"Sir, the body that came in had nothing of the sort on him."

Petrakis frowned. "Tell me what you found on him exactly?"

"Exactly? Okay, I can do that. Nothing. Just the clothes he was wearing."

"No wallet or badge or pistol?"

"No, nothing like that."

"Damn," he shouted and hung up.

Did the Russians take Samaras's ID after ambushing the ambulance? And if so, do they have Anna with them?

Why take Samaras's fiancée, though? What would be their end goal? Killing a cop would get every police officer and law enforcement agency on Greek soil after them. Abducting Anna would ensure those officers would kill them on sight.

He blinked, still staring out the windshield without seeing anything.

Unless they were using Anna to negotiate something in the future.

However, there was no proof they abducted her. An empty apartment and missing ID weren't enough to make such a huge leap.

This was out of control. They weren't big enough on the small island of Rhodes to handle international crime syndicates. They needed some sort of team from Athens to take over, and not just Inspector Kokkinos. He'd end up getting himself killed.

Things were too fucked up already.

He grabbed his phone once more and called the chief.

When he answered, he said, "Chief, this is bigger than all of us."

"What are you talking about?" The chief spoke with disdain. He obviously didn't like Petrakis.

The inspector told him everything that had happened since yesterday, summarizing it all in the most abbreviated manner possible, as the chief wasn't much for talking on the phone to begin with.

"We are dealing with a criminal element of a scope that we lowly inspectors can't manage on our own, Chief. I'm sure it was the Russians who murdered Officer Samaras. They're the ones who attacked the ambulance, and now they may have abducted his fiancée."

The chief had remained silent for the past few minutes as Petrakis spewed forth all the tension and anger he'd been dealing with.

"Petrakis, go to the airport. Leave now. Pick up Inspector Kokkinos. He was able to get an earlier flight. In the meantime, I'll inform the port authorities and airport security to keep an eye on all Russian nationals trying to leave in groups, but Petrakis, listen to me."

"I'm listening," he said, his hand tightening on the steering wheel.

"Without proof, without evidence, you're giving me nothing to go on, nothing to act on, and you know that." The chief took in a big breath. "You know, Inspector Petrakis, just because Anna isn't home means nothing. She could be at work, staying at her mother's place, a heavy sleeper—who the fuck knows. Look, we aren't used to this type of crime, nor are we equipped for it—"

"So, in other words, we're a glorified clean-up crew. When the bodies fall, we clean them up and *appear* to be investigating the alleged crimes, is that it?" He had to corral his anger, or it would cost him his job.

"That about sums it up, Inspector. Now, when Kokkinos gets there, relay everything to him, write up your reports, and take a day off. You deserve it. Then report back to me, and we'll see where you're needed. We may have wrapped everything up by then—"

Petrakis hung up. He'd had enough. It was either that or telling his boss to go to hell and fuck himself with a stick covered in barbed wire.

He started the car and got moving down the road, intent on going back to the hotels to confront the Russians as soon as he picked up Inspector Kokkinos at the airport. Whatever business the Russians had here in Rhodes, it was over. It needed to stop, or he'd make calls above his chief. He'd call Athens and get any available special forces team they had to come and stop them. The mafia, or whoever the hell they were, were not above the law.

When his phone rang again, he didn't look to see who was calling. It had to be the chief ready to ream him out for hanging up in his ear. Placate the man and stay on the case for another day, or tell him to fuck himself and transfer off the island?

Choices, choices …

"Petrakis," was all he said.

It sounded like someone was crying on the other end of the phone, but no one said a word. He looked at the screen. The number came up as PRIVATE CALLER. He put the phone back to his ear.

"This is Inspector Petrakis. Who's calling?"

"They killed him," a woman gasped, crying through her words. "They're going to kill me, too." She screamed as the distinctive sound of flesh smacking flesh came through the phone.

"Who is this?" Petrakis shouted into the phone, swerving on the road. He tapped the brake and eased to the side.

"You made a mistake," a man in a heavy Russian accent said.

The man from the hotel room. The one in charge.

"What mistake?"

"I told you. Do not interfere with my business."

"So, what, now you're going to murder cops?" he shouted into the phone. "Fuck you, I'll kill you myself."

"You left my hotel room in one piece. Then you take my comrade in ambulance. This is not acceptable. Now you and your family and that pig cop and his bitch will be cut up and fed to my pigs. Tonight, we dine with swine, *svin'ya*."

"Wrong, asshole. Tonight, you're all out of Greece, or you're all dead. And since I have the port authorities and airport security watching for Russians, it looks like you'll be buried on Greek soil. See you soon, you piece of shit. And that woman had better be alive when I get there, or you'll have nothing to negotiate your pathetic life with."

Petrakis hung up and slammed the gas pedal to the floor.

Chapter 28

FAYE HAD NO IDEA how much time had passed.

She was still locked in the closet of her neighbor's hotel room, and the Russian guy had crawled onto the bed and fallen asleep roughly an hour ago, maybe two.

She had lowered herself to the closet floor—standing in one spot was too hard—and waited until the guy was in a deep sleep to leave quietly, but he kept stirring and moving.

She pushed up carefully to get back to her feet, then peered through the slats. It was getting darker as the sun moved west. The bathroom was directly across from the bedroom, and that light was on so she could still see most of the room's interior.

The man seemed to be in a deep sleep now, his arms and legs splayed. Getting past him and out of the room before anyone else came shouldn't be too hard, but if she woke him and he was armed, things could get dicey.

Maybe she should exit the closet and drive her fist into the guy's throat while he slept. Hit him multiple times with as much force as possible. There was no way he'd be able to shoot her or chase her—he'd be too busy trying to breathe with a collapsed trachea.

Either way, she couldn't stay hidden in the closet until they vacated the room—they could have booked it for a week, and eventually, they'd want to check out of the hotel, which meant packing their things, which meant opening the closet and discovering her. And the other reason she couldn't stay hidden for much longer was she had to pee—bad.

Without contemplating it much longer, she eased the door open as slowly as possible, then stopped to stare at the man.

The door hadn't made a sound, which was great, and the man was still sleeping.

She exited the closet and approached the bed. A pair of scissors or a knife would work well to end his life, but she rejected the idea—too much blood, and she wouldn't have time to clean it or clean herself off.

The Russian man shook as if he was dreaming, and she jumped back out of reflex.

Watching him sleep was a waste of time. If she wasn't going to harm him, then she needed to leave immediately.

Faye moved toward the bedroom door, exited it, and then placed her hand on the door to exit when a beep sounded on the other side. Someone swiped a key card on the lock and was about to enter.

She dove back into the bedroom, lost her balance, hit the floor, and, without thinking, rolled under the bed.

The door opened hard, banged against the wall, and the

bed vibrated above her all at the same time.

"What was that?" the guy on the bed asked.

Footsteps entered the main room, signaling many more than one person.

"Get up," a man said in English. "We are just getting party started."

The man on the bed placed both feet on the floor to her right, hesitated a moment—probably staring at the open closet door, wondering why it was open now—then stood and exited the bedroom.

She was alone in the bedroom now.

The person who was grunting and moaning in the other room sounded like they were gagged.

Faye listened as furniture moved in the room and thought, *didn't they just tidy things up earlier*?

"I will take off tape. You promise no shouting?"

She moaned a *yes*.

"Good." A short cry of pain followed the sound of the tape being torn from flesh.

"Fuck you," the woman said in Greek. "You'll pay for this."

"You insult us?" the Russian said in English. "Knowing we want you dead? This is stupid idea."

"Go fuck yourself," the woman added.

She heard the woman spit from where Faye was hidden, making her want to laugh.

That woman had balls. Good for her.

"Tell me, where is the USB?" the Russian asked.

USB? What USB?

"I don't know," a man said.

Was that George from the beach? Did they bring him

here?

Then she heard what sounded like a slap.

Seconds later, "I don't know anything about anyone or any *fucking* USB. I'm on vacation."

"You must think we are idiots. You came for information on USB stick, no? We know agreement you Greeks have with the French. We have ears everywhere. You don't need to pretend to be hero. What will all this mean when you are dead? Your government pigs will abandon you, no?"

Another voice jumped in. "Will you speak, or we make you?"

Silence followed.

Faye didn't want to hear any more, but she had no choice unless she wanted to join those captive individuals.

There were more angry words spoken in Russian. Now and then, she would catch some words in English, but she couldn't understand what was happening.

A minute later, the door opened again. Someone else entered the villa, then the bedroom. She watched their feet. Three people were in the room. Two men and a woman by the size and shape of their footwear.

The woman kicked and grunted, but they were stronger and tossed her on the bed above Faye. When the woman landed on the mattress, the underside pushed down on Faye's cheek.

They fumbled with something on the bed above as the woman moaned and fought back, and then both men exited the room, closing the door behind them.

Faye guessed they tied the woman to the bed.

As the door closed, the woman struggled like an animal, the bed vibrating above Faye, but it was all in vain.

There was a commotion outside the room, and from the muffled sounds, Faye guessed they were beating the Greek man she'd met on the beach earlier, the man whose drink she'd spilled.

Slowly, risking her own health, she crawled out from under the bed and peeked over the edge to look at the woman.

Ropes secured her to the bed, and a hood had been placed over her head.

Faye leaned in close and whispered, "Don't be afraid." The woman jolted and stopped moving. "I want to help you."

The woman nodded her head vigorously.

Faye couldn't decide how to help except to untie her, so she grabbed the ropes securing the woman's left wrist, then stopped because footsteps pounded near the bedroom door.

She released the ropes, dropped to the floor, and rolled under the bed again.

The door opened. A man entered and moved to sit on the bed next to the woman.

If they touched her inappropriately while she was tied to the bed, Faye would have to cut their balls off with an ax.

The others were laughing outside the room, but she couldn't hear the Greek man anymore. He had to be unconscious now or dead.

Then she heard the patio door open. They were stepping outside. Maybe it was break time from all the torture time they'd been dealing with.

The man on the bed above whispered something to the woman, then stood and left the room.

Faye waited until the door was closed, then eased out from under the bed again, glanced back at the tied-up woman, whispered she'd get help, and slowly approached the door.

After taking a few seconds to listen at the door, she eased it open and peeked out into the main part of the hotel room.

Sure enough, the Greek man was secured to a chair, his head down, his face ruined. Unconscious or dead, she couldn't tell. All other occupants of the room were out smoking on the patio.

Time to leave. She grabbed the doorknob, twisted it to open it, and was about to pull on the door when the bathroom door clicked and started to open, which was strategically right beside her.

She dove through the bedroom door and leaned up against the wall.

When no one chased her, she slid back under the bed and waited again.

This was getting maddening.

She needed to piss like a racehorse. If she didn't get out of this room soon, her bladder would burst.

Footsteps came and went, but no one entered the bedroom again.

Faye eased out and got back to her feet. This was it. No more hiding. If she had to fight one or two of them, she would.

To reassure the woman, she eased back the hood and whispered, "Shhhh," then looked down into the beautiful woman's wild eyes. Tape covered her mouth.

Running for help might get this woman killed before Faye got back. Two women were better than one, and this woman had balls. It might be better to untie her and run with her instead of coming back.

So, Faye did what she thought was right. She whispered her plan, eased the tape off the woman's mouth, and removed the rope from each wrist and ankle in under a minute.

Faye moved to the wall by the door and motioned for the woman to follow.

Frantically, the woman didn't just follow. She ran from the bedroom, grabbed the main door, and ripped it open.

"Wait," Faye said in a forced whisper.

Someone shouted in Russian, but the woman was already out the door.

"For fuck's sake," Faye muttered, shaking her head. Then she ran for the open door.

But she didn't make it.

She had one foot outside and one foot inside when something smacked into the back of her head.

She was unconscious before she met with the ground.

Chapter 29

THE RECEPTIONIST AT THE front desk had received a package from the Russian embassy for the hotel owner and had called him to come receive it.

Markakis had told them to *call* him and claim it was a message from the embassy if they needed to get ahold of him, not ship something.

Even though the stupid Russians had done it their way, he wasn't about to leave the package at the front desk.

He retrieved it and sequestered himself in one of the meeting rooms.

Finally, alone, he peeled back the tape and opened the package. Inside, a small object was surrounded by bubble wrap.

He exhaled in relief. At least it wasn't something bloody and gross. Receiving human organs would've been quite unpleasant.

Carefully, he eased the package out of the box and unwrapped the second layer of paper around it. For some reason, they'd shipped him a gray brick with a card on top that read OPEN FIRST.

When he pulled back the flap and exposed the inside of the envelopes, he heard a faint clicking sound, and an LED screen lit up in red on top of the gray brick.

"What's this?" he muttered to himself.

From head to toe, his body was bathed in a cold sweat. Opening the top of the envelope triggered some sort of countdown screen.

He stared at the readout as it hit the number ten, then nine.

He set it on the table in a panic.

Eight …

He'd read about explosives being shipped to people. Was this a brick of C-4?

Five …

Four …

If it was, running was pointless. He stared at the screen, paralyzed with fear.

Two …

One …

Someone knocked on the door.

Markakis jumped and screamed, then stumbled and fell to the floor. His heart raced in his chest, and his eyes didn't leave the box on the table that had reached the end of the countdown.

It hadn't blown up.

"What …" he mumbled as the door opened behind him.

Mr. Diakos stepped into view. He glanced at the box,

then back to Markakis.

"Are you okay, sir?" he asked, gawking at him.

Markakis didn't answer. He tried to get to his feet, faltered, and dropped back on his ass. Then Diakos grabbed him under his arm and helped him into a chair.

Markakis held the table's edge to stand as he willed his heart to calm down. He actually thought he was a dead man moments ago. Who's to say the bomb wouldn't still blow in seconds? He needed to get it off his property, call the bomb specialists, run for his life—something, anything, but stand there.

Staring at the fucking thing was spiking his blood pressure.

There was a paper shoved in the side.

Diakos was saying something, but he ignored the blustering manager and grabbed the paper. He unfolded it and read.

You did nothing to help us. You didn't supervise the villa properly. A witness escaped. You have twenty-four hours to make it right and find our USB.

That C-4 didn't explode because it was a fake. The next one won't be fake if you don't get my USB. Nothing will be left standing. If you run, we will find you. This is something you do not want.

His hands trembled as he folded the paper and set it on the table. He tried to find his voice, but all he could manage to say was, "We have to close the hotel."

Diakos leaned closer. "What did you just say?"

"Close the hotel." His voice was firmer, stronger.

Diakos shook his head, color rising in his cheeks. "Sir, we had a deal. The hotel stays open. My wife and I have jobs here. You do not want to fuck with me, or you'll leave me no choice."

Markakis eyed him like he was a stranger who'd wandered into his house. "No choice? What the hell does that mean? Did you even look inside that box? This was a warning. I won't have the blood of innocents on my hands."

Diakos grabbed his lapel and shoved him back, then released him. The manager seemed overtly furious, more so than Markakis had seen in anyone for quite some time.

"If you even whisper that you'll close this hotel, I will be forced to show the photos I have to your wife. Are we clear?" His teeth were tight together, and veins corded in his neck.

Markakis, drenched through with the sweat of fear, could only gape at his manager open-mouthed.

Diakos's face contorted into a smile. Then he patted him on the shoulder in a friendly manner.

"It looks like we finally understand one another." He opened the conference room door and stopped to look back. "The hotel stays open. It will not close." Then Diakos stepped out into the hall and slammed the door shut behind him.

The photos Diakos had on him meant nothing if he was dead. Diakos had been blackmailing him for so long now he'd actually forgotten about it. The man was the hotel manager, and that was it. No one questioned it any longer. And when Diakos fucked up, he was reprimanded like anyone else, but he always kept his job.

There had been many times when Markakis would've fired the guy for sleeping with the guests—especially after two complained and threatened to sue—but Diakos reminded him of the dirt he had on him and promised to be more discrete.

Yet, all of that paled in comparison to Nadia.

She was the only woman who could tell him what to do.

She was the one who sent him the package.

Nadia ran the Russian men in the area, brought in the drugs, and responded to requests by her bosses in Russia. Betray her at your own risk, and that was something Markakis could never do—not to mention the hotel was still operating because of her.

Stupidly, he'd borrowed money from her to keep things going during recessionary times a few years ago. He was still paying it back due to her high-interest rates. No banks would touch him back then. Yet, Nadia was there to help. And so what if he had to pay back almost double what he borrowed? At least he still had a hotel and could provide for his family.

Yet, it would seem that this arrangement was getting dangerous—too dangerous to continue—and there was no way out.

Stumped on the next course of action, he exited the meeting room, trudged past the reception area, and stepped outside the building to catch his breath.

There was a wetness on his jeans. He leaned against the wall and glanced down at his thigh. He'd pissed his pants and hadn't noticed—how disgusting.

Cursing under his breath, he pushed off the wall. Instead of walking back through the lobby, he moved away from the front entrance to circumvent the hotel by walking around the exterior until he got to his room, where he could shower and change. He'd decide what to do after that.

Five minutes later, he fished his master keys out and approached his door when he heard a sound.

Frozen to the spot, imagining Nadia sent her men to communicate more messages to him personally, Markakis slowly turned and peered in the direction of the sound. A dark figure tried to remain concealed in the bushes to his left.

He lowered his keys and stepped toward the figure who had just retreated deeper into the bush.

"Wait, I won't hurt you," he said.

The person stopped moving. Something about the person's size and shape made him think it was a woman, but he couldn't tell in the waning light.

"I own this hotel. Is there something I can help you with?"

"I need help," the woman said in a shaky voice.

"Okay," Markakis said, holding up his hands. "I'm safe. It's okay, come on out."

After a moment, the figure rustled around in the bush, then stepped out and remained on her knees, looking up at him.

"I was kidnapped from my home by some Russian guys." She broke into tears. "I thought," her shoulder hitched, "I thought they'd kill me. Or worse, rape me and kill me." She brushed at her tears.

He glanced around to see if they were being observed. "Did they hurt you in any way?"

"No." She shook her head.

"What's your name?"

"Anna. I'm Officer Samaras's fiancée."

"And where is Officer Samaras right now?"

"They claimed to have killed him."

Markakis stopped and frowned. "They killed a cop?" He couldn't believe it. Had Nadia completely lost her mind? And if so, he was now financially in bed with cop killers.

She nodded. "That's how they knew where I lived, well, where *we* lived. They showed up with his wallet and badge and gun."

He shook his head to clear it. "Okay, do you know where these men are now?"

"Yes, in a room over there." She looked up at him, her hand gesturing to the right. "But I'm not going back there."

The room where he helped arrange the fucking furniture.

"No, I wouldn't ask you to go back there, but we need to call the police, and they'll want to know where these people are."

Anna nodded. "I can do that. I'll tell them."

"Follow me," he said and turned away.

Anna took a few steps, then stopped. "Where are we going?"

"To get you out of sight."

"No, I need to leave. The Russians are in this hotel. They have a man tied to a chair in one of the rooms and another woman, too. She helped me escape."

"How long ago did this happen?"

"Twenty minutes, maybe less."

He faced her, the ring of master keys dangling from his hand. "Here's the thing. Since you escaped them, they'll probably leave the hotel. They wouldn't stick around waiting for the police to arrive. So we have to be quick. We must call the cops and get them here quickly."

He fished out his keys and opened a door at the back of the building leading to the basement boiler room, hoping the woman would follow him. He needed to get her out of sight immediately.

"We can call from in here." He waved. "Hurry, in case they're looking for you."

Markakis stepped inside and held the door. She hesitated, looking around while hugging herself. He could tell she was trying to decide if she could trust him.

Then she took that one step forward and moved to the doorway.

"There's a phone in the boiler room," he said. "No one has access without these." He held up the ring of keys. "You'll be safe until the police arrive."

That sold her because she nodded and entered the building.

He looked outside, saw no one, then closed and locked the door.

She waited just inside the door, her whole body shaking.

"Follow me," he said, brushing past her. "Let's do this fast so they can get here and arrest those bastards."

She grunted her agreement and followed him dutifully.

He led her through a series of hallways that fed into the deepest part of the bowels of the hotel. At this hour, all of the maintenance staff had gone home, and unless there were a complaint about hot water in a room or an electrical failure, no one would venture this deep except security guards on a routine walk-through sometime after midnight.

They entered the last room, which had a large HVAC unit running. He turned around and pointed at a small bench on the side for her to sit on.

"Take a moment to rest," he said. "You went through a lot."

Anna stared at him, her wild eyes rimmed in red.

Markakis eased his cell phone out of his pocket, his own hands trembling still from the shock of that package and warning from Nadia.

"You have a phone …" she said, barely audible over the machine running.

He set it on a side table far from her grasp. When he faced her, she was frowning, looking more afraid than earlier.

"Why?" she asked. "Why bring me down here if you had a phone this whole time?"

He moved closer, and she leaned away from him, her eyes skirting toward the door.

"Because, my darling, you aren't going anywhere."

Markakis swung his fist with as much weight behind it as he could, hoping to knock her out. He hadn't hit anyone since a fight in high school, yet he connected with her cheek, knocking her head back so hard that when she smacked into the steel beam that was the framework of the HVAC unit, her eyes rolled back in her head and she slumped onto the bench, then slid to the concrete floor like she was made of rubber.

Even though it wasn't the punch that knocked her out, he achieved what he wanted.

He shook his hand in the air several times as her cheekbone hurt his knuckles.

"Ouch, fuck, that hurt."

He ran to the utility drawer and found a small section of rope and duct tape. Within a few minutes, Anna was bound and gagged.

He wiped the sweat from his brow and shook out his pant leg. That cold feeling of urine on his leg was annoying, but if everything worked out tonight, it was worth it.

He couldn't believe his luck.

The one woman, a cop's future wife, that the Russians had abducted had escaped, and she'd fallen into his lap. What were the odds?

And since he wasn't anyone's puppet, Nadia had a new problem on her hands.

He was a desperate man, and desperate men did desperate things.

Watching the sleeping woman, he picked up his phone and dialed Nadia's number by heart.

"Russian Hills," someone answered.

"It's the blue dolphin," he said, then hung up.

They'd call him back once they got to a secure line.

Seconds later, his phone rang.

"I'm here," he said.

"What do you want?" Nadia asked. "I'm busy. Speak fast."

"Your little games are over. I will no longer be your pawn."

There was a moment of silence on the other end of the line. Then he heard two words. "Be careful."

"You threaten me and my hotel with your little fake bomb, and you want me to *be careful*?" He spoke loudly to be heard over the noise in the room, but now he was shouting. "I have Anna with me, that cop's fiancée. She and I will go to the police. She's a perfect witness who just happened to escape. This woman knows enough to have every member of your little mafia club arrested. So, leave my hotel and take all of your comrades with you. Otherwise, I'll take her to the police, and she will relay everything she knows to them. You won't be able to hide anymore. It's over,

Nadia. Get out. You're no longer welcome at my hotel."

"You are in no position to make demands."

"Stop and think before you piss me off."

"Mr. Markakis. I am a businesswoman. When money doesn't work, violence fills the gap. When that becomes ineffective, I murder those who oppose me. Call the police. I don't care. That woman will not survive the night. If two cops, five cops, or twenty police officers arrive at your hotel tonight, I will have my men execute every last one of them. Am I making myself clear? Nothing you can say or do will make me comply with any demands." She paused, and Markakis waited—not because he wanted to hear more, but because he was stunned into silence. "But now that you've raised the stakes and proven you're my enemy instead of a friend, I have already planted explosives throughout your precious hotel. Very soon, there will be nothing left of this place but ash. No one threatens me without penalty."

She had out-maneuvered him, out-threatened him. He'd not only assaulted Anna in his presence, he'd used her as bait to get Nadia to do his bidding, and it backfired.

Or was she calling his bluff? Would she really blow up an entire hotel?

She had to be lying.

So he said the only thing that came to mind.

"Do whatever the fuck you want, bitch. I'm insured. You'd be doing me a favor. Hotel gone, large payout to me, loan to you, finished. Thanks for the money, you fucking cow. Also, you have a few hours to *check out* of my hotel, or every law enforcement agency this side of the FBI and Interpol will be hunting your sweet ass. Think about it, Russian whore."

Markakis slapped the end button, disconnecting the call.

Then he dropped to the floor, his legs too weak to support him, adrenaline spent.

He groaned at the wetness on his leg.

He really needed to change his pants soon.

But not until his heart was back in his chest.

Chapter 30

Petrakis tapped his foot while waiting for Inspector Kokkinos at the airport. He didn't know what to do with himself, and his patience had all but disappeared.

In the airport bathroom, he'd been able to get the little amount of Samaras's blood off his hands, but he couldn't remove the vengeful feeling raging through him. The way that Russian man had spoken to him and how he'd taken Samaras's life so casually was driving him insane.

People like that didn't belong in cages. They belonged in the dirt. There was no place in this world for men who could kill with such impunity.

Kokkinos's plane had landed ten minutes late. It had taken the passengers another half hour to deplane and collect their luggage.

If the inspector weren't out in the waiting area within ten minutes, Petrakis would leave without him. The man could take a taxi.

"Tired?" a man said behind him.

Annoyed, Petrakis spun around to see Kokkinos standing behind him.

He got to his feet, nodded at the inspector, and started for the parking lot without offering to help with the luggage.

Kokkinos followed him in silence.

Evidently, their dislike for each other was mutual.

At the car, Petrakis popped the trunk and then dropped in the driver's seat. Kokkinos put his things in the trunk, then sat crookedly in the passenger seat.

Petrakis started the car, got them underway, and headed back to the hotels.

"Where are we going?" Kokkinos asked.

"To Hell."

"Oh really?" Kokkinos watched him drive. "That bad, eh?"

"That bad."

After several minutes of silence, Kokkinos rested his head back. "You want to tell me what's going on? Or are you just a glorified taxi driver with a badge?"

Petrakis shot him a glance, then looked back at the road.

Over the next ten minutes, he told the inspector everything. Since at least one of them would die tonight—probably both of them—Kokkinos had a right to know what he was walking into.

"What the fuck?" Kokkinos said when Petrakis had finished his explanation, including the threat that the Russian was coming for him. "Are you insane?"

Petrakis tightened his hands on the steering wheel.

"Probably."

They rode in silence for a few kilometers again.

"We need more men," Kokkinos said. "We need backup."

"You're it. We've got a small team doing interviews and asking questions, but they're more bean counters. You're the backup."

"What does that mean?"

"I asked the chief for help. I told him what was happening. He sent you."

"Well, that's not good enough."

Petrakis tapped his brakes and eased the cruiser to a stop on the side of the road. "Get out. You can stay here and walk to a hotel in the area. Tell the chief I kicked you out."

Kokkinos stared at him without moving.

Petrakis leaned across Kokkinos's lap and opened his door. "Get out. You will die if you come with me to the hotel."

"These guys really got under your skin, didn't they?"

Petrakis met his gaze. "They are ruthless, disgusting men. They will stop at nothing. No amount of handcuffs will secure these assholes. I'm going back, and it's likely more people will die, but I'm going to do everything in my power to arrest those responsible for Samaras's death, then walk away from it all."

Kokkinos hadn't moved, his door still sitting open. After a moment, he closed it and nodded at the road. "I'm in. Drive."

Petrakis watched him a moment longer, then eased the car back onto the road.

It's your funeral.

Petrakis didn't speak again until they had arrived at the hotel entrance.

At the front reception desk, he asked for the manager, Mr. Diakos, or the owner, Mr. Markakis. After several calls, it was determined that neither man could be located.

From the corner of his eye, two men were coming down the side stairs. The elevator opened, and two more men stepped off, then stopped to stare at them.

Kokkinos frowned and turned to Petrakis. "These your Russians?" he whispered.

"No, I don't recognize these men."

Four men stepped in through the front lobby doors, and one single man strode toward them from the restaurant doors.

It was the single man, walking alone, that caught Petrakis's eyes. He'd seen him before.

Then it clicked. This was the man staring at him when he parked out front after sending the ambulance off with Samaras and the Russian.

This couldn't be good.

These men were big, thick—American military-type men. They looked like they pumped iron and ate their enemies for lunch.

As all nine men drew closer, making a circle around the two inspectors, the door behind the reception desk closed. Evidently, the front desk clerk had gone to hide.

Petrakis eased his hand inside his jacket but stopped when the man approaching from the restaurant shook his head and clicked his tongue.

"I wouldn't do that," he said from two meters away.

An American English accent.

Petrakis looked around them. The other eight men had their hands in their jackets, large bulges pushing out the sides of their suit jackets.

These men were all hardened criminals, like something he'd see in American movies with Sly Stallone or Jason Statham.

And they were obviously heavily armed.

"What do you want?" Petrakis asked, doing everything he could not to have his voice crack in fear.

Kokkinos wasn't saying a word. In fact, Petrakis caught a glimpse of the man shaking like a leaf in his peripheral vision.

Why the fuck did the chief send me that asshole?

"We need a word," the man said. "Follow me."

The man stepped away, and Petrakis followed—what choice did he have? Kokkinos moved in close behind, with the rest of the men following them.

Did they actually just walk into a trap to be killed like one would swat a housefly?

Wouldn't his mother be proud of him now?

Chapter 31

Nadia set the phone down in a rage.

They were done with this hotel, this entire USB business. Viktor had failed her. He wouldn't leave the island alive. Even if he made it out to their boat, she would have him executed.

She stared at the desktop, hands clasped together, not wanting to move until she caught her breath. Getting up too fast, releasing her hands too quickly, only meant she'd pick up her weapon and kill someone—anyone—whoever was closest to her.

Viktor was the one who needed to die. He had that Greek agent, George, in his room. That man had to know where the USB was. Then Viktor had that fucking cop's woman, Anna. He allowed her to escape, and now Anna was with Markakis. That bolstered Markakis into thinking he could threaten Nadia.

This had turned into an amateur night at the resort hotel —everybody thought they qualified for the tough-guy competitions.

Viktor supposedly threatened that inspector after he was caught snooping around, but the inspector still took Boris away in that ambulance, which forced their hand. They had to take out Boris and that cop. The inspector left her without options.

So, in conclusion, Viktor was useless and would pay. The owner of the hotel just guaranteed she would destroy his place of business now, and once *she* collected on his insurance, she would kill him herself.

Markakis would be surprised to see her on the day the insurance company transferred his payment. Nadia would start with Markakis's wife by cutting off small pieces, like her ears. Then she'd work her way up to fingers and toes. Mr. Markakis would transfer the entire insurance settlement into her accounts way before Nadia had to cut off major organs. Then she'd put a bullet in each of their heads, but not before reminding Mr. Markakis that no one threatens her and walks away from it.

The only thing holding her back was that damned USB stick.

The people back home who sent her here to obtain that stick outranked her. Without the USB, she wouldn't live out the week. She had employed Viktor, her most trusted lieutenant, for this job, but he hadn't gotten her the needed results. Her superiors were the ones who had specifically requested her for this job, and she'd taken much longer to get results than anticipated.

She picked up the phone instead of her weapon and

called Viktor. He answered immediately.

"*Da?*"

"Execute everyone involved. I'm finished with this fucking island. Then, meet me on the boat. Find that cop's bitch. Kill her. If you see the hotel owner or his wife, kill them. I don't care who you kill. Just make sure it's as many as possible. Make sure that the inspector dies screaming. They fucked with us enough. Then, set the charges and leave the island. No more talking, no more searching. If we can't get the USB, then no one gets it. Understood?"

"Understood. ETA for the boat?"

"I will give you two or three hours, but no more. Be on the boat or miss the boat. The mood I'm in, I don't care. See you in Mother Russia."

She slammed the phone down so hard it cracked the outer casing.

The two men standing guard by the room's door flinched, but neither man looked directly at her.

Good, they stay breathing for a little bit longer.

Aware her temper had to be reined in, she inhaled and exhaled slowly, then got to her feet.

"Prepare to leave. I want off this island and to the boat within the hour."

Both men nodded, opened the door, and disappeared around the corner.

She picked up her gun now that she was alone, checked that one was in the chamber, and then slipped it in the back of her pants.

There was something about murder—even if someone else was doing it—that pleased her.

Viktor was expendable. She'd execute him herself, then

toss his body over the side before embarking for the other side of the Mediterranean. Once in Egypt, she'd have to decide whether to fly home without the USB or fly somewhere else to hide like a common criminal.

The only thing that could save Viktor's life—and perhaps her own—was finding that USB before they left.

She shook her head at the futility of it all, knowing that wouldn't happen.

Because Roxanne Dupont hadn't just disappeared.

She'd taken off.

And so Nadia would have to run, too.

After Roxanne …

Chapter 32

PETRAKIS FOLLOWED THE AMERICAN to a meeting room at the end of a long hall. How this man had a key mystified the inspector.

Once the door opened, six of the nine men entered the room and took positions around the windows and door. The others remained outside the room, presumably to guard the door, Petrakis surmised.

"We have a problem at this hotel," the man said.

"I've gathered that," Petrakis responded, unsure where this was going or whether the men were friend or foe.

"Firstly, do you know why this man"—he pointed at Inspector Kokkinos—"was sent here?"

Petrakis frowned and looked from Kokkinos to the American and then back to Kokkinos. Finally, he shook his head. "I understood it as another inspector to aid in the investigation."

The American shook his head. "He's here because the Greek government is doing a diplomatic favor for the French government."

"A diplomatic favor?" Petrakis jerked his head back. "What?"

Kokkinos faced Petrakis and nodded. "I'm here to take Roxanne Dupont into custody."

"That's it?" Petrakis asked.

Kokkinos kept nodding. "The rest of these shenanigans will remain your case."

"Shenanigans? Is that what you're calling it? When the Russians execute a good cop like Samaras, you're calling it shenanigans?" He couldn't keep his volume under control.

The American stepped forward, his hands out. "Petrakis, you'll have to keep it under control until we're through here. Calm the fuck down."

He stared at the American. "Who the hell are you guys anyway?" Turning, he took them all in. "What is this? An American black operation on Greek soil?" He fixed his attention back on the man in front of him. "Is this sanctioned by my government?"

"Sanctioned?" The man smiled. "Inspector, are you asking the Russians the same questions?" The American waited a heartbeat, then added, "I didn't think so." He pulled out a chair by the long conference table and dropped into it. "Please. Sit."

Once Petrakis took a seat, Kokkinos followed, but he sat three chairs away.

"I'll explain what's going on as quickly as possible, with as much brevity as possible." The American paused, and Petrakis nodded. "Roxanne Dupont is a French intelligence agent. She works for the DGSE."

"The what?" Petrakis leaned back and crossed his arms.

"The Directorate General for External Security. The French equivalent to MI6 or the CIA."

"I'm guessing you know why a French intelligence agent is masquerading as an artist on Greek soil?"

The American nodded. "She's not masquerading. She's a real artist and uses that as her cover."

"Then why is she here?"

"She came to meet with a buyer. A woman named Nadia is arranging the sale and using Viktor to do the tough lifting. Viktor is the man you met in that hotel room."

Petrakis's stomach flipped a few times. He placed a hand on his abdomen, hoping to calm things. This was getting way out of control.

"I'm guessing again here," Petrakis said, looking from the American to Kokkinos, then back to the man, "but Roxanne is here to sell sensitive information, right?"

The American nodded again, his eyes moving from Kokkinos to Petrakis.

The inspector turned to Kokkinos. "And you're aware of all this?"

It was Kokkinos's turn to nod.

Petrakis shook his head, heat rising to his collar. "You know a cop was killed, right?"

"That was unfortunate and unavoidable," the American said. "We were busy attempting to locate where the Russians were taking their captive, a Greek agent."

"This Greek agent, what's his business here?"

"He's been watching the Russians, waiting for the sale to take place."

Petrakis blinked a few times. "Wait, let me get my head around things." He leaned forward and placed his elbows on his knees. "Is Roxanne *actually* missing?"

The American nodded. "We find her; this ends. A man was watching her before we arrived, but I lost him."

"Lost him? How?"

"Probably the Russians. There's blood at his last known location, and I understand you found his body parts strewn in several dumpsters around the hotel."

Petrakis sat up straighter. "That's your guy?"

"Unfortunately. He was a good soldier."

Petrakis glanced around the room at the men, then refocused on the American. "Who are you guys anyway?"

"I'm your liaison. You won't ever need to speak to my men. Consider us an interested party regarding that sensitive information."

"What should I call you?"

"You've heard of survival of the fittest? The phrase that came from Charles Darwin's evolutionary theory?"

Petrakis nodded.

"That's what we're dealing with here, so you can call me Darwin."

"I'm assuming that's not your real name?"

"Of course, it is," the American said dramatically.

"Yeah, right." Petrakis stood up. The men at the door moved fast, getting to within a foot of him by the time he turned back. He raised his hands. "I'm cool. I just wanted to stretch my legs."

Darwin nodded at the men.

They eased back toward the door.

Petrakis caught sight of Kokkinos's white face. He may

be here as a favor to the French, but this man was scared shitless.

"So, Charles Darwin, what next?"

"Just Darwin."

Petrakis rolled his hand in a gesture to carry on.

"We must locate the owner of the hotel."

"Why's that?"

"Because he has abducted a woman named Anna, the fiancée of your dead officer."

Petrakis stopped moving and stared sidelong at Darwin. "What did you just say?"

"Inspector Petrakis, there are a lot of things taking place at this hotel that you're not aware of—"

"Evidently."

"That Nadia and Viktor are desperate. They *need* this USB, and we can't let them acquire it. Roxanne brought it here with her, but then she disappeared. They snatched the Greek agent watching them, and now he's dead. They took Samaras's woman to prove a point to you for fucking with them, and then *another* woman helped her escape. Markakis took her somewhere and hid her, then called Nadia and threatened her."

Petrakis shook his head as if to clear it.

Darwin continued. "Apparently, Mr. Markakis owes Nadia a lot of money. She loaned him cash to keep the hotel afloat some time ago, and when she arranged for the sale of the USB, this hotel was chosen because of how pliable Markakis would be."

"How do you know all this?" Petrakis asked in a half whisper, staring at Darwin.

Ignoring his question, Darwin said, "So, now we must

locate the woman who helped Anna escape and ascertain her role in all of this, then find the USB and destroy it, and everyone can go home."

"All in a day's work, I guess?" No one responded to Petrakis's sarcasm.

Darwin pushed up from his chair and moved to the window. After a moment, he turned back and glared at the Greek inspectors.

"We must find that USB and destroy it, gentlemen."

"What the hell is on this USB? Weapons plans? Government secrets? Banking information?"

"The USB contains raw data on mercenaries, men who have altered their appearance, changed their ID, and gone into hiding. People who served their country decommissioned spies retiring on an island somewhere. The USB is purported to contain over five hundred names, service records, actual locations, and proof of ID of these powerful people. The international clusterfuck of this data reaching the hands of the Russians would be a nightmare."

"How did Roxanne get it? Surely, someone else has a copy somewhere."

Darwin shook his head. "Her boyfriend hacked it. Then he wiped the data, cleaned his online presence to disappear effectively, placed the information on a USB, then arranged the sale."

"The boyfriend?"

"His body was discovered recently, sliced up like a slab of meat."

"The original computer? Storage disks?"

Darwin shook his head again. "There's only one in existence. Once they compiled the information on the USB she had on her when she arrived at this hotel, they destroyed any trace of the hacking. The boyfriend Peter took a hammer to the computers they used, then burned them in a fire. I assure you. There's only one USB in existence, one piece of death floating around here somewhere, and some very powerful people are attempting to acquire it."

"And your interest is purely professional?" Petrakis paused after a new thought hit him. "Or personal?"

Darwin looked away, checked his watch, then turned back to Petrakis.

"My involvement is personal. I work for no one. My tracking systems were pinged a month ago when Roxanne searched for this information in her home office. That office has now been destroyed, but not before she garnered some of my details. I hurt the Russians bad back in Toronto about eight years ago, and they've been looking for me and my wife ever since." His jaw clenched, the muscles in his face at the back of his jaw flexing. "You understand, I can't let the Russians get this USB. If they obtain it before I do, my life is forfeit, along with several of these men."

Everyone stared at each other for several heartbeats as Petrakis pieced it all together. Darwin had said *wife*, which meant he had something to lose. Calling this personal was an understatement. If his story was to be believed, the man was only breathing because this USB hadn't been located yet.

"What happens to Roxanne Dupont when we locate her?" Petrakis asked. "I mean, she will have seen the information she placed on the USB. She could possibly identify you."

"Miss Dupont, unfortunately, put herself in this position. She cannot be allowed to walk away."

"You'd kill a woman?" Petrakis's voice rose, and then he chastised himself. Of course, they would. They're mercenaries.

"Inspector, she is an enemy first, a woman second—"

Petrakis's phone rang. "Can I get that?"

Darwin gestured. "By all means."

Petrakis retrieved the phone from his pocket and smacked the answer button.

"Inspector Petrakis."

"Sir, I was told to call you."

"Who is this, and why are you calling?"

"Sir, we have a body in the water by the Lindos Palace Resort Beach."

"I'll be right there."

He almost dropped the phone as he jammed it in his pocket.

"What happened?" Kokkinos asked, his voice weak like he'd suddenly come down with a cold.

Petrakis stared at Darwin when he answered.

"Someone just found a body floating in the water by the beach."

Darwin nodded at the men near the door.

They swung the conference room doors open and stood to the side.

Darwin gestured. "After you. Let's go see who else is dead."

Chapter 33

FAYE SNAPPED AWAKE, AN unbearable headache making her scrunch up her eyes.

Her wrists and feet wouldn't move. They had to be tied to a chair as she was in a sitting position. A moan escaped her, but her mouth didn't open as it was covered with something, probably duct tape.

She opened her eyes to slits and took in the bright room. This wasn't the hotel. There was a subtle movement below her feet.

Were they on a boat? If so, how did they pull that off?

When she focused on the man in front of her, he was watching her intently, his hand resting on his lap, a gun in it.

Why couldn't she just sit in her hotel room, read a book, and leave well enough alone? Or maybe go swimming, drink excessively, find a random guy to fuck, and enjoy her vacation like everyone else?

No, she had to get involved in the craziness, inserting herself right into the bad guy's lair.

Voices conversed nearby, but she couldn't determine what they were saying.

The door opened, and two others entered the room.

She'd seen them before around the hotel. One of them approached her and grabbed the edge of the tape covering her mouth.

She braced for the pain, and then the man tore it away.

She moved her mouth around, loosening her jaw. "Thanks for the hair removal," she said, then laughed briefly before squinting in pain.

The Russian studied her like he hadn't seen a woman in years.

"You're an insane bitch, right?"

The others laughed at his wit and charm.

"Are you a cosmonaut?" Faye asked in English. "One of those Russians who has his head in the clouds?"

The Russian slapped her.

"I ask questions. Not you."

Now it was Faye's turn to burst out laughing.

"What you find funny?" He raised his hand, poised to slap her again.

"When this is over," Faye said, trying to get her laughter under control, "I will end up killing you, your friends, your children, and your fucking dog if you don't untie me."

The three men looked at each other, mouths open, then laughed.

The Russian slapped her again, knocking her head sideways so severely she heard her neck bones crack. The sudden movement flared her headache.

"How you get into our villa?" the man asked.

She shrugged, then spit blood onto their carpet. "I entered the wrong room. Simple really. Oops, big mistake."

"The Greek said you're working together. He confessed everything."

"What? Oh, George?" She shook her head. "Not me. You got the wrong girl."

"You don't want to save your life? He told us everything we needed, and now he drinks vodka with the captain. Do the same and live."

She shook her head slowly. "No, he told you everything you wanted to hear. And since I just entered the wrong villa, untie me before I get angry."

"Where is the stick?" he asked.

"Probably up your ass."

He moved to strike her again.

"Wait!" she shouted. "I have no idea what you're talking about. I was just in the wrong place at the wrong time." The Russians looked at each other and shrugged. It would be a long night.

He grabbed her hair and yanked her head back. She had to admit, that really hurt.

"My boss is out of patience." Then he tore at the top of her jeans, trying to open them. "Maybe we fuck it out of you."

"Yes," she moaned the word. "Please, do it. Fuck me hard until you all die of AIDS." She glanced over at the others sitting on the side. "Come on, guys. Tag team me. I can take more than one cock at once. How do you think I got AIDS in the first place?"

The man, tugging at the button on her jeans, let go and

stepped back. Under his breath, he said something in Russian that sounded like he swore to himself.

"Filthy bitch. You're lying." He slapped her again.

"Only one way to find out. Whip out your dicks and let me wet them between my legs."

The Russians seemed to be taken by surprise. Blood oozed out of her mouth. She spit on the ground, and the man closest jumped back, bumping into the wall.

One of them pulled a condom from his back pocket and then opened it in front of her.

"We fuck tonight," he said.

The man approached, already pulling his pants down.

When he was close enough, Faye collected the blood from the inside of her cut cheek and horked it at his face, covering him with a splash of her bodily fluids.

The man took several steps backward, wiping at his face. He seemed to panic, frantically slapping at the wet goo on his face, spitting onto the floor.

"What kind of woman are you?" one man whispered, staring at her in stunned disgust.

One of the Russians left, cursing under his breath. Another followed him, and the latter stayed to watch her from afar this time, not getting close enough to be spit on.

He glanced at the roll of tape, probably thinking of sealing her mouth closed, then fucking her.

But fear won out, and he didn't approach her.

They remained there for the better part of an hour, just watching each other as the boat swayed at anchor.

How the hell would she get out of this now?

She rolled her wrists, twisted her fingers back, and tried everything to loosen the ropes, but nothing worked.

Faye would remain attached to the chair until they were good and ready to release her.

Chapter 34

Darwin watched as they hauled the body closer to shore. Two divers had suited up and jumped off the Greek coast guard vessel. Apparently, they'd been on site within twenty minutes of the discovery.

Behind Darwin, the inspector was talking to the two teenage girls who had decided to do a little night swimming when they discovered the body floating in the water. Darwin listened while he watched the divers moving closer, dragging the unidentified body with them.

"Ladies, I'm Inspector Petrakis," Darwin heard over his shoulder. "I understand you two called in this discovery."

Darwin glanced back as the young blonde one pointed at the water, then wiped at her tears with her other hand.

"We saw the body in the water," she muttered through her tears.

Darwin considered that this body could be the missing

woman, Roxanne Dupont. In all his years, he hadn't killed a foreign intelligence agent—a female—and he didn't want to start now. But what choice had Dupont left him? This was a dilemma he would have to face sooner rather than later—unless she was already dead.

The girl's friend hugged her, and they sobbed together.

"I'm sorry," the brunette said, her face buried in the shoulder of the other girl. "I forced you to swim when you didn't want to."

Petrakis moved toward the water's edge to stand beside Darwin. The girls needed time to calm down, and it was likely other officers would take their statements.

"You think it's Dupont?" Petrakis asked.

"You can never really tell with the Russians who will be killed next or where they'll dump the body." He kept his voice low so the teenage girls wouldn't hear him.

Darwin's men had formed a semi-circle in the darkness of the beach to secure the immediate area. They were relatively safe as long as they stood there on the sand. No one would approach with stealth without one of his men informing him. The only threat would come from a sniper, but he guessed Nadia hadn't elevated her hit list to killing the inspector—yet. They'd already murdered a cop named Samaras. Anyone could be next.

The divers were taking their time, easing the body closer to shore. Another ambulance was en route to pick up the body for the coroner.

Darwin found it interesting that in Greece, ambulances were called to pick up dead bodies instead of a coroner van. He thought ambulances were only called when someone needed medical care or emergency help—but not in Greece.

The ambulance was the dead-body delivery vehicle for the coroner, and they had a limited supply of vehicles and staff on an island about a ten-hour boat ride from the capital city, Athens.

Darwin's earpiece clicked that a call was coming in on his encrypted line. He tapped it once to accept the call.

"Speak to me," he whispered.

When Petrakis glanced his way, Darwin raised a hand and stared at the ground to indicate he was listening to someone in an earpiece.

"I'm monitoring Nadia's line," Rosina said. "That device Sergei planted just recorded something."

"Have you played it back yet?"

"Not yet, but I'll have it all in one minute. Hold the line."

He faced Petrakis. "My wife."

The inspector nodded and stared back out at the approaching divers.

Men with flashlights approached them from the side, a backboard in hand. They were here for the body.

The divers were ankle-deep in the water now, ready to lift the body onto the backboard.

Petrakis moved into the water and stood over the body, his shoes soaked through.

"Roll the body over," Petrakis said. "I need to see the face."

The divers did as they were instructed.

Petrakis leaned down using his phone's flashlight app. When he stood upright, he turned away and stepped out of the water to stand beside Darwin.

The men were loading the body now.

"So, who is it?" Darwin asked.

Petrakis glanced at him, his eyes hard, expression cold.

"Miss Roxanne Dupont was just found dead in the water."

Darwin scoffed. "Was that intentional?"

Petrakis frowned. "Was what intentional? That she's dead and in the water?"

"The phrase you used, 'dead in the water.'"

Petrakis shook his head. "No phrase. I meant it literally. She was found. Dead in the water."

"Got it. Well," he waved a finger at the body as the men lifted it on the backboard. "Check her pockets. Make sure she doesn't have the USB on her."

"Here? Now?"

Darwin nodded. "Absolutely. If she goes to the morgue with that USB, a trail of murdering Russians will follow and kill anyone in their way. You don't want that on your conscience if you could've just grabbed the USB right now."

Petrakis nodded and stepped away to stop the men carrying her body.

"Darwin," Rosina whispered as the line was still open.

"Yeah?"

"We have a problem."

"What sort of problem?"

"Nadia just called Viktor."

"And?"

"She's ordered the murder of everyone involved, then she wants him to blow up the hotel and meet her on the boat."

"How much time do we have?"

"She said two hours or so. Maybe less."

"That's not enough time."

Petrakis was walking back to him after a small war of

words with the coroner's men.

"Honey, give me a second." Darwin turned to Petrakis. "Did you find the USB?"

Petrakis shook his head. "Nothing on her. If she was carrying it, that USB is now on the bottom of the sea."

"One second," Darwin said, holding up a finger. "Honey, can you send me the file with Nadia's voice? I want the inspector to hear it."

"Doing it now. You'll have it in under a minute."

"Okay, I'll call you back soon."

Darwin clicked off.

"What is going on?" The inspector moved closer. "More trouble with the Russians?"

"We just intercepted a phone call that Nadia made from her room in the hotel."

Petrakis jerked back, tilting his head. "Intercepted? How can you do that?" Then he held up his hands. "You're doing illegal wiretapping?"

"I think we're beyond that, Mr. Inspector."

Petrakis glanced out at the water, then looked upward. "You're right. We are. Tell me how you did it, though." He turned back to Darwin. "I'd still like to know."

"Sergei helped us." Darwin smiled. "He helped us a lot."

"And who's Sergei?"

"He works for Nadia. In fact, he's one of her personal security detail."

"And why would he help you? These aren't the kind of men you can threaten with a beating or jail time."

"We took pictures of as many of Nadia's men as we could, covertly, of course. Well, my guy Miller did before they killed him and placed his body in the dumpsters."

They started walking up the beach and headed back to the hotel.

"And what did you do with these pictures?" Petrakis asked.

"My wife did facial recognition on most of them. She was able to identify seven out of ten men. Of those seven, we researched their families and girlfriends, even hacked personal records to see where they traveled recently, and found several weak spots for a few of them."

"Weak spots?"

"Things I could use against them to coerce compliance."

"Compliance with what?"

Darwin glanced sidelong at him. "You're a clean cop, through and through, aren't you?"

Without pause, Petrakis nodded. "Is there any other way to be?"

They turned to the right to use the pathway back to the hotel as Darwin opened his cell phone. There was no message from his wife yet.

"Well," Petrakis said. "You were talking about compliance."

"We needed a man on the inside. Someone to plant listening devices." Darwin patted the inspector on the shoulder. "You handled Viktor quite well when you barged into their room at the other hotel. They were interrogating that Greek intelligence officer—"

Petrakis stopped walking. "If you were listening into that, why not break the door down and stop them?"

"Because I needed the information the Russians were trying to get out of George. Everyone is here to locate that USB stick. If they find it first, my life is forfeit. If I find it first, their life is forfeit. George knew what he signed up for. He wasn't professional enough when tracking them. They spotted him quite easily. So they sent Kokkinos to take in Roxanne Dupont."

Petrakis's breathing rate had increased, even though they weren't doing any serious exercise. If it wasn't so dark, Darwin was sure he'd see the man's neck and face colored in anger.

"If it makes you feel any better," Darwin said, "I had a team waiting to launch a full attack on that room and extract George the second he told them where the USB was. Once I knew its location, we had planned to get him out of there safely. I was in the room next door, listening to everything."

They started walking again. "Okay, then tell me how you got Sergei's compliance."

"He has a French girlfriend waiting for him in Paris."

"That's it? You threatened his girlfriend, and he believed you?"

Darwin shook his head. "Not exactly." He slowed as they approached the front access doors to the lobby. "This conversation ends there, so we finish it here."

Petrakis nodded. "Please, I'd like to hear more before sending that file to your phone."

"I have contacts in many European cities and some in Canada and the States. I simply called my contact in Paris. They visited Sergei's girlfriend. She's seven months pregnant."

Petrakis leaned forward to grab Darwin, his hands moving quickly.

Darwin saw the advance and easily grabbed the man's wrists, spun them in a circle, one wrist over the other, which twisted the inspector's body away from him, and then he shoved the man. Petrakis stumbled and caught himself before he face planted the ground.

"Mr. Inspector, that wasn't wise. If I didn't push you away, one of my six men trailing us would've taken a shot at you."

Petrakis stood four feet away, rubbing his wrists and glancing at the darkness surrounding them.

Two of Darwin's men had emerged from the shadows, weapons in their hands.

"Your men would shoot a cop?"

"Without hesitation. My men don't care what job you may have. We're all men with an agenda. Yours may be deemed more noble than ours, but at the end of the day, we're all the same. You're a man, you're armed, and you'd kill with that weapon to save your life or the lives of others around you. My men do the same but are paid one hundred times more than you. Be clear, draw on me, or touch me again; there will be consequences. Don't lose sight of who is in control on the street. I assure you, it isn't the authorities. They are only left with the illusion of control."

Petrakis nodded, the look of disdain easy to see on his face. "So, tell me, did your Paris man hurt a pregnant woman?"

"Not at all. What kind of men do you think we are?"

Petrakis rubbed his wrists. "Then I'll ask again. Please explain this compliance thing."

"My man arrived and gave her a fake story about being Sergei's friend and that since Sergei was on a dangerous job in Greece, he'd asked my guy to come and keep her safe until Sergei got back. That's what she heard, and she's happy for the company. He's still there, in fact. They're having a blast. No harm done."

"What did Sergei hear? No way he likes that."

"Sergei heard that my guy would stay with her and kill her slowly, then mail her body parts to Sergei piece by piece if he didn't do as we say." Darwin raised his hands. "Before you respond to that, Inspector, we're not animals. We would do none of that. But Sergei had to believe us, so my man set up a video call from inside the apartment when Sergei's girlfriend was sleeping. What was of utmost importance is that he believed us, and he was compliant. That's how I know so much about what's going on. I'm listening in everywhere."

"And I'm supposed to believe you just walked up to this Sergei guy and showed him a video, and he shrugged and said he'd do it?"

"Believe what you want, but that was the easy part."

"How so?"

"Petrakis, abducting someone off the street, placing a hood over their head, securing them to a tree in the woods, and negotiating is what we do. We left him there with the hood on, then drove off. The ropes that secured him were loose enough that he could free himself and walk back to the hotel before Nadia noticed him gone."

Petrakis shook his head and moved closer again. "I have no idea how you do what you do and sleep at night."

"I'm actually doing what you're doing, but without your rules. We're all making the world a better place, no?"

Petrakis shook his head. "Whatever you say, Mr. Charles Darwin."

Darwin's phone clicked in his ear. "That's the file. Now

we will listen to what Nadia said about five minutes ago."

He opened the file, took a quick look around them to ensure no one was too close, then handed an earbud to Petrakis and stuck the other one in his ear before pushing play.

After two seconds, Nadia's voice came through the earbud loud and clear. It was so clear it sounded like they were on a phone call with her.

"Execute everyone involved. I'm finished with this fucking island. Then, meet me on the boat. Find that cop's bitch. Kill her. If you see the hotel owner or his wife, kill them. I don't care who you kill. Just make sure it's as many as you can. Make sure that the inspector dies screaming. They fucked with us enough. Then, set the charges and leave the island. No more talking, no more searching. If we can't get the USB, then no one gets it. Understood?"

There was a pause, and then Nadia said, *"I will give you two or three hours, but no more. Be on the boat or miss the boat. The mood I'm in, I don't care. See you in Mother Russia."*

The earbud dropped from Petrakis as he stepped away and looked skyward.

"You okay?" Darwin asked.

"How does the world have people like that?" He turned to face Darwin. "How could someone be so evil?"

Darwin had a soft spot for the man. This wasn't his fight. He'd originally come to the hotel to investigate a missing woman, and now she'd been found. Sure, several other bodies had piled up, but that could be dealt with when Nadia was dead or off the island. Staying here any longer was too dangerous for Petrakis.

"Inspector, you have to leave. Go get Inspector Kokkinos and take him back to the airport, then go find a hotel, pay cash, and stay hidden for a day or two. This'll all be over by then."

He glared at Darwin. "I'm not running from these people. They killed Samaras."

"Then you'll die. Do you have anyone who would care if you died? If not, stick around. But let me tell you something. I know people who were on the Russian's hit list. I know the lengths they'll go to when a kill order has been placed. You will die in the worst way possible by tomorrow morning if you don't run now."

That redness Darwin had detected earlier when Petrakis seemed angry was all gone. Now, the man's face was as white as old yogurt.

"Run, Inspector. Now. Leave this hotel with Kokkinos within the next ten minutes."

"How will I explain that to Kokkinos?"

"He came here to apprehend Miss Dupont. You just identified her body. Inspector Kokkinos's job cannot be completed as Miss Dupont is dead. Explain that to him and run. Or stay and die."

They stared at each other for several heartbeats, then Petrakis nodded. "Fuck it. I'll go." He stormed past Darwin, headed for the lobby doors, then stopped before entering. "Are you going to kill any of them, Mr. Darwin?"

Darwin waited a moment, then nodded. "I'm afraid I may have to."

"And what about the charges they've set? Will you let this hotel burn to the ground?"

Darwin shook his head. "Nothing will happen to the

hotel, I assure you."

"Well, I don't feel too assured."

Darwin said, "Sergei told us about the charges and gave us their locations. Once they were planted and set, my men removed them. Unfortunately, we couldn't diffuse them as none of my guys are bomb experts, but they are no longer on hotel property. Nothing will happen to this place, but the Russians don't know that yet."

Petrakis smiled. "Maybe we are on the same side after all." He sounded despondent but resigned to his own fate. "Good luck, Mr. Darwin."

"Here's my cell number, Inspector." Darwin handed him a slip of paper. "Call me once you're free of the area so I don't have to worry about you."

Petrakis eyed him. "You care about me now? Or you don't want to worry about me being here because of the homicides you're about to commit?"

Darwin stared back at him for a long moment. "I'm not concerned with the lengths I will go to protect myself, my men, or my family. You shouldn't be concerned about me, either. Now, grab Inspector Kokkinos and leave through the back. Sneak around to your car and be out of here as soon as you can. Don't remain anywhere public."

Petrakis was about to enter the hotel when he stopped and turned back. "Why's that?"

"I can think of several reasons. If you're in a public area with hotel guests around, there could be collateral damage when Viktor and his men try to kill you and Kokkinos. Also, a more public area is where Viktor would expect you. The chances of being seen are greater. Just stay at the back, stay unseen, and get off the property. You're increasing the odds of staying alive that way."

Petrakis stared at him with what seemed like a renewed sense of respect. Then, with an almost imperceptible nod, he pushed open the doors and entered the lobby, the doors closing behind him with a sense of finality.

Darwin wished him well but had a bad feeling he hadn't seen the last of the inspector.

Chapter 35

MARKAKIS HAD SWEAT SO much that his shirt was drenched, and his mouth was parched. The girl had stopped trying to get out of her restraints, and that irritating crying and moaning thing she'd been doing for the past half hour had subsided.

Something else was bothering him now, though.

He was thirsty. Beyond anything he'd ever felt before. His pants were still soaked through with urine, and it felt like he needed to take a piss again.

All of this could be handled within ten minutes of being in his room. A shower, a change of clothes, and a large water bottle. Then he could remain with Anna for the night down here. He could even bring her some water.

By morning, before the sun rose, he'd have to move her, though. Staff would access this room. They'd see her, and he couldn't allow that. As soon as the Russians left his hotel, he'd release her and explain he kept her captive to save her life. He had personal dealings with Nadia, and knowing Anna had escaped that Russian woman's clutches, all Markakis did was keep her safe until the morning.

Whether the authorities believed him or not, that would be his story. His word against a Russian criminal. Or his word against a woman who was abducted from her home by violent criminals. Of course, they'd believe him. *And* he was the one walking her into the police station. That had to give him some credit.

He got to his feet and approached her. The woman, who appeared to be in her mid-forties, had woken up from his punch a few minutes after he hit her. This was good. He didn't want her unconscious all night. What if she needed medical attention?

That cop had chosen well when he picked this woman, but he was dead now, and this poor woman would need comfort for that loss.

Towering over her, he watched her, then knitted his brow as she twisted away from him.

"I'm not the enemy," he said, using a soft tone. "Because of me, you will live. I've saved you from those mafia thugs."

She moaned two words that sounded like *fuck you*.

"You may be upset now, but when this is over in the morning, and that bitch has left my hotel, her tail between her legs, I will drive you to the police station myself. You'll see. They'll thank me for taking care of you."

She moaned several more words and, this time turned to glare up at him.

After a head shake to show her he had no idea what she was trying to tell him, he got down on his knees to be at her level, then wrapped his arms around her.

The woman's body went rigid. It was as if she held her breath.

"It's okay, no need to worry. I'm here for you."

His right hand had inadvertently gone under her armpit and was on the side of her breast. Warming to the idea that she needed comfort, he adjusted his arms to hug her tighter to him.

"I'm sorry for your loss. At least you'll make it out of this alive and can mourn properly."

His right hand fully cupped her breast now, and a stirring in his loins made him not want to let go. Maybe they should get to know one another in the hours they had left until the morning. Since she was single now, perhaps she needed a man's strength and warmth to feel safe again.

But before getting close to one another, he needed to change first. She would not be *that* friendly with him at the moment as he stunk of rank piss.

With one final squeeze of her breast, he released her and got to his feet, a gentle smile on his face.

"I'm going back to my room for a shower and a change of clothes. I'll get us some wine, water, and snack food for the evening." He withdrew the keys from his pocket. "No one has access down here but me, so you'll be safe."

She wasn't just glaring at him now. There was an anger in her eyes that seemed menacing.

"I understand," he said loud enough to be heard over the HVAC system as he moved toward the door. "You don't want to be left alone." With a wave of his hand, he gestured at his soiled pants. "But I had an accident, and if we're going to spend the night together, it should be more pleasant for you as well." He opened the door, peeked along the empty corridor beyond—relieved it was empty—then looked back at her.

Now, a tear slipped from her right eye.

"Don't cry, Anna. I'll be back to comfort you. We'll hug and hold each other for hours. This is a trying time for both of us. This room can get pretty warm, too. Even if we lower the lights and remove some of our clothes, it'll help to adjust for the temperature." He smiled at her. "I'll make sure you're safe and warm. We're in this together. We should do everything together."

Markakis closed the door, his erection already building. He had no idea how erotic it was to have a woman waiting for him, gagged and bound as she was, with the need for comfort.

Of course, a woman needed comfort. She was obviously distraught, and he was a nice guy. He'd never hurt her or do anything she didn't want to do. Even if offering comfort tonight just meant holding each other all night, she'd understand if that aroused him. She was a woman. They were intuitive with that sort of thing. And if something developed, then that was the natural order of the species, wasn't it?

If anything happened through the night as he hoped they would, when the morning came, and he took her to the police station, the story would remain the same.

She escaped the clutches of the Russian mafia, and he hid her overnight. The only reason he kept her bound and tied was for her own good. He couldn't have her running around the hotel while they searched for her.

Being intimate with one another was what adults did. She could *claim* it wasn't something she wanted, but it would be her word against a reputable businessman in the community. After all the free rooms he'd given to local cops in the past, there was no way they'd consider him inappropriate in any way. With a body like hers, how could she ever convince the guys that she wasn't begging for it? She even claimed the Russians wanted to rape her, and he saved her from that.

At least he'd be gentle and kind, which isn't rape in anybody's book.

But first, he had to get to his room, change into something like track pants, grab a bottle of wine and snacks from the kitchen, and then get back and lock them inside for the rest of the night.

Ten minutes, maybe fifteen max.

The last problem to deal with—what would he tell his wife? The stupid old hag always sat around complaining like he didn't give her the life she currently enjoyed. The money, the fine cars, the roof over her head. The lazy bitch was all take, take, take, and then she would whine about how things weren't being handled well or there wasn't enough money. Why couldn't she just be happy, go and have a spa day, and drink herself to sleep? What did he care as long as she stayed out of his way?

At the end of the hall, he opened another door with his key that led to a stairwell.

Another empty corridor.

He considered himself lucky, even though no one should be roaming these halls at night except maybe security.

Even that prick Diakos would've gone home by this hour.

Markakis ascended the stairs and made it to the last door. This one led outside. Then it was a hundred meters to his room, a shower, and back to Anna.

The anticipation of a quiet evening with her while sipping wine as they waited until the coast was clear felt like a reward for all the stress he'd been dealing with.

God had arranged the details. It had to be God, the universe, or whatever people believed in today. There was no other way to see it.

He was a good man. He wouldn't hurt her. So, of course, fate had put her in his path. Whatever forces were at work had brought them together, and they would see it through together.

Anna was young, willing, and ready for him. He smiled to himself. Maybe they could do it several times throughout the night.

The last door required a key. He inserted it slowly, his stomach filling with knots as the lock clicked.

This was where the entire night could be ruined. If just one of Nadia's men were waiting for him or saw him, he'd have to call the police and let Anna go. There would be no other option.

So, he had to do everything he could to stay out of sight.

The door opened silently on well-oiled hinges. Internal praise flooded him for the employees who did their jobs well and kept things like doors quiet.

Once outside, he locked the door and slipped the ring of master keys into his pocket.

Keeping to the shadows near the row of bushes, Markakis moved toward his room about ten doors down toward the beach. They always took the bridal suite when they came to see how Diakos was doing.

Which reminded him—those pictures Diakos had over

his head would need to be dealt with. No more blackmail, no more shit. Even if his wife found out and left him, then fuck her. He could make it on his own. Then he could fuck whomever he wanted, whenever he wanted, and as often as he wanted instead of sneaking around like a teenager in high school. How did it come to this, that as a grown-ass man, he had to hide his lascivious ways?

He passed door after door without anyone seeing him. No one was out walking in the dark at the back of the hotel. A lighted concrete path wound its way to the water, but he preferred to stay in the shadows near the bushes.

When he stopped in front of his room door, he eased the keys out and moved from the shadows.

Nadia must've left and taken her men with her. No one was around. The place was as quiet as a tomb.

Calming now, feeling safer by the second, he slipped the key in the door and turned it.

After one last look left and right and seeing nothing, he pushed into his room and closed the door behind him.

"Honey?" he called, moving into the living room part of the large suite. "Diakos is so busy with the investigation and the police presence that I thought I'd give him a hand tonight —" He stopped talking when he saw the living room was empty. "Honey," he whispered. "Are you still awake?"

He could only hope she'd drank too much wine and passed out in their bed. Then he'd grab fresh clothes, shower in the guest room, and be out of here and in Anna's arms within fifteen minutes.

The bedroom light was off, so he moved that way, making sure to be quiet. He'd left earlier to pick up that package at the front desk, then opened it, called Nadia, and bumped into Anna. All that took some time, so it wouldn't surprise him if his wife had fallen asleep waiting.

He slipped inside the bedroom door and waited for his eyes to adjust, but it was just too dark, so he slid sideways along the wall to the en suite door to turn on the bathroom light.

When he hit the switch, he nearly jumped out of his skin.

Two men stood in the room supporting his wife. Her eyes were closed, and blood ran from the side of her face.

"What's this?" he asked, his stomach so sick instantly that he was concerned he may vomit.

Someone pushed him from behind. He stumbled forward and dropped onto the bed.

So there were three of them. One had been hiding in the bathroom behind him.

The man who pushed him stepped around to face him and then pointed at Markakis's wife.

"To save her life, where is Anna bitch?" the man asked. "You get one chance."

Markakis opened his mouth, gaped like a landed fish for a moment, then said, "Anna?"

The man nodded once.

They plopped his wife in a chair, and then one of the men yanked out a knife that had to be more than a foot long and was lowering it to his wife's neck when Markakis shouted, "Stop."

But the man didn't listen.

The knife slid across her neck, wedging deep.

Markakis stared in horror at the sight. It wasn't possible. His brain didn't register what the man had done because there was no blood right away. The man had taken the knife away from his wife's throat when the first traces of blood started.

She opened her eyes now, fully awake from whatever had happened to her before.

Miles of regret overwhelmed him. He should never have threatened Nadia. He'd made a huge mistake. Was there a way he could barter his life, give them Anna, and apologize? Even give Nadia the hotel if that was what she wanted?

"You have one more chance," the man was saying as Markakis stared at his dying wife.

She slipped from the chair, blood gushing from her neck now, her face whitening in the room's dim light. Gurgling sounds filled the room as she breathed through the canyon that the monster had carved into her neck. It lasted a full minute until she was laid out on her back on the floor, blood pooling all around her upper body, eyes wide in death.

As much as fear consumed him, there was something about watching them murder her for no reason at all that made him angry. And now fury overrode his fear, and he faced the man asking questions.

"How could you?"

"We ask the questions, asshole. Last chance. Where is the girl?"

"Fuck you."

"Wrong answer."

The men moved forward, knives coming out.

The interrogator raised a hand, and the men stopped their advance. He stared at Markakis, tilted his head, and looked into his eyes.

"You are a curious man. One who knows business and negotiation, yet you don't save her life."

"I didn't know what you would do," Markakis said, his voice cracking. He'd almost stuttered the words as shock settled over him.

"I won't ask for Anna anymore, but I will say this."

When the man didn't speak for a moment, Markakis shouted, "What? What will you say?" He'd started to cry and knew it was an ugly cry among such strong men.

"If you tell me where she is voluntarily, I will instruct my men to make it quick. For information, I offer mercy."

Markakis frowned. "Make what quick?"

The man motioned to his men, and they advanced.

The two men locked his arms up while the interrogator secured his legs. He squirmed, but these men were strong.

He opened his mouth to scream, but a dirty rag was shoved so deep he thought he would gag and vomit into it.

Then the pain came to him.

They were doing something to his right hand, but he couldn't see.

After a moment, the pain rose to an overwhelming white-hot scream, and then they lifted his hand and showed it to him.

His fingers were all missing.

"Do the other hand, then his feet. Then, cut off his balls. Then take his eyes, his tongue, his ears. Mutilate and carve the man until he tells us where Anna is."

Markakis screamed the HVAC room name and shouted that the keys were in his pocket, but no one could tell what he was saying through the cloth stuffed in his mouth.

Then his eyes rolled back in his head.

He recalled coming up from a fiery pit of pain and hell and whispering something about the HVAC room.

Someone tapped his shoulder, then the pain started again.

Before passing out, he opened one eye in time to see a knife come down into that eye, blinding him and forcing the last breath from his lungs.

Chapter 36

Inspector Petrakis made it back to Kokkinos's room and explained how they found Dupont's body in the water.

"I can confirm it was her. They've taken her to the coroner."

"And so you just want me to pack up and leave?"

"Well, you were here to take her in, and she's been found dead, so your job is finished here."

Kokkinos stared at him. "What's really going on?"

"Nothing," Petrakis nearly shouted. "We need to leave. Now." Petrakis opened the room door and peered out into the night. The area was clear.

"I still don't understand what the rush is," Kokkinos said. "Since Roxanne was found dead and I was supposed to be here to escort her back to Athens, then effectively, I don't have a job here anymore. At least let me sleep the night in the hotel room they provided for me."

Petrakis spun around and faced the man, animosity rising to the surface. There was a dark side of him that wanted to leave Kokkinos alone. Let him stay the night and see if he can survive it.

But he couldn't let another fellow officer be put in harm's way, not after what happened to Samaras.

He frowned when he noticed how thick Kokkinos's shirt was.

"Inspector Kokkinos. Are you wearing a vest?"

The man nodded.

"If you want to spend the night on the island, that's fine with me. Spend a couple of nights a week. I don't give a fuck. But that won't happen at this hotel. I have been apprised of credible intel that aims a bullseye on your back and mine. We are to leave immediately. This investigation will be wrapped up tomorrow by someone else."

Kokkinos frowned. "Bullshit. Who's taking over? You're just trying to get rid of me because of how I outed you on that last case. You're afraid I'll embarrass you again."

Petrakis glanced at his watch. He ignored the man's words because if he didn't, he'd end up decking the guy or pulling his weapon and ordering him off the premises at gunpoint.

"Inspector Kokkinos, we do not have the time to debate this further. If you're unwilling to leave now, then I'll leave without you. Stay at your own risk."

Kokkinos narrowed his eyes at Petrakis. "This is about what happened months ago in that case. You're afraid I'll take over and embarrass you again? Look, you can relax. My orders have nothing to do with your case or any homicides that happened here. I'm here for Roxanne Dupont as a favor to the French—"

"I know why you're here," Petrakis shouted. "But we're leaving now."

"Fine," Kokkinos grunted as he lifted the single bag he brought with him.

Petrakis glanced outside the room again, then swung back to Kokkinos. "You armed?"

The inspector nodded and patted the back of his pants. "You expecting trouble?"

Petrakis held the man's gaze for a moment, then nodded. "Yes. Stay alert. We'll walk around the back of the hotel, which will take us to the parking area. Then we'll take Samaras's car out of here."

Petrakis stepped outside and walked across the path until he reached the row of bushes lining the back of the property.

Kokkinos shut the room's door, eased down the steps, then strode over to Petrakis.

"What's with all the stealth and secrecy? You're acting like we're on the run from international spies. Like James Bond meets Jason Bourne or something."

"You keep thinking like that—"

"And what?" Kokkinos cut him off.

"You'll stay alive."

Kokkinos scoffed. "Oh, come on. We aren't dealing with those sorts of folks. This is Greece, for fuck's sake. The worst you get here is pickpocketed. What, a couple of homicides per year?"

"That's so far from the truth, it isn't even funny." Petrakis started along the bushes. "Follow me and stay hidden. Then I'll drive you to any hotel you want. Let's go."

He moved slowly and only stopped a few doors down

when an inebriated guest wobbled toward a room. Once the man fumbled with his keys, inserted them after the third try, then accessed his room and closed the door, Petrakis started moving again.

To Kokkinos's credit, he followed close behind and was relatively quiet.

When they reached the back of the main building, there was a rustling in the bushes ahead.

Petrakis stopped and held up his hand for Kokkinos to stop.

Kokkinos didn't see him in the dark and walked right into his hand.

"One second," Petrakis whispered. "Someone is just ahead."

Kokkinos leaned out and glanced up the path. "I don't see anyone."

Petrakis lowered to his haunches and waited, scanning the area for movement of any kind. Maybe it was an animal. He was wasting time when they needed to get lost and be gone.

He slowly got to his feet again, staring at the back of the building now. Something glinted in the warm breeze near one of the back maintenance doors.

When he squinted, he saw keys sticking out of a lock in the back door.

He pointed at the door, and Kokkinos followed the direction of his finger.

Kokkinos shrugged. "Keys?" he whispered. "So what?"

"Someone was about to enter that door, heard us or saw us, then bolted for the bushes and left the keys dangling."

Kokkinos tilted his head, closing one eye when he looked

at him. "You sure, Mr. Detective? Are people that afraid that they'll run at the very sight of us?"

"Then explain the keys and the sound we heard."

Kokkinos stepped out of hiding. "An illusion," he said, his voice at normal volume.

Petrakis raised his hands to silence the man, to get him back to their hiding spot, but it was obvious Kokkinos was done with the cloak and dagger games.

"It's all an illusion you're telling yourself, Petrakis. I'll go to another hotel tonight because I want privacy when I call our superiors in Athens and try to explain whatever the hell you're up to here."

Movement in the bushes up ahead stopped his rambling.

They glanced up the path as three men moved into view, then stopped a few feet from the back door, holding the keys. All three men faced them.

"What's this now?" Kokkinos asked, then looked back at Petrakis. "You set this up?"

Petrakis reached for his weapon. It was dark, but he could still recognize the man standing in the middle, flanked by his soldiers.

It was the man from the hotel room, the one who spoke to him of warnings and pig roasts.

The man Darwin called Viktor.

He recalled that woman's words from the recording Darwin played for him.

Make sure that the inspector dies screaming.

This wasn't good, and it was about to get worse.

"Kokkinos, we must turn around and go the other way."

Petrakis was already stepping backward when Kokkinos moved toward the men.

"Why would we do that?" Kokkinos asked him, then faced the three men as he took another step their way. "Gentlemen, what's going on this evening?"

Before Petrakis could yell a warning, the men moved their hands quickly and then opened fire.

Kokkinos jerked and vibrated as bullets hit him—a macabre dance that drove him to the ground. He moaned and grunted in pain as he rolled onto his side and then into a ball on the ground.

The weapons turned toward Petrakis, but no bullets hit him. A few punched the ground in front of his feet, while others smacked leaves in the bushes beside him.

The barrage ceased, the noise going with it.

Had Kokkinos just been hit in the vest? Or had bullets entered his flesh?

"Inspector," the man in the middle said, moving toward him. "We meet again."

Petrakis raised his hands, his eyes on Kokkinos, who still moaned on the ground, dark spots already forming on his shirt in several places.

Bullets hit his flesh. That was blood spreading.

"I need to call an ambulance," Petrakis was able to squeak out. It was the first thing that came to his mind. His life was about to end, and he was thinking about calling an ambulance.

Then, an odd thought struck him—how many times had he called for an ambulance from this hotel in the past day alone?

"There will be no need for ambulances," the man said, now two meters away. His men still pointed an Uzi at Petrakis. "This man will die from those wounds," the Russian continued. "And you will die as well." He glanced down at Kokkinos and shook his head. "It's unfortunate, really." He met Petrakis's gaze. "Messing around in things that aren't your business."

"We were just leaving—"

"So soon? I mean, didn't you just bring this man here to help you in your *investigation*?"

Kokkinos's moans were weakening. There would be no ambulance, no hospital. How fair was life when men like the trio in front of him killed without regard? How does one prepare for death? Shouldn't he be angry? These men executed Samaras, and now Kokkinos was dying, and all he felt were the minutes ticking by for him as well, with each breath he took.

"We're in over our heads," Petrakis said, with the intent to keep them talking. Anything to stave off the inevitable. "Please, I'll leave and get him the help—"

"Shut up, you fucking pig." Viktor spit on the ground. "We will take you down to Anna, Samaras's bitch. You may die together. Slowly."

Petrakis frowned. "Where is she?"

"Through there." The man pointed at the door with the keys still dangling in it. "We were just about to go inside after the hotel owner so graciously told us where he hid her."

Petrakis was frowning again. "The owner? You mean Markakis hid her?"

Viktor nodded. "He had balls, but he's dead now. He crossed Nadia, and you crossed me. So, we take you down to Anna and execute you together. How does this sound? Lovely, no?"

"Markakis is dead?" the inspector repeated the words out

loud. These people were monsters. They took a life like it was a random act, as random as which restaurant one might choose for dinner.

"He died screaming, in pieces."

While Viktor spoke, his comrades nodded and smiled.

Petrakis lowered to his knees on the cool grass. He couldn't possibly hold himself up any longer. Going for his gun would be a death sentence, and he couldn't outrun bullets. It was over. It was truly over. His life meant absolutely nothing to these men.

"Take him," Viktor said. "Bring him with us."

The two bodyguards advanced as Viktor turned away to attend to the door with the keys.

A weapon discharged—multiple times.

Petrakis dove sideways to lie beside Kokkinos as he withdrew his weapon and aimed upward.

But he was too late. Both men had fallen, new holes in their foreheads.

Petrakis aimed at the retreating image of Viktor and fired, but he'd already jumped away from the door and was running for the corner of the building twenty meters away.

When Petrakis saw who had shot those two men with such precision, he was stunned.

Wounded, blood oozing out of his right side, Kokkinos had curled into a ball and was playing the role of a dying man while hiding the weapon in his hands. In order to keep the shot as accurate as possible, Petrakis figured Kokkinos had waited until the men advanced and were nearly standing right on top of him.

Taking those shots had saved Petrakis's life, but sadly, not Kokkinos's life.

"I tried"—he coughed blood—"to get all three."

"Take it easy," Petrakis said. "I'll call for help."

"It's too late." Each word came out with effort, Kokkinos's face tightening with the strain. "I should have listened to you."

"No, don't talk." Petrakis held the man's head. "I'm so sorry."

"Just—" Kokkinos cut himself off with a bout of coughing. After a moment, his breathing labored like he was on his last few breaths. He looked up at Petrakis and said, "Just get the bastards for me."

For the second time that day, a fellow cop died in his arms, and Petrakis was filled with the urge to scream and the rage to kill to avenge their deaths.

This had to end.

He eased Kokkinos's head to the ground—feeling like a complete shithead for hating the man so much when he just saved his life—and got to his feet.

After removing Kokkinos's vest from him, he slipped into it. Those keys would take him to Anna, Samaras's fiancée. He would get her out of there and make sure she was safe. Then he would find that crazy guy, Darwin, and tell him he's staying until the end.

But he wasn't staying on to arrest people.

He was staying to kill them all and explain it away later.

Chapter 37

FAYE COULDN'T TAKE ANOTHER punch. Her jaw wasn't broken yet, but it would break soon. And that meant wiring it shut and eating with a straw for months. Although her nose was certainly broken. She had to breathe through her mouth, which kept filling with blood.

Since they were worried about her threat of contracting AIDS, one of the men got dressed in a makeshift HAZMAT suit. The thick gloves that were duct taped to his wrists were what beat the shit out of her while they asked ridiculous questions.

It was in these moments when she wished she'd just kept her mouth shut. A bad mouth was a dangerous thing to have.

Both cheeks were now swollen to double their regular size. Blood oozed from the inside of her cheeks where her teeth had cut them, and she wondered if she had internal bleeding or was the pain in her chest from a broken rib?

She leaned forward on the chair as much as the binds would allow, hoping to feel some sort of resistance.

Maybe sex with multiple partners would've been better than this. They were still going to kill her, so why not fuck her way out of this life?

In the end, what did she care? She'd killed so many people. It was bound to happen to her one day. If there were a chance she'd get out of this alive, she'd take it. But if not, then she'd accept that and move on to the afterlife—if there was such a thing.

Two men stepped into the room, balancing as the boat swayed on the water.

An odd thought about the wind picking up crossed her mind, and she wondered why she had random thoughts that meant nothing. Like deciding randomly to walk into the water until she drowned and died. Why? To see how it felt? To see what was on the other side? How stupid! She could've died, and now she was fighting to stay alive.

She never made sense to herself, so how could she be expected to make sense to others?

"Hey boys," she slurred, then gasped as her cut lip protested that slight movement of her mouth.

"We're gonna hurt you more."

"Yay, me."

"Hurt you *real* bad."

"Oh …"

"Like start taking off body parts. Watch you pass out, wake you up, make you pass out again." The man bent over and placed his hands on his knees to stare into her face. "You think that would be fun?"

"No, can't say that sounds like a party I'd attend."

"Then tell us where is USB."

"I wish I could, fellas, but I have no clue what you're talking about."

"We come here for one purpose." The man stood back up and looked at his friend. "Meet Dupont bitch and make sale. But someone killed Dupont, and now we fucked."

"Dupont?" Faye whispered. "The artist? Roxanne Dupont?"

"You know of her?"

She had their attention now.

"Yes, she's one of my favorite artists." Faye struggled to lift her head and look at the two men. "Why would you people want to meet an artist?"

"You dumb cunt." He leaned back in close to her face. "For the USB."

"Roxanne had a USB?"

"Damn, are you stupid?"

"And she wanted to give it to you?" Faye was stunned. Could all this have been averted?

"No, idiot. She wanted to *sell* it to us. Then we leave Rhodes, and she heads back to France rich. No one gets hurt, no one dies."

"But ..."

"But what?" the man said. Even the other man leaned closer.

"I killed Roxanne," she whispered.

The man stared at her, eyes widening. "What did you say?"

"I killed Roxanne Dupont."

They exchanged a glance, then stared back at her.

"Go on."

"I watched her art show, then followed her outside that night. She was headed to the beach—"

"To meet my people." The man's voice rose.

"You sound angry," Faye muttered. "No more violence, okay?"

"We decide when it ends. But I can hold off hitting you again as long as you're talking."

Faye nodded and lowered her head until she stared at her lap. "I tried to talk to her. She rebuffed me—"

"What is this, *rebuff* mean?"

"Pushed me away. Declined my advances. She didn't want to talk to me."

"Because she was about to make big money with sale of USB."

"How was I supposed to know?" Faye said, her voice raising now. "I followed her career, flew out here to see her, and then when I wanted to wish her well and tell her how amazing I think she is, the woman pushed me away. And she wasn't nice about it, either."

"Why kill someone for that?"

"Haven't you heard that song, "Stan" by Eminem? I am a fan. I have certain rights with a celebrity. When I pay money to support your art, then I travel to see you. At least thank me and move on. Push me away—and I mean she pushed me, literally—that was just way too much." Faye shook her head. "Nobody pushes me."

"So you killed Dupont?" The disdain in his words was stronger than his accent. "How did you do it?"

"How? What do you mean *how*?"

"She had to be hard to kill. The woman was a French intelligence officer. Trained in weapons and with her fists."

Faye shrugged. "Well, come to think of it, she was a bit of a fighter. I surprised her with several punches. Thought that would be the end, but she came at me. We ended up on the sand, rolling around. I shoved a fistful of sand in her mouth, then covered her mouth and nose with my hand until she stopped resisting." Faye shrugged again like it was no big deal. "She stopped squirming under me because she stopped breathing. Few people can breathe and swallow when there's that much sand in their throat and lungs."

"You killed her because you're a stupid cow, that's why."

"She's not the only one I killed." Faye glanced up and saw both men staring at her, hanging on every detail. "I saw the hotel cameras and wondered if security would hand the footage over to the police when they came to look for the missing artist, so I met with the head of security, a man named Kallonis, but he wouldn't listen to me either."

"You were the one who killed Kallonis?" The men looked at each other again, seemingly dumbfounded. "Nadia has been confused all this time about that security man. Wait until she hears what this bitch is saying."

"Of course, I killed Kallonis. I tried to seduce him, but he rebuffed my advances—"

"That word again, *rebuff.*"

"—so when nothing was working, I killed him. In the end, I just hoped and prayed that the footage would be grainy and no one would see me well enough to know."

"When you killed Dupont on the beach, did you take the USB?"

"Now who's the stupid one?" She gawked at them for a moment, blood and snot tickling her chin as it dripped off her face. "If I had your fucking USB, don't you think I'd give it up by now?"

The boat swayed to the left, and the men adjusted by grabbing something nailed down. Her weight shifted, and her chair felt like it was lifting, but then she settled back as the boat righted itself.

"We must call Nadia," the quieter man of the two said.

The one who'd asked all the questions nodded. "Call her."

They stepped from the room and closed the door. A second later, the lock clicked.

The boat swayed the other way, and her stomach protested.

What just happened was good and bad at the same time.

Good because the beating had stopped. Bad because now that they knew what she had done, essentially, she told them everything, and they had no further use for her.

She suspected when they returned, it wouldn't be to beat her anymore.

No, when they returned, it would be to kill her.

Chapter 38

DARWIN STOOD BACK AND watched the security screens before him, undaunted by the crying coming from across the hall.

It was for their own good.

With Nadia's order to kill anyone involved and then raze the hotel, getting as many staff hidden away in the basement as possible until Nadia and her people left the premises was a smart play.

It was also something Petrakis wouldn't have liked, which was one of the reasons he needed Petrakis and Kokkinos off the property. The inspectors would claim some law was being broken, and they'd be right. But Darwin's way *saved* lives, Petrakis's way, not so much.

"Roll that part back," Darwin said, staring at a woman who appeared to have been following Roxanne.

The lone hotel security man filling in for Valentine did as he was told.

"Pause it there," Darwin said as his phone rang. It was connected to his earpiece, so he tapped it without looking to see who was calling.

"I'm listening." When the security man looked up at him, Darwin pointed at his ear and mouthed the words, *phone call*.

"Where are you?" Inspector Petrakis asked.

The inspector would only ask that if he was still on the property and looking for him.

Darwin motioned to the security man that he'd be back, then stepped into the corridor. As soon as he exited the security room, one of Darwin's men, who had been guarding the door, slipped inside to watch the security guy.

"Inspector, please tell me that you both got away safe?"

"We did not."

"Where are you now?" A sinking feeling hit his stomach.

"I snuck into the manager's office. I'm in the lobby."

Darwin's mouth popped open. "You're still here and in the office by the reception desk?"

"Yes, and why is everything closed? The restaurant, everything is down for the night. What happened to everybody?"

"Petrakis, that isn't your problem anymore. Walk outside to your vehicle, take Kokkinos with you, and drive away. It's too dangerous for you here."

"I can't."

Darwin paused, afraid to ask him why but more afraid for the man's life. He had too much to handle without having to protect the inspectors.

"Kokkinos is dead," Petrakis said.

He'd spoken so softly Darwin almost asked him to repeat it, but then the words registered.

Darwin ran a hand through his hair and stared at the end of the hallway where two of his men flanked that access door.

"What happened?"

"We were headed to the parking lot along the bushes at the back of the building when we bumped into Viktor—"

"Viktor? And you're still alive?"

"Yeah, it was him. He had two gorillas with him. They shot Kokkinos and were about to kill me when Kokkinos drew on them, and before he died, he killed the two guys with Viktor."

"Did Viktor get away?"

"Yes."

"And Inspector Kokkinos is dead?"

"Yes, and I have Anna now. Samaras's woman."

"What?" Darwin raised his voice, then he reined it in. "How do you have Anna?"

"Markakis had abducted her after she escaped from the Russians. He had her tied up in the HVAC room. Viktor was on his way to her when we bumped into them. Oh, and the owners of the hotel are dead, too. They killed Markakis and his wife."

The world got smaller, the walls crushing in on him.

"Petrakis, do exactly as I tell you. Understood?"

The man's breathing came over the line like he held the receiver at the base of his nose.

"What do you want me to do?"

"Come to the camera room one floor below. Bring Anna. Make sure no one sees you. Can you do that without getting killed, or should I send up a couple of my men?"

"On my way."

Darwin tapped the earpiece, and the line died. He

motioned at the men at the end of the hallway.

"Inspector Petrakis and a woman are on their way down. Let them in. The woman goes in there"—he pointed at the room where seventeen staff members were being held—"and the inspector joins me."

The men nodded and looked back at the door.

Darwin shook his head and stepped back inside the security room. His merc eased around him and moved back to his position at the door.

"That woman," Darwin said, pointing at the screen. "Who is that woman? She looked like she was following Roxanne."

The security man shrugged. "I don't know the guests, sir."

"Print her photo."

The security man typed on the keyboard. Moments later, the printer whirred into action, a full-color photo coming out slowly.

"Take me to the cameras that cover the staff quarters within a half hour of when Kallonis was killed."

As the security man navigated the equipment, Darwin snatched the photo from the printer and stared at it. He'd seen this woman before. From the grainy photo of the paused camera, he was sure she was the one his men had seen talking to that Greek agent, George, on the beach. Then, she followed George toward his hotel.

What was she doing following Roxanne?

After he watched the Kallonis footage, he would take the photo in the other room. One of Diakos's people had to recognize her. One of them would know what room she was staying in.

"We're almost there," the security man said, the camera on fast forward in front of him.

The echo of a door closing filled the corridor. Footsteps bounded toward him as Petrakis and Anna were escorted his way.

He watched what the security man was doing in front of him while he listened to what was happening in the hallway.

A door opened. The sobbing got louder. A female protested, and then the door slammed shut and was locked again.

"What is this?" Petrakis shouted.

Then he grunted and was manhandled into the security room.

"You wanted to see the inspector, sir?"

Darwin turned to see that Michaels had wrapped a forearm around Petrakis's neck, holding him in place.

"You going to behave?" Darwin asked.

The inspector nodded, unable to speak yet.

"That look in your eyes tells me otherwise."

Petrakis jerked his head back and forth, but only as much as the man's hold on his head allowed.

Darwin nodded, and Michaels released the inspector.

Petrakis gasped in air, rubbing his neck. "What the hell?" His voice was raw now, heavy as if he had just woken up. "What's going on down here?"

"We are keeping people safe," Darwin said, turning back to the cameras.

The security man sitting at the console had stopped to watch the inspector's entrance. He probably hadn't seen this much violence in the past year or even in his lifetime.

"The camera," Darwin said, twirling a finger.

The security man understood immediately and spun back to the console.

Petrakis's breathing was calming as he moved to stand beside Darwin. "Where did you get this footage?"

"A Greek agent stole the main unit using the name Valentine."

"I was there," Petrakis snapped. "He stole it right out from under me."

Darwin half turned and smiled at him. "We stole it back and haven't had a chance to view the footage yet. My guy hacked their cloud and grabbed everything by transferring it to our own cloud. Now theirs is empty, and ours is full."

"Holy shit." Petrakis looked him up and down.

Darwin held up the woman's photo. "Do you know this woman?"

Petrakis studied the photo and then handed it back. "I've seen her around but don't have a name."

"After the art show, Miss Dupont left her room that night. She was headed toward the beach. This woman was outside her room door." Darwin tapped the photo. "This woman followed her. She's either the last person who saw Miss Dupont alive, or she's the person who killed her."

"Got it," the hotel security guard said.

Darwin leaned down and watched the screen as the head of security, Kallonis, strode along the path, a woman following close.

"That's the same woman from the photo in your hand," Petrakis said.

Darwin didn't acknowledge the comment as he watched Kallonis turn and address the woman on the TV screen. They looked like they were arguing about something.

When Kallonis turned away to enter a door, the woman snatched something off the ground and ran at him.

She struck the back of his head by leaping up and coming down brutally hard with whatever was in her hand.

Kallonis dropped, his body shaking like he was having a seizure. The woman hit the back of his head a couple of more times, then tossed the object—likely a thick rock—into the adjoining bushes.

"Print the best screenshot of her face from that incident," Darwin said.

The security man looked sick, but he hadn't stopped the camera. The woman had walked off the screen, and now the footage was of Kallonis lying there, no longer moving or vibrating.

"Hey," Darwin said, smacking the security man's shoulder.

He jumped, snapping out of his trance. "Apologies. I've never seen anything like that before."

"Print me a screenshot of her face. Then erase the footage so no one else has to watch it."

"You can't do that," Petrakis said. "There's proof of a homicide on that—"

"Step out of the room." Darwin pushed Petrakis, and he stumbled backward.

Darwin's men surrounded Petrakis, then moved around him and into the security room.

"Michaels, get me the photo he's printing," Darwin said as he moved past the men.

"Are you going to tell me what's going on down here?" Petrakis asked when they were standing across from each other in the hall.

"You heard the same recording from Nadia that I heard."

"And, this is your response? To lock the staff away instead of letting them leave to go home to their loved ones?"

"Look what happened when you tried to leave." Darwin waited a moment. "I'm sorry you lost another good man, but these people are safe here. Nadia believes the hotel will be razed and blown up, but as I told you earlier, we took care of the explosives."

"What did you do with them?"

Darwin considered telling him, then thought better of it. The less the inspector knew, the less chance it would hurt his career—or conscience—when this was over.

"I'm sorry to hear about Inspector Kokkinos," Darwin repeated. "If there was another way …"

The inspector glanced away, obviously distraught.

"You can't hold these people." Petrakis nodded at the door.

"I'm thinking I can. And you should be in there with them."

"No," Petrakis shouted. "I stay and fight. Those bastards killed Samaras and Kokkinos. This has to end, and I want a hand in ending it."

"If you truly mean that, then stay on as an observer. If we need you, we'll tell you."

"Observer?" he blurted.

"That way, you stay alive, Inspector. And I don't want to kill your career over these assholes. Stick around, watch the ending of this particular party, but stay out of the way and try not to break any laws. Just keep clear of this mess."

"Sir?" Darwin's man stepped out of the security office with a photo in hand.

Darwin snatched it from him and saw that this picture was much better than the first one. He held it up for Petrakis to see.

"This is the woman who killed the head of security, and I think this is the woman who killed Miss Dupont and tossed her body in the sea. Now we just have to identify her and go pay her a visit." He turned to his men. "Bring that security guy to the room. Then, leave two men behind to make sure no one leaves. The rest of you, come with us."

His men nodded, and a moment later, the security man, white-faced and staring at the floor, was escorted into the room.

Darwin and Petrakis looked in at the Lindos Palace Resort Hotel staff. Many of them eyed Petrakis with a look of anger.

The manager, Mr. Diakos, pointed a finger at him. "This is your doing?"

"We have reason to believe," Darwin cut in, "that a terrorist threat will take place against you this evening. Losing Miss Dupont and your head of security was only the beginning. Inspector Petrakis has been pivotal in figuring it all out."

He felt Petrakis's eyes on him.

Darwin continued. "This will all be over within an hour or two. Then you'll be free to leave. In the meantime, someone must tell us who this woman is."

He held up the two pictures side by side, turning slowly so everyone in the room could view the photos.

"That looks like a woman named Faye," one girl said.

"Which department do you work in?" Petrakis asked.

Darwin let him have his moment. It added to the illusion

that he was the one in charge here.

"I'm often at the front desk," the girl said. "But I forget her last name."

"What room is she staying in?"

"She was in the room beside Miss Roxanne Dupont, but for tonight, she had asked to move rooms. I forget the number, but it's beside the group of Russians we rented to."

Darwin met Petrakis's gaze, then jerked his head toward the corridor.

"Thank you for your help," Petrakis said, stepping backward into the hallway.

Darwin's men closed the door as several voices rose, asking for water and food.

"Beside Roxanne's room?" Darwin said, leaning close to Petrakis. "Now, besides the Russians?"

"Go figure," Petrakis said. "Through all this, a random woman shows up and kills the artist and the security man."

"There's a reason. She went after Kallonis to get access to the footage of her following Dupont to the beach, is my guess."

"We have to talk to her. Arrest her."

Darwin glanced around him. "I need six men with me. The rest stay and lock this basement down. No one in or out. Understood?"

His men nodded and broke into groups.

"Follow me, Petrakis."

They headed for the door with the EXIT sign over it.

His phone rang.

He tapped his ear and caught his wife's worried voice, making him slow to a stop before exiting the corridor.

"What is it?" he asked.

"I just intercepted Viktor calling Nadia."

"What did they say?"

"A woman they have with them on their yacht just admitted to killing Dupont and Kallonis. I'm sorry, they didn't offer her name. Viktor said the USB is lost, gone."

Relief flooded through Darwin, but it wasn't over. Having the USB in his possession was absolute—that's what ended all this. Without the USB being destroyed in front of him, he'd always worry it would surface one day.

"Is that it?"

"No, Viktor said he killed the inspector."

"He did. Inspector Kokkinos is gone."

"Fuck," Rosina spat. "Bastards."

"I know. Anything else?" He wanted to hear it all, but he also wanted to get to Faye's room. "Wait, did you say they have that woman?"

"Yes, on their boat in the harbor."

He watched Petrakis, who could only hear Darwin's side of the conversation.

"Anything else?"

"Yeah, Nadia upped the timetable. They aren't waiting any longer."

"How much time do we have?"

"None. They're leaving now. They got a call from a Greek police informant. Someone called the chief locally, and a six-man, heavily armed team is en route to the hotel. They'll be there soon, very soon. They already know about Kokkinos being killed. The order to lock down the hotel came from Athens. More men are coming, but that'll take a few hours."

Darwin glared at Petrakis, then checked his watch. "Now,

as in, they're running for their boat."

"I'd say so. Then they'll hit the charges. Hey, at least they're leaving."

"Which means we're leaving, too. I'll call you back when it's over." He clicked off.

"What's happening?" Petrakis offered him a deadpan stare.

"You called your boss?"

The man hesitated, then nodded. "I asked for backup."

"Heavily armed backup."

"And what of it?"

"You have six men on their way, sanctioned by Athens, with many more coming."

"Great. We can shut this shit down. Viktor can't get away."

Darwin shook his head. "So much for being an observer."

He turned to his men. "Wait thirty minutes, then release everyone and meet the rest of us at the rendezvous point."

His men nodded, and then Darwin spun around and sprinted out the door, taking the stairs two at a time.

Petrakis stayed on his heels as he exited out into the night.

"Where are we going?" he asked.

"For a stroll along the beach."

"A stroll along the beach? What the hell for? I thought we were going to find this Faye woman."

"The Russians have her on their boat."

"Don't we still have a few hours before they leave?"

Darwin shook his head. "That's why my wife called. Nadia ordered an immediate retreat. Nadia knows the Greek authorities are coming. There's an insider. It's all over."

Petrakis grabbed Darwin's arm and tried to spin him around, but Darwin shot his arm up and shoved the inspector so hard the man lost his footing and landed hard on his ass.

Darwin lowered his hand to help him up. The inspector hesitated, then took it.

"Stop touching me, Inspector. That was the last time. Do it again, and I won't be so nice."

Petrakis brushed himself off. "I was about to say that since they're leaving, this is truly over. We know who killed Dupont. We know who killed Kallonis. The Russians killed your man in the dumpster. What else is there?"

"I need to see their vessel. I need to watch Nadia and Viktor's board. Not until I confirm they've left the area can I relax."

Darwin started toward the beach again.

Petrakis caught up with Darwin while several of Darwin's men followed behind them in a protection formation.

"What about that USB thing?"

"Miss Dupont had it and was killed before she had a chance to sell it. So, either she still has it somewhere in her belongings, or that Faye woman stole it from her. As soon as the Russians leave, I will continue my search without threat of violence or, worse, death since the bastards are running."

Petrakis glanced back at Darwin's men, then stared at him as they walked side by side. "Searching for a USB in this hotel after everything that happened with men like those guys behind us is a highly unlikely scenario once my men arrive."

"Well, we'll have to see about that."

Darwin picked up his pace, moving ahead of the inspector as their shoes hit the sand.

Chapter 39

The boat was moving.

Faye opened her eyes. No, she was moving.

Two men were carrying her while she was still bound to the chair. Her fingers and toes had long since gone numb. She wondered how long before they would do damage she wouldn't walk away from.

Had she dozed off? Did they drug her?

Hey, at least they stopped beating me—for now. There's that.

Probably, no one wanted to get dressed up in that makeshift HAZMAT suit again, so they opted to forgo any further beatings.

"Where are you taking me?" she mumbled.

"To die." The man by her head grunted the words.

The chair was tilted at a forty-five-degree angle. One man carried her by the shoulders, and another held the legs of the wooden chair. Too bad the chair wasn't the kind often found in old schools. They were made of rickety wood. She could squirm, and they'd drop her, and the chair would disintegrate under her hundred and forty pounds. Not this chair, though—sure, it was wooden, but it was too sturdy.

"You're leaving me tied up to die?" she asked, watching the man who held the legs.

"Yeah," he said. "Swimming is more difficult while hands and legs don't work."

Her stomach dropped. She didn't want to drown now. Tried that. Didn't like it.

"Oh, okay, so we're going swimming. This should be fun."

The men exchanged a glance.

A door opened behind them, and she glanced around. They were on the top level of a massive boat, a yacht.

"Holy shit, how big is this thing?"

Neither man answered her as they set her down. The men collected their breath and whispered Russian as she glanced around.

It was pitch dark out toward the sea, but the land was lit up in patches along the shore. Where a hotel extended close to the beach, pathways, and cabanas were lit. In the distance, several large hotels stood out in the darkness, several floors lit up where late-night guests were drinking, partying, and having fun.

Not Faye. She was stuck to a chair on a boat full of Russian thugs, waiting until they tossed her in the water.

"Hey, can you throw me toward the shallow part?"

They both looked back at her but said nothing.

"C'mon guys, I'm just thinking out loud here. How about

a fighting chance if you're supposed to leave me tied to the chair while throwing me overboard? Toss me to a shallow area. Worst case, I'll stay tied to the chair until morning when swimmers might find me. This way, you did what you were told. I'm found in the morning, and no one will be the wiser."

"Shut your mouth. We don't throw you overboard here."

"Oh." She raised her eyebrows. "Where are you planning on tossing me overboard?"

"We are leaving soon. Maybe fifteen minutes. Once we're out to sea, we toss you, and you become food for the fishes."

"Fishes?"

The men nodded.

"That's only a word when referring to multiple species of fish. Otherwise, the plural of fish is simply fish—"

The man shot out his hand and whacked her hard, then realized he'd touched her with his own flesh and spastically wiped his hand on his jeans.

She spit blood but didn't take on any more pain. That side of her face was still too numb.

"You stay up here," the man said, still wiping his hand. "Watch the land disappear. Then you go swimming. Until then, shut up, or we knock you out and throw you overboard while you sleep."

Faye nodded, not sure she'd be able to speak without saying something snarky.

One more test of her binds confirmed she was stuck to this chair until someone released her, or she died.

She was starting to think she would die in this chair.

She should've gone with the sex option.

At least dying would've been more fun.

Chapter 40

DARWIN TOOK UP A position on the beach behind a closed beach bar building.

Petrakis sidled up next to him. "Why are we stopping here?"

Darwin glanced back over his shoulder. "I wouldn't want us to be slaughtered on the sand."

"Slaughtered?" Petrakis reared back.

"Nadia's people are making a run for it. They're heading toward their boat. We walk out there and expose ourselves, and they use automatic weapons on us."

"How will standing behind Yorgos's Beach Bar building stop the Russians from leaving?"

"We aren't *stopping* anybody from leaving. They're free to hop on their boat and take off."

Petrakis stepped away from him, glanced over at the dock about a hundred meters away, and then looked back at

Darwin.

"You mean to tell me that the dock right there, not a football field from us, has the cop-killing Russians escaping, and we're going to do nothing about it? Just let them go?"

"Inspector Petrakis, step back into hiding." When Petrakis didn't move, Darwin eased his weapon out. "Do it now."

Petrakis's eyes skirted down to Darwin's hand, then back to his face. "What, you're going to shoot me? An inspector with the Greek police?"

"If your antics expose our position, then you put the lives of my men and myself at risk. I'd rather lose you than all of us."

Petrakis remained where he was standing—several feet from the shelter of the building—for a few heartbeats, then moved to the building wall.

"It's obvious we aren't working toward the same end goal."

"Whatever goal you had in mind, end or otherwise, won't happen today. You can't *arrest* these kinds of people. They'd be out within a day, and you and your family would be targeted for execution. A jury gets assigned to their case, and half the jurors are threatened or killed. One year to trial? Are you kidding? It would end in an acquittal or a hung jury. These are the sort of people who die in their line of work. That's it. That's the life they chose to be in the brotherhood."

"How do you know so much about them?"

"I've been hunting and hunting them for over a decade."

Petrakis's eye twitched. Darwin couldn't tell if it was anger or fear that the inspector was dealing with.

"Hunted? Like a man would hunt deer?"

"Exactly like hunting deer, but more dangerous. The deer aren't armed."

Petrakis cleared his throat. "How many men have you killed?"

Darwin stared at him for a long moment. "Are you looking for my résumé or deciding whether to arrest me?"

When Petrakis didn't answer, Darwin turned away and watched the dock.

Two people strode along it, then hopped onto the huge yacht at the end of the dock. Water was already churning at the back end of the boat. The engines were on as they geared up to leave.

"Michaels," Darwin said into his earpiece. "Pass me the binoculars."

Seconds later, a man materialized out of the bushes several feet to their left, a pair of binoculars in his hands.

"Where did he come from?" Petrakis asked, obviously startled.

"My men have the perimeter secure. They are trained to form a circle or half-circle around us and to remain unseen. I've also got men watching the docks. We're all connected to the earpiece right here"—Darwin tapped his right ear—"and everything you and I say, they hear. Unless I take a phone call. My phone's connected to the same earpiece, so when my wife calls, I'm off their signal temporarily."

"Wow, I had no idea that sort of technology existed."

Darwin lifted the binoculars and focused in on the yacht. "It exists, Petrakis, it exists."

The large boat had two levels, then an upper deck. On the main level, men with machine guns were stationed in each corner, pacing several meters to the left and right while watching the shoreline. On the next level, the same thing was happening in each corner. But when Darwin raised the binoculars to the top deck, he saw only two men who appeared to be unarmed. They were standing near a woman who was sitting on a chair.

He tried to zoom in to get a good look at the woman in the chair, but she was turned away from him, staring out to sea.

"What next then?" Petrakis said. "We just sit here behind Yorgos's Beach Bar, up against the wall, surrounded by at least six to eight mercenaries who remain hidden in the bushes and watch the bad guys run away on their boat?"

"Yes," Darwin said, pushing the binoculars against his eyes, still focusing on the woman. "That's what we do."

Then the woman half-turned. She was facing the shoreline. After a heartbeat, she angled around and looked directly at the dock.

"Holy shit," Darwin whispered. "They've got Faye."

"What?" Petrakis said as Darwin handed him the binoculars.

"On the upper deck. Looks like she's tied to a chair." Darwin grabbed his phone and dialed Rosina. After a moment, she was on the line. "Honey, are you sure, in all the chatter you've recorded and listened to, that you didn't hear anything about the USB?"

"The Russians don't have it if that's what you're asking."

"So, at this point, there's no confirmation of its location?"

"That's right. All we have is the original arrangement Dupont set up, the Russians arriving to make the purchase, the meeting that was supposed to happen but didn't happen on the beach after the art show, and then Roxanne's death. I thought they'd taken the USB and killed her for it, but Nadia does not have it. She's confirmed as much on multiple occasions."

"We saw a woman on security camera following Dupont to the beach that night. The same woman who we see killing the head of security. We have our murderer but no USB."

"Then that woman would have it, logically."

"And that's where this gets interesting."

"How so?"

Darwin snuck a glance at Petrakis, who was still using the binoculars.

"That woman is tied to a chair on the roof of the yacht the Russians are boarding to leave. Her face has dark splotches on it, but it's hard to tell what those splotches are in the dark."

"Blood," Petrakis said beside him. "Looks like they beat her."

"Inspector Petrakis suspects they beat her. Probably for the USB, but you're sure they still don't have it, right?"

"After reviewing everything here, I can tell you that, at this point, the USB is lost. Their words."

"Okay, I'll call you back." He clicked off. "Give me those."

Petrakis handed the binoculars back. "For the record, we've got them on so many charges their heads would spin. Even abduction charges. I mean, that woman up there is tied to a chair. What happened to her? What are they going to do to her?"

"There is no 'for the record' Inspector. Everything we do is *off* the record."

"I didn't sign up for '*off* the record.'"

"That's right," Darwin said, focusing the binoculars. "You didn't sign up at all. You're here as an observer only." He focused the binoculars toward the dock and saw the queen herself—Nadia—surrounded by worker bees as they escorted her along the dock toward the boat.

It was almost over. No more threat of being killed.

They'd come, created their mess, and left without the USB. It was a half-win, but he'd take it. A total win would be to locate that damned USB, but he couldn't think of where it would be.

They'd gone into Dupont's room after the Russians had ransacked it, but he couldn't find it. The Russians still claimed they didn't have it. No one else had claimed it, and the French wanted it back.

The only people who ever saw the data so far were dead. Dupont's boyfriend had done some sort of hack that had popped up on Darwin's radar, and then Dupont arranged the sale. She killed her boyfriend, came to the Lindos Palace Resort Hotel, and then she was killed here. If that USB is at the bottom of the sea, having slipped from Dupont's pocket, then all the better. It would be gone forever because Darwin and Rosina erased Dupont's boyfriend's hacked data.

But if someone else had it and was being quiet about it, sleeping at night would still be a problem.

The best way to end this was to locate that USB.

Could Faye have stolen it and refused to tell the Russians about it?

That left one item on his agenda once the Russians were gone. Search Faye's room, and then they'd leave.

The bushes rustled beside them.

Darwin lowered the binoculars, clipped them to his belt, and withdrew his weapon.

A Greek police officer in riot gear with his hands on his head materialized from the bushes, Darwin's man right behind him.

"Sir, we have six men," Darwin heard in his earpiece.

"Good work. Disarm them and bring them all to the beach bar where I am."

"What's going on?" Petrakis snapped, his jaw tight, teeth clenched. "That's a Greek police officer." He moved toward Darwin's man, who raised his weapon and placed the tip against Petrakis's cheek.

"Back off me, man," the mercenary said, his voice deep, gruff.

"I'd advise you to do what you're told," Darwin whispered. "These men are the best of the best. Elite fighters that saw action in the deserts of Afghanistan. Insurgent fighters. The kind of men who yank the Osama bin Ladens of the world out of their holes in the ground. Everyone is an enemy. Doesn't matter color, age, ethnicity, or whether you're wearing a badge. So step off the man."

Petrakis raised his hands chest high, then stepped back. "Okay, take it easy."

The bush moved as more men pushed through. Soon, all six Greek police officers were disarmed and sitting cross-legged on the sand, their hands on their heads.

"Charles Darwin, you can't do this." Petrakis pointed at the yacht as its engines revved. "You're immobilizing the authorities, the only men who can legally stop the Russians while letting the Russians get away. I'll call the Coast Guard and have them surrounded. You can't stop me."

"How did these six men hear you?" Darwin said, gesturing at the police officers on the sand. "Was your phone on? Were they listening in the whole time?" Darwin nodded. "I heard you tell them about the beach bar we're behind at least twice. The dock, the yacht. You tried to get me to talk about how many men I've murdered." He slapped Petrakis's jacket. "Still listening? Is anyone still listening?"

Petrakis stepped back, mouth open.

"You're the only one still standing because I respect you. Otherwise, I'd have my men place you on the sand with those six men. Attempt to betray me again, and I'll put a bullet in your forehead. You underestimate the playing field you're on, the sport you're playing, and the opponent you're engaged with. In my line of work, mistakes like that are often fatal."

The yacht's engines revved loudly.

"Now," Darwin said, turning away. "I've got a short phone call to make." He pulled out a burner phone and then dialed Nadia's personal line. The yacht was a dozen meters from the dock now and gaining speed.

A man answered. "*Da!*" He barked into the line.

"Got the USB?" Darwin asked.

There was a pause, and then the man said, "Who is this?"

"You want the USB? Put Nadia on."

Something muffled the sound as people spoke in the background like the man had placed his hand over the receiver.

"Is this who I think it is?" Nadia asked.

"The one, the only."

"I'm happy this drew you out of hiding."

"Leaving so soon?"

"Where are you? We should meet. Talk."

"I'm in the hotel, one floor down in the security room. Come join me."

"Wait for me. I'll be there in five minutes."

The line died.

Darwin slipped the phone away. "They do not have the USB, and she plans to blow up the hotel within five minutes."

"How could you know that?" Petrakis said.

"Because I told her I was in the security room back at the hotel. She said she'd meet me there in five minutes and to wait for her there." He pointed at the yacht as it continued to move away from the shore. "It doesn't look like she's on her way."

Petrakis stared out at the boat as its lights were all that could be seen in the dark.

"You're going to have to shoot me." Petrakis slipped a hand in his pocket, and three weapons moved upward to train on him from three different men. He stopped moving instantly. "My phone. I'm getting my phone."

Darwin nodded, his weapon still in his hand, and his men lowered their weapons.

Petrakis eased his phone out, then took a deep breath. "You sure know how to start a guy's heart."

"Who are you calling?" Darwin asked.

"The Coast Guard. They killed Samaras and Kokkinos. You do what you want, but I refuse to let them just float off into the sunset."

Darwin lunged forward and smacked the phone out of Petrakis's hand. The man looked up at him, eyes wide, mouth open.

"First of all, there is no fucking sunset, you dick, and

secondly, you're not listening well. You *do not* arrest people like this."

"So what? They get to kill cops and get away with it?" Petrakis shouted as his hand jerked back to his weapon.

Darwin raised his silenced weapon, the sound suppressor already screwed onto it, and aimed at Petrakis's heart from three feet away. He dropped into a shooter's stance.

"What are you doing?" Darwin asked. "Pulling a weapon on us guarantees you die."

"I'm going to take my weapon, run to that dock, find a boat or steal one, and go after them. They *cannot* get away with this."

"You will do no such thing."

Petrakis took a step backward. "Then you'll have to shoot me."

Two Greek officers sitting on the sand leaned back to be out of the line of fire. One mumbled something that sounded like a prayer in Greek.

"Let me ask you something," Darwin said, his gun not wavering yet. "If you're going after a boat filled with Russian mafia hit men, are you at least wearing Kevlar? Is that what's under your shirt?"

"Of course I am. I took the one Kokkinos was wearing. He wouldn't need it anymore."

"Okay, good."

Darwin fired two bullets into the center of Petrakis's chest from five feet away in rapid succession.

The man jerked back and dropped hard onto the sand, moaning and squirming in pain.

"Holy," Petrakis moaned the word, then added, "fuck." He tried to lift his head and look at Darwin but jerked it back to the sand.

"Why?" the inspector gasped, then coughed and cried out.

Darwin slipped his weapon away, leaving the sound suppressor attached, and stared down at the Greek officers.

"If anyone moves, shoot them."

All six men on the sand had blanched at the sight of Petrakis getting shot. Now, they tried to act like statues, with two of them appearing not even to be breathing.

Darwin glanced out at the retreating lights as Petrakis squirmed on the sand.

"You don't listen well, Mr. Inspector. I said you *don't* arrest people like Nadia and her crew. I *have never* said I'd be letting them go."

Darwin checked his watch. He'd called Nadia about four minutes ago. The lights were even farther away as the yacht made a run for it.

"Any second now …" he muttered to himself.

Then, a fiery orange ball lit up the dark horizon as the yacht exploded. The center of the huge boat burst outward, and then a succession of blasts tore into the fore and aft areas, with one more blast tearing apart the top.

In mere seconds, the entire boat was torn apart. What was left of it was on fire in the water or already sinking about five hundred meters from shore.

Nadia, her crew, and everyone else on that boat—including Faye—were gone. No one could survive that blast.

It was over, truly over.

Darwin turned to the men on the sand. He studied their faces, then glanced at Petrakis, who watched the flames in the distance while he squirmed in pain.

"I told you the explosives were removed from the hotel. We were storing them on the Russian yacht."

He strode past Petrakis. "Gentlemen, escort those police officers back to town. Your fees are being wired to you. Petrakis, join me if you want. There's one small task I must still do before I leave."

Darwin stepped into the bushes and shoved his way through until he popped out on the other side.

"Michaels and Smith, you're with me," he barked over his shoulder.

Then he headed back to the hotel.

Chapter 41

When the earth blew up, and everything disintegrated with it, something shoved her ass into the air like she'd been shot out of a canon.

Then, she lost consciousness.

Lucky, though, because she hit the water several dozen meters from the wreckage with most of the chair torn apart under her. The blast did something to the legs and back of the chair, but it also did something to her left ankle.

Twisted back from the blast? Landing wrong in the water?

Either way, it didn't matter. Her left ankle was useless and in such pain that she was wide awake after sinking a meter underwater.

Hands freed from the confines of that horrid chair, she thrust upward and was able to break the surface without filling her lungs with salty seawater.

Faye gasped, clenched her teeth at the pain, and inhaled blessed oxygen.

The bastards were bombed out of the water and had no idea that by placing her at the top corner of the boat in a chair, not only would she be propelled from the boat with the initial shock wave, but the chair would protect her flesh from most of the blast's heat.

Treading water, her aching ankle dangling useless, she turned toward the blast site. Flames licked several pieces of debris, but no one appeared to be alive.

What the hell happened? How did the thing blow?

Whatever it was, she didn't want to stick around and ask questions.

Faye thrust forward toward the lights onshore as her face cried out in pain. The saltwater had gotten into her open cuts from the beating. Parts of the chair were still attached to her right leg, and both wrists still had duct tape wrapped around them, with her left forearm still connected to a broken chunk of wood.

Once on the sand, she would remove the pieces and then find help. By morning, she'd have her ankle cast, and that would be the end of it.

At least, she hoped so.

The shoreline wasn't too far, she kept telling herself as her arms weakened with the effort.

The pain throbbed in her ankle, but the cool water seemed to soothe it. Maybe it wasn't too bad after all.

A girl can hope.

She paused to tread water, turning back to ensure no one was chasing her.

The water behind her only had debris. No one else

survived that blast. All the bastards were dead.

She twirled back to face the shoreline and saw movement along the beach to the left.

At least six men, maybe eight, were walking away, headed toward the hotel in the distance.

She squinted to see them better and was sure she had caught sight of the uniforms.

Greek police?

Did they fire some kind of bazooka or RPG at the Russian boat?

Shit, if the Greek police were here and they watched the yacht explode, then they were well aware of what was happening. Weren't they?

That meant the authorities would know her role in everything that happened. She never did get the security footage from Kallonis, so someone had it.

Faye angled toward the shore and kept swimming, but she swam toward the right this time.

There was no way she could go back to the hotel now.

Her small luggage in the room was history. That *fucking* mirror she thought was Roxanne's was gone now, too. She was ecstatic. No more illusions or dreams or whatever the hell she had been seeing in that mirror.

In fact, if the authorities saw her on that boat, they'd assume she was dead. She'd used her real name at the hotel, and when she never turned up to check out or gather her belongings, that would guarantee it—she died in the explosion.

Several engines fired up by the docks about two hundred meters away to her left.

Men were loading into boats to race out and look for

survivors.

Her limbs were tiring, but she couldn't be picked up. Playing dead worked for her. She could heal her foot and move to the next hotel, but this time on a different island. Maybe Naxos or Mykonos. She'd had two husbands die on her, leaving a small fortune behind, so maybe she could splurge on Santorini.

Boats were headed her way.

Faye lowered herself in the water until her eyes were above the surface. They wouldn't see her in the dark, even with the huge flashlights they were using.

When they got close, she took a large gulp of air, dropped below the surface, and listened for them to zip past her location.

Waiting a few moments more, she rose to the surface slowly, then gasped a breath of air, the pain from her cuts intensifying after having been under the salt water.

Both boats were closing in on the explosion site behind her as she pushed onward toward the shore again.

Taking routine breaks, Faye could touch the sand with her right foot about twenty minutes later, several hundred meters down the shore from where she'd seen the Greek police and the dock where the boats had come from.

She crawled up on the sandy beach in a dark area and rested on her back for several minutes.

Then she risked a look at her left ankle.

It was swollen to twice its normal size.

"Shit."

That'll put a damper on her travel plans.

She rolled onto her stomach slowly, pushed up to her knees, then stood and balanced on her right foot.

With one last look at the Lindos Palace Resort Hotel in the distance, Faye Olympiou wobbled away to get her foot set and cast. Then she would be off to another island where she would check in to some other expensive hotel and see what sort of carnage she could get involved with.

There were always hotels with people waiting to be fucked with.

And there was always someone who needed to die.

Oh, what fun she derived from taking a life.

Maybe she'd avoid Russian types in the future, though.

They were dangerous, and dangerous people scared her.

Chapter 42

THEY APPROACHED FAYE'S HOTEL room with caution. Darwin's men had taken the Greek police back to their vehicles, and they'd all left the site together. Now that the Russians were all dead, there was no need to employ nearly a dozen mercs anymore, so only Michaels and Smith stayed with him.

Finding Faye's room had been easy since they'd surveilled the Russians in their room for the past few days, and hers was the unit beside it, according to the staff locked in the room across from the security office.

Once Darwin had gained access, his men went to work, tearing everything apart and tossing her luggage upside down. Petrakis had stayed with him, which he didn't mind as he wanted to see how the inspector was doing after having to shoot the man.

"Feeling better yet?" Darwin asked as he checked under

the bathroom sink, running his hands along the back of the pipe.

"You broke several ribs," Petrakis said, trying not to breathe too much or expand his chest. "I'm going to feel it for weeks." He winced.

"That is the point of the vest." Darwin glanced at the inspector. "It saves your life, but it hurts like a bitch doing it."

"You didn't have to shoot me."

Darwin got up and lifted the toilet bowl lid off the back. "Oh, right, I could've told you they were going to kill themselves with the explosives they thought they'd left at the hotel. And you wouldn't have tried to stop it?" He snuck a glance at the inspector.

"Placing those devices on their boat and causing their deaths ..."

"Blah, blah, blah. At the end of the day, all we did was find a dangerous item they had left behind at the hotel and run over to give it back to them." He stopped what he was doing and faced the inspector. "Are you sad the bastards are dead? Would you prefer another outcome?"

They stared at each other a moment, then Petrakis shook his head. "I might agree that it's better this way and less costly to the taxpayer for a long trial."

"Oh, come on, admit it. You're happy they're dead, and you had nothing to do with it because I kept the information from you. Therefore, you're not complicit in any way. Tomorrow, you and your career remain intact, and the rest of us disappear." Darwin moved out of the bathroom, leaving the door ajar an inch or two, then pulled open the small dresser drawers. "How about a thank you? That could work.

Case closed, case solved."

"I learned a lot on this one."

Darwin looked away in order to search the dresser. His men had tossed her bed and the luggage and were working on the chairs and cushions on the other side of the room by the patio door.

Petrakis headed that way, stopping at the glass door that led to the outdoor patio. "I learned that this is one sick hotel."

"Oh yeah? How sick is the hotel?" Darwin was on the third drawer of six.

"Evelyn Diakos, the manager's wife, was sleeping with Kallonis's wife, the man Faye killed. Mr. Diakos was trying to fuck Roxanne." Petrakis glanced back at Darwin. "Apparently, he made a habit of fucking his guests."

Smith and Michaels stopped what they were doing, stared at Petrakis, then went back to work.

"Well," Darwin said, shaking his head. "I can tell you that Roxanne Dupont was also fucking Evelyn Diakos. My guy Miller was here days before we arrived. He snapped photos of Evelyn entering Dupont's room the night before she went missing. They argued about something, but Miller didn't catch it all."

Petrakis snapped his fingers, then grunted with the pain from vibrating his chest area. After several deep breaths, he leaned against the wall, his face a deeper red.

"That all works with what I learned. I'd never figured out whose jacket was in Roxanne's room that night. And the room service guy from the kitchen said he delivered enough food for two. Diakos's wife must be going after as many women as Diakos himself went after, even competing for the same guest at times." He stared out into the night. "Bunch of sick fucks." He turned back to Darwin as he was yanking out the last drawer, the hope of finding the USB fading quickly. "Diakos was blackmailing the owner, too. He has photos in his office taped up under his desk. I imagine that's all over now. This hotel will go to whoever is in the Markakis's will."

Darwin pulled the empty dresser from the wall to look behind it when the glass door Petrakis was standing beside blew inward. The inspector shot forward into the room, stumbling to stay on his feet before smacking into one of the plush chairs and tumbling to a stop on the floor, face down, eyes closed.

Darwin dove between the bed and the wall as both Michaels and Smith grabbed their weapons and took up a position to the left of the broken glass door.

"How did we miss this?" Darwin shouted at his men. "Who the fuck just shot the inspector?"

Rapid fire raked across the room, punching huge holes in the wall above Darwin. He curled into a ball and waited for the barrage to end as small chunks of wall rained down on him.

One of his men returned fire.

More glass shattered.

Darwin already had his weapon in his hands and was twisting the sound suppressor off the tip when he heard Petrakis grunting by the wall.

He glanced down the length of his body and saw Petrakis's face. The man fluttered his eyes but wasn't able to push himself up. However, many bullets just hit his vest and had to have broken more ribs.

Then darkness engulfed the room as the lights went out. They were covered in a black blanket for a heartbeat before emergency lighting bloomed by the room's door, casting an eerie red glow throughout the room.

"You all suffer now," a man shouted in Russian-accented English.

Viktor.

The man had been on the hotel grounds the entire time. Darwin hadn't seen him go for the yacht. He didn't even think to check because Nadia had ordered everyone to the boat.

And Rosina hadn't told Darwin that someone was staying behind. Viktor had to have called Nadia en route with the change of plans.

Sergei had planted listening devices in Nadia's rooms, not on their individual devices. Darwin would not have been privy to it if a call had been made at the last minute.

"You all die, *svin'ya*," the man shouted, closer now.

More bullets punched into the walls above Darwin. He grabbed the side of the mattress and eased it over him by about a foot, offering him a fraction of coverage.

Then, one of his men shouted something unintelligible, grunted, and opened fire with his automatic weapon.

Darwin leaned up to glance over the edge of the bed.

Smith was dead, and Michaels was hiding behind Smith's body, blood oozing from several places, but still alive.

"Motherfucker," Michaels shouted.

He pushed Smith off him, got to his feet, then aimed the tip of his weapon out the door and fired randomly, keeping it mostly hidden behind the wall.

The loss of life if people were out wandering the path would have been too high a price, but it was nearing two in the morning. At worst, this riotous noise would only rouse guests from sleep.

Even though he was hidden, bullets punched into Michaels, shaking his body violently.

All weapons ceased firing. Michaels stumbled backward, then dropped to his knees, gurgling blood before falling face-first onto the hotel room carpet.

Petrakis still moaned on his stomach, injured and unarmed—they'd taken his weapon earlier, so he wouldn't try anything stupid.

Darwin wasn't hit, but he only had one handgun.

The rest of his heavily armed men—all ten of them—had escorted the Greek police back to town and were probably on their way to their private escape routes—chartered planes, chartered boats, and villas where they'd hide out until the next job.

He was alone with Viktor and woefully low on ammunition, with no escape route or plan.

There was no choice. Wait the man out. Wait until he got close for a kill shot. But with the weapons Viktor was using, Darwin's odds of survival were extremely low.

His mind raced with possibilities as he placed his hands on the side of the mattress again, gripped the cloth handle, and eased it over him a little more.

Something clattered to the carpeted floor beside his leg.

Faye had left a *fucking* handheld vanity mirror on the bed, and now it gave away his position.

Unless Viktor weren't in the room yet, then it wouldn't matter.

Darwin held his breath and listened. Someone shouted outside somewhere. Petrakis moaned softly like he was about to go to sleep.

Darwin snuck another look at Petrakis. The inspector was on his stomach, his forehead on the floor, and his nose pressed into the carpet. He was breathing through his mouth, trying to manage whatever pain he was enduring.

Two-handed, Darwin held his weapon and waited.

Glass under someone's foot crunched as they entered the room through the broken sliding door.

Darwin averted his eyes to the mirror on the carpet beside his thigh.

On the other side of the wall to his right was the bathroom. Viktor had probably watched four men enter the room. Smith and Michaels were dead. Petrakis was on his stomach at the end of the bed.

The Russian would be cautious as he looked for the fourth man—Darwin.

He may have a chance if he could make Viktor think he was in the bathroom.

Slowly, as another foot crunched glass on the other side of the room, Darwin picked up the vanity mirror and held it by the handle.

He'd get one shot at this. It would have to work.

Gun in one hand, mirror in the other, Darwin edged along the side of the bed, barely concealed by the overhang of the mattress. He stopped when he could see the bathroom door. It sat slightly ajar, just like he'd left it after searching for the USB in there.

Another crunch of glass.

Darwin couldn't risk looking up over the bed now. He only had one play.

So, he curled his arm across his abdomen as if he was about to throw a Frisbee, then whipped the handheld vanity mirror at the bathroom door.

It was a direct hit.

The bathroom door opened halfway with the force of it being thumped, and the mirror vanished inside the bathroom, where Darwin heard it break into pieces on the tile floor.

Viktor shouted something in Russian, then stomped across the floor toward the bathroom.

Darwin calculated the man's steps as they drew closer to his position. Closer, closer, then Viktor was at the end of the bed.

As he passed Inspector Petrakis lying face down on the carpet, Viktor fired twice into the inspector's back.

The man grunted with each impact, then lay still.

When Viktor was in Darwin's line of fire, he squeezed his trigger, aiming for a chest shot.

The impacts hit Viktor, but then Darwin saw the thick chest—Kevlar—and knew they weren't fatal.

Viktor dove and Darwin adjusted his aim before he lost sight of the man.

He fired two more times.

Viktor spun sideways, hit the wall, and dropped to the floor.

Before the man had fully settled, Darwin pushed up off the floor, weapon out in front of him. He fired again, but only one bullet exited his weapon, and the magazine was empty.

That bullet grazed Viktor's jawline, making a dark-colored gouge on the side of his face.

When he fell, the Russian had dropped his gun. Darwin couldn't grab it and swing it toward the man because it was strapped to his body, and Viktor was now lying on the strap.

So he jumped on him without thinking, knees landing in

Viktor's midriff. Stunned from the bullets hitting his vest and the cut on the side of his jaw, Viktor had taken several seconds to recover, to orientate himself.

Darwin landed half a dozen blows on Viktor's face before the man registered Darwin on top of him. The man's arms squirmed, and Darwin fought to secure them.

When he did, he felt the rigid steel hidden in a sheath on the side of Viktor's leg.

After two more stunning blows to his face, cracking cartilage and bursting open the man's bottom lip, Darwin fumbled at the clasp that held a twelve-inch blade to Viktor's hip.

Before the Russian could stop him, Darwin had the blade unsheathed and up against Viktor's neck, ready to slide it sideways.

"Stop squirming," Darwin shouted in the man's face. "Your carotid will open nicely with this blade."

Viktor's eyes blazed with hatred under him.

Darwin had a dozen questions, none of which they had the time to entertain. Sirens were already wailing in the distance.

Realistically, there wasn't more than a minute left.

"Why did your men kill Brian Miller?"

The Russian spit blood in Darwin's face. It made him blink, but Darwin applied pressure to the blade, ready to slide it without hesitation if the man attempted to shove him off.

"That American bastard was going to buy USB. We could not allow that."

"You fucker, he was here to *stop* the sale, not buy anything."

The sirens were even closer.

A rage built inside Darwin as he stared down at the high-ranking member of the Russian *bratva*, the brotherhood. Viktor had made it personal by staying behind, which saved his life as he wasn't on that boat—well, until now.

"Now you'll die," Darwin whispered, leaning in close to Viktor. "And for what? Your country?" Darwin scoffed. "No, they won't remember you or honor you. You will not die for Nadia, either. You die because of your ego. I will cut your throat like the pig you are, and there will be blood, there will be a lot of blood—"

A weapon fired, and Darwin was jerked sideways, the blade knocked from his hand.

Stunned into action, he scrambled to the side and spun around, holding up his empty weapon.

The sirens had to be at the front of the hotel now.

Inside the room, it was still dark but for the red glow.

No one was standing by the door broken patio door. Everyone was still in the same position, Michaels and Smith dead by the broken glass door, and Petrakis on his stomach, grunting with each breath.

When he stared at the inspector, he saw a weapon in his hand.

Petrakis tilted his head to look up at Darwin.

"His …" he said, more grunt than word. "Hand …"

Darwin scrambled over to Viktor.

Half of the man's head was missing. He had died, eyes wide with rage, a small gun in his right hand.

Darwin saw the hidden pocket on the right side of Viktor's parachute pants. When Darwin had been holding the knife to Viktor's throat with his legs securing Viktor's arms, the man had somehow been able to withdraw the weapon and aim it upward at Darwin. If Petrakis hadn't shot him in the side of the head, Darwin would've taken a bullet—or more than one—in the abdomen.

"Where did *you* get the gun?" Darwin asked, too stunned at the close call to thank the man for saving his internal organs and probably his life.

"You didn't—" he winced, inhaled deeply, then added, "search me. Just took my service weapon."

"I'll be damned."

He glanced back at Viktor. He'd stopped bleeding when his heart had stopped, but until that happened, an enormous amount of blood had leaked from the man's destroyed cranium.

"You weren't lying," Petrakis managed to say.

"About what?"

"You told him, 'there will be blood' because—" Petrakis winced, holding his breath. "Oh, fuck it hurts." He breathed in and out, then said, "Because you were going to open him up like you would a pig."

Darwin got to his feet, his legs wobbly, and leaned against the wall.

"Don't try to move. I'll get emergency services down here. They'll tend to your wounds."

"He killed—" Petrakis moaned, then said, "Samaras and Kokkinos." He inhaled and exhaled twice while Darwin waited. "It felt good to kill him."

"It should. Men like Viktor only belong in one place— the ground."

Petrakis exhaled loudly as if he wanted to laugh but couldn't.

Darwin turned to open the room's door when something

in the bathroom caught his eye.

Faye's broken mirror lay scattered on the floor in pieces. Up against the wall, he saw something that made him gasp.

Behind him, Petrakis grunted again, then swore.

Darwin entered the bathroom and picked it up.

When he examined the broken handle of the mirror, he saw exactly where it had been hidden and how Roxanne Dupont had done it.

"You won't believe this, but Miss Dupont was a genius."

"What?"

The sirens outside had been cut off. Help had arrived, and sirens were no longer needed.

"She hid the USB in the handle of her mirror. We thought this was Faye's mirror. It must've been Dupont's, and Faye snatched it after killing her." Darwin stared at the elusive USB for a few more seconds before depositing it into his pocket. "I'll be a motherfucker," he whispered to himself. "It's finally over."

Darwin opened the door, stepped outside, then stopped and looked back.

"Thank you, Inspector Petrakis. You did an amazing job. I'll direct paramedics to you, but I fear we shall never meet again."

Petrakis was able to lift his gaze far enough to stare at Darwin.

"Wait—" he was reduced to a painful bout of coughing.

"No time to wait. I need to disappear again. I'll always be eternally grateful for what you just did for me. I'll be in touch one day. Perhaps I'll find a way to return the favor."

Darwin spun on his heels and walked away from the room. Seconds later, he entered the bushes that rimmed the back of the hotel property as four cops, followed by paramedics with orange kits, headed toward Faye's room, the cause of all the early morning noise.

Ten minutes later, he was headed to the airport, where he would don a disguise and exit the country under his assumed name.

He dialed Rosina in Italy and told her he had the USB in his possession.

"It's over, honey."

"See you soon. Oh, wait."

"What is it?"

"Sarah called. She just got back from New York, and Aaron and the boys are missing. She wanted to know if you could look into it."

"I'll do one better."

There was a pause on the other end of the line.

Then Rosina said, "Want me to book you a flight from Athens to Toronto?"

"See, that's why I love you. Predictive thinking."

"I'll let Sarah know you're on your way."

"Gotta run," Darwin said, cutting off the line and hitting the gas.

There was a lot of blood, and he'll probably have to spill more in Toronto.

But that was the way of things in this world. That's who they were.

And when he settled back in Italy with his wife, and Petrakis was out of the hospital and resting at home, he'd send him a thank-you gift for saving his life.

Something to remember their brief time together.

Something to remind the inspector that, for a moment, he

was on Darwin's side of the fence regarding the law.

Sometimes, the garbage had to be taken out, and the court of law wasn't always the best arena to perform that task.

No, sometimes people just have to die.

It was the only way to end their reign of abuse and terror. It was the only way to silence their voice.

Especially if they were cop-killing thugs, they seemed to be the best kind of people to kill.

The best kind …

Afterword

Dear Reader,

Writing a book with another author can often become a daunting task. In this case, Rania was a wonderful author to work with. Her ideas were fantastic, her plotting stellar, but most of all, I love her dark side.

Originally, Rania came up with most of this novel idea after having traveled to Rhodes. She visited the hotel that inspired this book. The hotel we used is entirely fictional, as well as the characters, which were people she encountered or did business with—such as Inspector Petrakis (Hadjialexandrou Andreas), Mr. Adonis Diakos (Alexandros Mortzos), the art critic Nikolas Kovac (Nicholas Koveos), and the head of security, Kallonis (Palonis Giorgos). Last but not least, Faye Olympiou was named after one of Rania's beta readers (Faye Griva).

When I read the first draft of her manuscript in early development—about 40,000 words of this 80,000-word novel—we began the conversation of writing it together. I was quite taken by the details surrounding an investigation at a hotel and all the inner workings of that hotel and wanted to include Darwin from the Sarah Roberts Series.

We discussed the plot at length, Roxanne Dupont's role, Faye's insanity—psychopathy—and who was fucking who at this Lindos Palace Resort Hotel.

By the time I got to Faye hiding in the closet and then under the bed in the Russians' hotel room, I was in love with this book. We discussed Darwin's role, and Brian Miller was introduced.

The information on that infamous USB would now hold Darwin's personal data, and we went from there. Rania wrote the first half of this novel in Greek and translated it into English. I reread the translated English, added my bits and pieces, cleaned it up to some degree, and then wrote the book's second half, which included all the Darwin scenes.

For those caught up with the Sarah Roberts Series, Sarah just finished *The Unknown*, book 29, in New York. She's about to come back to Toronto for *Wrath*, book 30. Then there's *The Damned* and *The Game*, all the way to book 34, *The Disappearance*. So many more are coming.

At the end of this novel, Darwin and Rosina discuss Sarah and how she had just landed in Toronto. She had called for Darwin, and now he was on his way to help her. You will revisit that call early on in *Wrath*.

I hope you enjoyed our collaboration as much as we enjoyed writing and revising it.

We've worked on another collaboration called *The*

Soulless. It was released in mid-2022.

In the meantime, check out Rania Stone's other thrillers, *The Unjustified* and *The Sun's Chariot*.

Thank you for everything, dear reader. We have so much gratitude for you.

Keep reading, smiling, and caring for yourself and each other.

Until next time.

Blessings,

Jonas Saul

Rania Stone

The Sarah Roberts Series

Dark Visions (One)
The Warning (Two)
The Crypt (Three)
The Hostage (Four)
The Victim (Five)
The Enigma (Six)
The Vigilante (Seven)
The Rogue (Eight)
Killing Sarah (Nine)
The Antagonist (Ten)
The Redeemed (Eleven)
The Haunted (Twelve)
The Unlucky (Thirteen)
The Abandoned (Fourteen)
The Cartel (Fifteen)
Losing Sarah (Sixteen)
The Pact (Seventeen)
The Terror (Eighteen)
The Chase (Nineteen)
The Betrayal (Twenty)
Sarah's Return (Twenty-One)
The Hunt (Twenty-Two)
The Delivery (Twenty-Three)
The Trap (Twenty-Four)
The Ultimatum (Twenty-Five)
The Depraved (Twenty-Six)
The Condemned (Twenty-Seven)
Payback (Twenty-Eight)
The Unknown (Twenty-Nine)
Wrath (Thirty)
The Damned (Thirty-One)
The Game (Thirty-Two)

The Decoy (Thirty-Three)
The Disappearance (Thirty-Four)
The Whole Truth (Thirty-Five)
Alex (Thirty-Six)
Parkman (Thirty-Seven)
Darwin (Thirty-Eight)
Aaron (Thirty-Nine)
Remains To Be Seen (Forty)

The Jake Wood Novels

The Immortal Gene (Book One)
The Immortal Target (Book Two)

Standalone Novels

'Til Death Do Us Part
The Drowning
The Woman in the Woods
The Threat
The Specter
The Mafia Trilogy
A Murder in Time
Frequency of the Dead

Co-Authored Novels

Collision Course (Written with Gary Ponzo)
There Will Be Blood (Written with Rania Stone)
The Soulless (Written with Rania Stone)

Short Story Collections

Twisted Fate (Tales of Horror)

Jonas Saul

Twists of Fate (Tales of Hope)

About Jonas Saul

Jonas Saul is the bestselling author of the Sarah Roberts Series—more than two million sold!—and has written and published over sixty thrillers. After acquiring an agent, he signed several deals in Los Angeles, with MadRiver Pictures optioning his Sarah Roberts Series— over forty books!—(currently in development).

Jonas has often outranked Stephen King and Dean

Koontz on Amazon over the past decade. He's regularly invited to be a guest speaker, teacher, or workshop presenter at international writing conferences and film festivals worldwide. He hosts an annual writer's retreat in Greece, where he currently lives. He focuses his teaching on how to get tension and emotion in every scene, on every page, how he made it as a creator/writer, the path to success in this business, and the pitfalls to avoid. He also hosts a reading retreat in Greece with guest authors, yoga retreats, and hiking retreats. Visit the Imagine Greece Retreats website at www.imaginegreeceretreats.com, or email him directly to discuss an opportunity to join one of the retreats at jonas@imaginegreeceretreats.com.

Jonas is also a professional freelance editor. He works for several publishers and does private editing for clients, with many testimonials on his website at www.imaginepress.org, which details each author's response to Jonas's editing skills. Email Jonas directly for an editing quote at editor@imaginepress.org.

To book Jonas for a speaking engagement at a writer's conference/festival, to have him on your jury at a film festival, or even to say hello, email Jonas directly at jonassaul@icloud.com.

For updates on releases, hit the "Follow" button on Amazon or Bookbub, and join Jonas on Facebook, where he's most active.

Contact Jonas Saul

Linktree: Find me here

Email: jonassaul@icloud.com

Rania Stone Titles

Novels

What He Didn't Know (Translated to English)
The Lives Between Us (Translated to English)
There Will Be Blood (Co-written with Jonas Saul)
The Soulless (Co-written with Jonas Saul)

Children's Books (All in Greek)

A Walk In The Garbage City
The Magic Ring
The War Of Fire And Water Drops
The Well Of Colors
Adventures In Bunny Land
Adventures In Bunny Land 2
Melinda And The 100 Princesses
The Cursed Chest
The Christmas Reindeer
Melinda And The Magical Crystal Ball
Cat-Tales

About Rania Stone

Rania Stone is the author of five adult novels and eleven children's stories. She's a well-known author in Greece and has recently had several of her novels translated into English. Her first English release, *What He Didn't Know*, came out in late 2020.

She's been writing for over two decades and calls Greece her home.

Contact Rania Stone

Website: www.raniastone.com

Facebook: RaniaStone/Facebook

Bookbub: Rania Stone

Email: contact@raniastone.com

Instagram: Rania/Instagram

www.ingramcontent.com/pod-product-compliance
Lightning Source LLC
Chambersburg PA
CBHW031304210726
48287CB00005B/1409